Critical Praise for Triage

"Remarkable . . . riveting . . . surprise is a key element in Anderson's storytelling. . . . The shocking conclusion is both a dramatic and moral triumph . . . that such a thoughtful, provocative book also provides so much pleasure is a tribute to Anderson's already formidable talents."
—Dan Cryer, *Newsday*

"Suspenseful."
—*The New Yorker*

"Thrilling."
—Susan Salter Reynolds, *Los Angeles Times*

"A sensibility that understands the seriousness of love and life."
—David Nicholson, *The Washington Post*

"A brilliant, gripping new book . . . there are passages in the book that leave a reader's heart beating hard."
—Allen Salkin, *New York Post*

"*Triage* looks human savagery in the face and doesn't blink. . . . But this is not a despairing book, and that is what makes it so strong. . . . [Anderson] has crafted a story that is acute and moving, one that strips away obfuscation and illusion and tells powerful truths."
—Anthony Brandt, *Men's Journal*

"[A] searing debut novel."
—*Time Out*

"A study of love, death, and redemption in the finest style, and it is so good it is difficult to avoid a stream of vacuous superlatives. . . . To be unmoved by this novel is to be dead."
—Nicholas Fearn, *The Independent* (London)

"Written with the taut compression of a thriller, it's also an unflinching depiction of what happens to people in a war zone."
— Christina Patterson, *Observer* (London)

"A dark and devastating story of war and redemption."
— *The Times* (London)

"[A] gripping psychological thriller."
— Margaret Walters, *The Sunday Times* (London)

"A first novel of extraordinary depth and beauty . . . reminiscent of Hemingway."
— David W. Henderson, *Library Journal*

"A powerful exploration of war's effects on those who survive it. . . . A magnificent homage to the method, subject, and spirit of . . . Ernest Hemingway, that reads and feels like a contemporary *A Farewell to Arms.*"
— *Kirkus Review*

"Coupling a provocative premise with a fine moral sensibility, Anderson has produced a memorable tale of two eras."
— *Publishers Weekly*

"*Triage* by Scott Anderson is a war novel made all the more harrowing by its understatement. . . . Anderson builds a powerful narrative reaching as far back as the Spanish Civil War — and forward to the possibility of survival with dignity and sanity."
— Christopher Hart, *Bookseller*

"Anderson's account of a war photographer going to the brink of insanity stayed with me for weeks. From the brutal opening scenes in Kurdistan, to the startling, beautiful ending, Anderson truly captures how people face danger and loss. Only an experienced war reporter would have this story inside him, and only a first-rate writer would know how to tell it. Anderson is a rare combination of both."
— Sebastian Junger, author of *The Perfect Storm*

TRIAGE

Scott Anderson

SCRIBNER PAPERBACK FICTION
Published by Simon & Schuster

SCRIBNER PAPERBACK FICTION
Simon & Schuster, Inc.
Rockefeller Center
1230 Avenue of the Americas
New York, NY 10020

First Scribner Paperback Fiction edition 1999
SCRIBNER PAPERBACK FICTION and design are trademarks of Macmillan Library Reference USA, Inc., used under license by Simon & Schuster, the publisher of this work.

Designed by Brooke Zimmer
Set in Electra
Manufactured in the United States of America

1 3 5 7 9 10 8 6 4 2

The Library of Congress has cataloged the Scribner edition as follows:
Anderson, Scott Anderson.
Triage / Scott.
p.   cm.
I. Title.
PS3551.N3945T75   1998
813'.54—dc21   98-12821
CIP

ISBN 0-684-84695-0
0-684-85653-0 (Pbk)

FOR MY MOTHER
Barbara Joy Anderson
1928–1994

Acknowledgments

Writing a novel is a peculiar act of faith—a faith that, at least in my case, was largely borne by others. For their constant encouragement and sage advice over the many years and mutations that this book took, I wish to especially thank four people: Barrie Kessler; my mother; my grandmother, Louise Coonrad; and Rebecca Lee. As well, I feel deeply grateful to my agents, Deborah Schneider and Patty Detroit, for their ceaseless support; to my editors at Scribner, Scott Moyers and Gillian Blake, for their enthusiasm and fine editing; to Colin Harrison at *Harper's* magazine for his boosterism and big-brotherly advice (too late I discovered he was actually younger than me); to Connie Brothers and Frank Conroy of the Iowa Writers' Workshop for providing me with the environment to return to fiction writing; and to the Copernicus Society of America for helping supply the means to do so. Finally, to my friends—Rebecca Brian, Craig Cuny, John "Pinkie" Faherty, Pete Manno, Chuck Siebert, and Jen Wood—who, collectively, have helped remind me that to write is not enough, that the well-lived life also includes shooting pool, hanging out in seedy bars, and going on long road trips with no particular destination in mind.

ONE

He lay beneath a blanket of torn flowers. They were scattered over his chest, gathered about his neck like a garland. Occasionally, the wind found his resting place; stems shifted, loose petals took flight.

Above him, Mark saw a sky that was gray. He searched this sky for something to orient him—a patch of blue, a border of white—but the gray was unending. He thought of the land that surrounded him. It was brown and spread away for hundreds of miles, tumbled to ravines, smoothed to plain. He felt stone dust settle on his skin, licked it from his lips.

It occurred to him that maybe the flowers had caused it, that maybe here even flowers could destroy you. He envisioned the gunner, bored, gazing across all those empty miles beneath the gray sky, hour after hour, day after day, his eyes suddenly drawn to the colors Mark held in his hand. He imagined the joy the man must have felt at that moment.

At the outset, Mark had been thankful for the sky. Gray was the color of a good day in Kurdistan; the sun would not burn his skin, the glare would not hurt his eyes. Upon reaching the hilltop, he had stood on the highest rock and looked in all directions at the mountains. Not a building or a road. He had climbed down from the rock and begun picking wildflowers. The stalks were brittle, and he felt them snap beneath his fingers.

He didn't hear the artillery shell, but he believed he saw it. When it dug into the hill just below him, little bits of metal and stone had sprayed into the air like a fan. He had stood there amazed, watching the shards arc high before fluttering lightly down to earth.

But not standing, Mark now decided. He had almost certainly been flung to the ground at that very first instant—before sound, before sight. It was while lying beneath the flowers that he had watched the spray against the sky.

No pain. Only a vague, prickly sensation, as if his whole body was asleep. He lifted his head and looked over his chest. He saw that he rested on a large flat rock. His left arm was stretched out to the side, and he studied it carefully. There didn't appear to be anything wrong with it. The right arm lay on his chest, the hand rising and falling as he breathed. Mark watched the hand for a moment. The fingers trembled, and he felt their nervous little taps on a rib.

"Colin?" he called.

He lifted his head a bit more to see his legs. They were splayed over the rock, rigid, the feet turned out to either side. His left foot twitched back and forth. He was troubled by this movement, tried to make it stop, but the foot would not respond to his will.

A dripping sound close to his right ear. Mark twisted to see that his head had rested in a slight bowl in the rock. A pool of blood there. He felt it trickle through his hair, tickling his scalp. He watched it fall from him in quick droplets.

He lay back on the rock. Blood seeped into his ears. Mark took comfort in its warmth and looked up at the gray sky that was eating all sound.

He wasn't sure what to do. If he left the rock, it would only take a few minutes of desert air to dry his pool, and then all that would remain of him would be a small crucible of brown powder, a powder the wind would find and scatter. He wished to stay there, to protect the pool.

But after a time, he thought differently. He understood that if he stayed upon the rock, he would simply disappear as well. And so, he rose.

The sounds, the smells, the things that touched his skin that night, of these details, his memory would part with none. Coming down off the hilltop and across that empty valley, and Mark would remember every step, the slope of the ground beneath his feet, the weight upon his back, the brush of meadow grass on his fingers. A sky of infinite darkness — not a star, not a sliver of moon — and Mark would remember every time he fell to the ground and listened to the wind and imagined it to carry the voices of soldiers, every time he forced himself to rise again, to stand out of the soft, velvet safety of the grass and move on. Seeing himself as he would appear in the nightscope of a soldier's rifle, lit up, a chest and a head floating above the meadow, a target as big and white as the moon. Trying to raise a hand to show he was unarmed, that he was coming off the mountain in peace, trying to forget that none of that mattered in this war. Falling again, forcing himself up, moving on. After a time, the strength of his chant — "stay calm, stay calm" — giving out. Just a half-mad fugitive then, swollen hands sliced by sawgrass, leaden feet that tangled on unseen roots, a chest and throat choking under the weight of its tether, a mind emptied until all it held was the last plea of a thousand dead men — "I don't want to die here, I don't want to die here."

Another sound then, louder than the whispering grass or his shuddering breath, a roar, and Mark reached the bluff and the river lay black before him. He rushed into it, felt the ice water rise to his knees, his hips, and he would always remember that instant when the current caught him, the interminable, slow-motion moment of both sorrow and relief at his own helplessness. Feet slipping on smooth rocks, arms flailing for balance, spinning and down, into the river. Stunned by the cold on his chest, his temples, a light flash of shock and that was too long. Carried under, body hitting rocks, scraping along the riverbed, mouth gasping for air and finding only water, fingers scrabbling for something to hold but going too fast for that, dying now, the dead weight on his back pinning him down, sending him deeper and colder. The strap pulls taut against his neck, the weight is all on his throat, and he is strangling now, dying quicker, moving downstream, pinned to the bottom, the rocks sliding under his back, and the clutch on his throat won't loosen, won't even let him scream as the life is pinched out of him. Both hands clawing at the strap, no strength, almost finished now, and then he hits something in the water, hits it hard, and the force sends him sideways and the grip on his throat lets off for a moment, the strap goes slack, and Mark gets out and he is done with it and he is in the air again and he is free and alive and all alone, hurtling down this river beneath the deep blue dark of a coming dawn.

Reaching shore, the silhouette of a tree in the fading night, and Mark sat beneath its bare branches to lick the bloodwater from his hands, from his arms, like a dog. Not a shadow of wind then, not an insect or a bird or a swaying reed, only the running of the river. The sky softened to silver, eastern hills emerged from the night, and Mark rested his head against the trunk of the tree and shivered. Shivered from the chill of the wet clothes that clung to him. Shivered at having left the dark behind him, at seeing day break on the land before him.

He lay beneath a ceiling of stone. A yellow light played over the uneven surface, outlining its pits and gouges. Mark saw a series of straight, flat-tipped scars in the rock and recognized them as the marks left by pickaxes. He didn't know where he was.

Sound filled his ears. He raised his head and peered into a murk of smoke and dust.

A long narrow room lit by kerosene lanterns. A Pesh Merga barracks with men lying in army cots, two rows that extended along either wall as far as Mark could see. The aisle between the rows crowded with men sitting cross-legged, leaning their backs on the cot frames. Hundreds of men in the room, and they all seemed to be making noise—shouting, calling, muttering to themselves.

A boy sat in the aisle at the foot of Mark's cot. He was young—fifteen or sixteen—and the sleeves of his olive drab coat were rolled up over his thin arms. He appeared to be the only other silent one in the room. His hands were raised and cupped below his chin, and he stared into his palms. The boy was so transfixed that Mark thought he cradled something—a small animal, perhaps, or a baby bird fallen from a nest—and he felt an urge to call to him, to ask what he held. Then he saw the hands were covered in bandages from which blood was seeping.

Mark looked about the room again. Now he understood the voices, knew where he was. He lay his head back and heard straw crinkle by his ears.

The Harir cave. A forty-bed ward and an operating theater carved out of solid rock, with no ventilation, no running water, no medicine. During his five weeks in Kurdistan, Mark had made a half-dozen visits to the cave for a photo-essay he was thinking of calling, "The Worst Hospital in the World." Each time, he had been shaken by the sights, the stench, had counted the minutes until he could return to the air and sunlight that waited beyond the cave mouth. This desire now seized him with urgency. He tried to rise.

His arms and legs would not move. Mark stared at the wool blanket that covered him. He checked the sides of the cot, but there were no straps or ropes holding him. He again tried to rise. Nothing.

He looked to the ceiling and thought back to the river. Fragments of memory, of being shaken awake and looking into the faces of two Pesh Merga guerrillas, the sky gray above them, the ground cold beneath him. They had asked him something in Kurdish, but Mark couldn't remember if he answered before going back to sleep. Nothing after that, nothing until now.

Mark felt the first knotting of panic and tried to calm himself. He imagined crawling, out of his cot, over those filling the aisle, crawling until he had slipped beneath the black curtain and reached the outer world. But this was beyond him. Even falling to the ground was beyond him. He could do nothing but lie in the cot and wonder why his body felt made of stone.

The voices of the wounded rose in volume and tempo, took on a fearful edge. A sudden infusion of light in the far recess of the cave, and Mark knew what it meant even before turning his head. There, a mere silhouette against the brilliant light of the operating lamps,

Talzani stepped from the surgery room. The lamps were shut off then, but Talzani's white coat retained their glow as he made his way down the rows of wounded.

Triage. Mark had already seen it, photographed it. He felt fatigue wash over him, push him down toward sleep. He shook his head violently to keep it at bay.

To be alert, that was the important thing. You had to be alert when Talzani came for you, because triage was done quickly. If you were asleep when he came, if you were too slow with your answers, these could be taken as signs and the blue plastic tag placed on you. Your fate decided by the color of plastic. Get a yellow and be shunted aside. Get red and be treated. Get blue and die. On several occasions—when Mark had been a photographer in Harir instead of a patient—he had seen those given blues beg Talzani, cry to him, offer him money and houses and wives, but the doctor was incorruptible.

He turned to see the white coat draw nearer, just seven or eight beds away. The dark at the edge of his eyes grew, took more and more of his vision. Voices in the cave took on a flat clarity.

He tried to raise his right arm. A slight motion under the blanket. He lifted his left leg, then his right. The blanket shifted each time. His body was coming back to him. Talzani would notice this, surely. Mark took deep gulps of air to steady his breathing. In the corner of his eye he saw him, four beds away now.

The ceiling had lost its features, had become a solid mass of blanched yellow. It seemed to be descending, closing on him. Mark looked into a far corner. It was away from the light, the darkest spot in the cave, as dark as sleep.

"Salaam."

Mark jerked awake when the hand touched his shoulder. He stared with wide eyes, the face above him a blur. First the black moustache, then the thin, young face of Ahmet Talzani came into focus. He was smiling.

"Ah, Mr. Walsh," he said in English, "you've decided to visit me again. And to what do we owe the honor?" A holstered gun poked through a flap of his stained white coat. He drew closer, his smile easing away. "What happened, do you remember?"

[16]

Mark didn't answer, just stared up at him. The orderly, an aged, white-haired Pesh Merga, muttered something in Talzani's ear.

"They found you down by the river. Do you remember that?"

Mark nodded.

Talzani pulled the blanket back. He gazed at the bruises on Mark's chest and legs, whistled softly through his teeth. "Good heavens. Did someone beat you?"

"I fell crossing the river," Mark said. "I was swept down."

The doctor took a cigarette from his coat pocket and lit it, cocked his head to the side. "You were on the other side of the river? Where were you coming from?"

Mark watched the burning tip of the cigarette. "I went out hiking in the morning. I got lost. And then it turned dark."

Curiosity left Talzani's face, and he smiled again. "A dangerous area to go hiking, Mr. Walsh, so close to the contested zone."

The orderly became impatient and whispered in Talzani's ear once more.

"He says you can't walk. Is that so?"

"I don't know," Mark said. "I just woke up and—I think I'm just stiff."

Talzani handed his cigarette to the orderly. He put a hand on each of Mark's shoulders and pushed down. "Does that hurt?"

Mark shook his head.

"But you can feel it?"

Mark nodded. The doctor traveled down, pressing here and there, as if giving a desultory massage. He dug his hands under Mark's back, felt along the spine. He cupped the hip bones and kneaded them, rubbed around the knees, then went to the feet and squeezed hard.

"No pain?"

Mark shook his head again.

Talzani straightened and took back his cigarette. He stared at Mark's body, sent twin streams of smoke out his nose. "Can you move your arms?"

Mark bit his lip and slowly raised his elbows a little off the mattress.

"Your legs?"

He tried to lift his legs clear from the bed but couldn't; he brought his feet in, pushed the knees up a few inches.

"Very good."

The orderly muttered something else. Talzani raised his eyebrows.

"A head wound, as well? I don't think our rivers agree with you, Mr. Walsh." Holding the cigarette between his teeth, the doctor came forward and began turning Mark's head to the side, but then noticed the thin, straight cut across his throat. He frowned, traced it with a finger.

"A chafing wound. How did you get that?"

"I don't know," Mark said.

Stifling a sigh, Talzani twisted Mark's head until it was flat against the pillow, ran his fingers through the matted hair until he found the cut in back. Mark gritted his teeth as he felt it being spread open, the fresh blood spilling down his neck. A trail of cigarette smoke curled around his head to roil and disperse before his eyes. Talzani let go and stepped away. He flicked blood from his fingertips, took the cigarette from his mouth.

"Very lucky, Mr. Walsh—a flesh wound, maybe a concussion. Kurdistan isn't a good place for a skull fracture. You might want to get stitches though." Reaching into his coat pocket, he withdrew the stack of plastic tags. "As for the rest, it's difficult to say. Your body took quite a jolt, but you're not paralyzed and there don't seem to be any broken bones. You have some neural disruption but, God willing, it's temporary. We'll know soon enough."

The plastic tags were thin and Talzani held about fifty—yellows, reds, and blues. He cradled them in the palm of his left hand, brought up his right, and began to absently shuffle them.

"The legs will be the biggest problem. That's always the case. Legs, legs, legs. For every arm I've amputated up here, I've probably taken ten legs. Puzzling, isn't it?" He waited for a response, but Mark was watching the plastic, watching how the topmost tag changed with each shuffle: red, blue, yellow, blue. "I'm not sure why this is. I think human legs simply weren't designed for modern war."

Talzani stopped his shuffling. He looked at the tags in his palm and, with a careful surgeon's hand, reached in to pull out a yellow. He dropped it on Mark's chest. "Take it easy. Get some rest."

But Mark still stared at the plastic in Talzani's hand.

"You're going to be all right," the doctor said, leaning over, trying to meet Mark's eyes. "Do you understand?"

But Mark couldn't stop looking at the tags.

"You're going to be all right." Talzani turned and moved on to the next man.

He awoke to find he was being shifted onto a stretcher by two orderlies. They took him out of the cave, and Mark shut his eyes tight against the sudden light. He felt himself drift with the lulling motion of the stretcher—head rising and falling, feet rising and falling—and listened to the regular scrinching sound of the canvas each time his weight shifted.

They carried him to the recovery ward. At some time in the past, the building, standing on a level stretch of land sixty feet from the cave mouth, had been a shepherd's hut. Now it more closely resembled a beachside cabana, with a makeshift reed roof and only two walls, and it was filled with those who didn't require the cave's warmth to survive the cold nights. The orderlies moved several of the other wounded to clear a space, then hoisted Mark off the stretcher. They settled him on the stone floor, threw a thick blanket over him, and walked away.

Through the gaps in the roof, Mark saw a pallor of sun. He breathed the fresh air in deeply, but occasionally the smell of the cave came to where he lay. Each time, the stench of waste and disease lingered, seemed to cling to his clothes and nostrils. He would wait, taking short, shallow breaths through his mouth until he felt steady enough to inhale deeply once more.

In late afternoon, he heard the sound rise within the cave. It was low and indistinct at first, like the hum of a generator, but it grew in pitch until Mark could pick out individual voices, individual cries. Others in the recovery bay began to pray. Mark looked to the cave.

The orderlies brought the blues out on stretchers, lined them up in a neat row. There were five of them, and their mouths gulped at the sky like feeding fish. One could move his hands, and he used them to shield his eyes against the daylight.

The mullah from Harir came over the bluff. He went to the

stretchers and walked among them, squatting down to speak, leaning close to hear a whisper. Talzani emerged from the cave. With a nod from him, two orderlies lifted up the first stretcher. The mullah took a Koran from his robe and read aloud from the holy book as his right hand went out to touch the forehead of the dying Pesh Merga. Mark watched the procession move away, the mullah still reciting, still touching the man's forehead, Talzani following, his hands clasped behind his back, his head slightly bowed.

The prayers of the men in recovery grew louder. Mark closed his eyes. The report of a gunshot. Mark twitched but kept his eyes shut. Four or five minutes later, another shot. Then another. Another. After the last one, Mark opened his eyes and stared into the reed roof.

A shadow fell over him. Talzani. Holding the revolver at his side, he gazed down at Mark. His face was white and his eyes were clouded glass.

"Do you know what Pesh Merga means?"

Mark nodded, but Talzani seemed not to notice.

"It means 'those who face death.' A romantic name, don't you think? Poetic. I myself have never seen one face death; they all turn away at the end."

The doctor looked to the ground, ran a trembling hand through his short black hair.

"It's not so easy, is it?" he asked quietly. "Without your camera, it's not so easy."

He started back to the cave, holstering the gun as he went.

The cloud cover blew off that night. Beyond the reeds, Mark saw a thousand stars.

An afternoon cool and clear, the clefts of the surrounding mountains dark with the runoff of melted snow. Mark sat on the edge of the promontory, a hundred yards from the cave mouth, and slowly opened and closed his hands. It felt as if thin needles were being stuck deep into his joints, but the fingers were bending, straightening, coming back to him. He reached for his knees. Even through his heavy trousers he felt the swelling. He rubbed them until the pain made his eyes water. It had been five days since the explosion, four nights since the river. That morning, he had sent a boy to settle his account at the hotel and collect his things; his camera bag and knapsack were now in the shade of a rock outcropping beside the cave.

Below him was the road. It hairpinned down the mountainside to disappear amid the stone homes of Harir. At the far end of the town it reappeared, twisting past fields and hills before turning north to slip behind a mountain. Somewhere beyond that mountain, the Turkish frontier. The Jeeps would leave at nightfall. Mark was determined to be on one.

He tucked his feet under him, set his right hand on the ground, and rose again. His knees wobbled but held. He waited for the trembling to subside, then took a small step. His legs felt disembodied. Another small step, his body teetering to either side.

"You are doing well."

Mark turned to see Ahmet Talzani coming over the broken ground. In the daylight, his doctor's coat appeared splashed with brown paint. Mark looked back at his own feet and took two more timid steps. Talzani's feet scraped on the ground close by.

"Very good. Very good, indeed."

Mark stumbled and came down hard on his right foot. The pain shot through his hip, into his head. He inhaled sharply.

"It hurts today?" the doctor asked. "Excellent. Pain is always preferable to numbness."

Mark resumed walking and Talzani fell in alongside, watching the tentative steps.

"You should have crutches," he said.

Mark knew this wasn't an offer but an observation. "I'll be okay."

When he tripped again, Talzani caught him by the arm.

"You're overanxious, you're making mistakes. Here, rest." Talzani gently helped him into a sitting position on a boulder. He sat alongside and took a cigarette pack from his coat. "Maybe you should wait another day."

"No," Mark said, "I have to get going. I'm late as it is."

"Suit yourself." Talzani lit his cigarette with a small gold lighter, tilted his head back, and released a plume of smoke. He sniffed at the air. "Spring. A wonderful time of year here. Living in that cave, I would even forget there are such things as seasons if I didn't force myself to take these breaks." He held the cigarette up. "Breathe air, look at the world. And, of course, one reaches the point of diminishing returns; if I stay too long in there, I begin killing more patients than I save." He laughed lightly, looked to Mark. "And the other photographer, he is leaving with you?"

"Colin? No, he's staying a few more days."

The doctor nodded. "I haven't seen him come by. I would have thought he'd visit you after your accident."

"I doubt he knows about it. He left for the lowlands the day before it happened."

"Ah, that explains it." Talzani smiled. "Anyway, all you war people think you're immortal—probably not good for morale to see a colleague end up in Harir cave."

Mark smiled back. "No, probably not."

They fell into a comfortable silence. For some minutes, they gazed out at the mountains, Mark rubbing his sore hands, Talzani nursing his cigarette, raising it to his lips, rolling it between his fingers. "Still," he said, finally, "I trust you've had an enjoyable visit."

Mark studied the doctor's profile, realized he was serious. "Oh, it's been a real treat, Talzani. I can't understand why you don't get more tourists up here."

Talzani laughed. "Sorry. It's the Moslem in me—a point of honor with us to make sure strangers are content."

They watched a shepherd moving his flock up to pasture on a distant hillside. The sheep were white with black feet, and they looked almost dainty scrabbling over the rock-strewn slope. Talzani folded his arms over his chest, lolled back on the boulder.

"Probably the way the whole world was two thousand years ago," he said, "this kind of life, this kind of beauty. But a cursed place. Beautiful and cursed. I wonder sometimes how that works. Do we see its beauty despite the war, or because of it?"

Mark remembered other places. Afghanistan, Mozambique, Cambodia. Jungle, mountains, desert, savanna. In each one, he had found beauty. In each one, he had felt the land held something sacred. He was thinking of this when Talzani spoke again:

"We're about to be crushed," he said. "The BBC is reporting the Iraqis have expanded their offensive. Already they have taken most of the plains, and now they will come into the mountains. Every hour the news is worse. More dead, more wounded." He looked to the western horizon, as if for a sign of the invaders. "As you can imagine, the world is outraged. The Americans are giving speeches about it in Congress. The UN is debating a resolution of condemnation." Talzani sighed. "But that's okay, that's okay, it's not their fault. We've been losing wars forever; it's what we Kurds do best."

He stood up, flicked the cigarette out over the escarpment. He stepped to the edge and peered down.

"You know, in my lifetime—just my lifetime—we have fought eight wars: the Turks twice, the Iranians and Iraqis three times each. If you go back to my father and my father's father, you cannot even count them all—Turkey, Iran, and Iraq but also Syria, Russia, the British, the French, everyone. We are like the little guy at the bar who wants to fight all the big men. We get beaten up by one, then get up off the floor and go after another. Over and over. A lifetime of war. Can you imagine?"

"Why do you stay?" Mark asked.

Talzani looked to him and shrugged. "Where am I to go, Mr. Walsh? I am only from one place." He kicked at a large stone, as if try-ing to dislodge it from the ground. "Not that I always accepted that, of course. When I was studying in Michigan, I hated Kurdistan, hated the war, the leaders who always kept it burning. I wanted nothing to do with it. I was going to stay in America and have a good life. I was going to be a surgeon—a real surgeon—find a wife, live in a great big house." He chuckled, shook his head. "Great big house. If I had kept all the limbs I've cut off here, I could have built a mansion with them."

The rock was too large or the earth too dry. Talzani stopped his kicking and strolled back to the boulder.

"Homeland. It doesn't matter what you do or even what you believe, you never escape the homeland. It always keeps you. They talk of free will, but we are all just homing pigeons in the end."

With the doctor again beside him, Mark gazed down at the vil-lage. A breeze was coming up from the valley and it brought sounds—the tinkling of goat bells, a shouting child, a calling ven-dor—across the miles of air.

Mark saw a figure in black appear on the road below, leaving Harir and walking toward them. He sensed Talzani's attention fix on the figure as well. After a time, Mark recognized the mullah. He looked to the cave mouth and saw that a stretcher had been brought out.

"How many today?" he asked.

Talzani reached into his coat for another cigarette. "Just two. And one burial."

He motioned with his head toward the cave; off to one side was an odd-shaped bundle of dark plastic about six feet long, tied off at either end with white rope.

"They found it by the river this morning—badly decomposed but a man. I had it wrapped in plastic for the smell." Talzani rolled the cigarette back and forth between his fingers as he stared at the bundle. "A curious case. The feet were severed—very jagged wounds, the bones shattered, so clearly an explosion of some sort, a land mine, most likely—but then his hands were tied together. A bootstrap. Someone had tied his hands together like this"—Talzani crossed his own wrists—"with a bootstrap. I cannot account for this." The doctor looked to Mark, gave a quick, incredulous laugh. "You see? It's very puzzling, isn't it?"

"Yes, I guess it is."

Talzani flipped a hand in the air, as if shooing a fly. "Ah well, these little mysteries, morbid curiosities, war is full of them."

In silence, they watched the mullah ascend. He held a Koran in his hands and seemed to be reading from it. His black robe curled and billowed in the wind. Mark smelled the burning tobacco, heard its dry crackle when Talzani inhaled.

"What do you bring with you, Mr. Walsh?"

Mark turned to him. The doctor held the cigarette poised, close to his lips, as he watched the approaching mullah.

"What do you mean?"

"When you come to a place like Kurdistan, a dangerous place, what do you bring?"

Mark shrugged. "Cameras, some filters. The clothes depend on the climate."

Talzani shook his head. "No, no, I mean what charms?" He

looked to Mark with a tired smile. "Surely you carry some talismans to keep you safe."

Mark reached into his jeans pocket and brought out a small, silver-black coin. He held it out to the doctor. "An Indian head nickel. Over sixty years old. My grandfather gave it to me when I was a boy. It's been through every war with me."

Talzani took the coin and studied it, turned it over and over between his fingers. The mullah was passing just beneath them, almost to the crest. Talzani handed the coin back.

"I'll tell you something I've learned from being here, Mark. I think it might help you."

Mark felt himself draw back a little, his toes curling in his shoes; it was the first time Talzani had ever used his first name.

"There is no pattern to who lives or dies in war. Most of us, we can't accept that. We invent all kinds of explanations and superstitions for why things happen. 'He died because he lost his nerve, he died because he forgot his lucky coin.' None of it is true. In war, people die because they do. There's nothing more to it than that."

He reached into his coat pocket and took out the stack of plastic tags. He held them up, as if offering them to Mark.

"My little tags. A pattern, no? A scientific method to decide who lives and dies." Talzani withdrew the offering, cradled the tags close to his side. "If only it were so."

Mark remembered the evening in the cave, watching as Talzani had shuffled the tags.

"Would you believe that sometimes I am so tired, or the cave is so dark, I'm not even sure of the colors I give them? Would you believe that men have been given blues, have been set aside to die, suffering from nothing more than dehydration or a broken arm? Disturbing, I know, but it's true."

The doctor lifted the flap of his coat pocket and carefully placed the tags back inside.

"Well, those were simply mistakes, of course, but always there is this question of what is a blue, and this is not at all about science or medicine, just mathematics. In quiet times, when there is not a lot of fighting and I have more time, maybe even the man with a stomach wound has a chance. But then more wounded come in and he is out of luck, because now anyone who is going to take up two hours of my time to save is not worth saving. And then more wounded come in, and now the time is down to an hour, a half hour, twenty minutes. You see how it goes? Simple math. Math and luck."

He scraped his foot over the pebble-strewn ground, leaving a swath of cleared dirt.

"But don't imagine I lie awake at night thinking of these things. No. I sleep very soundly. My little tags are for them, because they need to believe there is a system. For me, I know it is all fate. Once you understand this, it makes life here much easier, for you are freed of this idea that you can prevent something from happening. Some live, some die, that's all."

The mullah reached the promontory. He started toward them, but Talzani motioned for him to wait. The mullah stopped, and Mark noticed for the first time that he was middle-aged, with a dark beard and very white skin; as he stood there, thirty feet away, staring at them, he seemed as impassive and still as a statue.

Talzani leaned closer to Mark, rested a hand on his shoulder.

"You were very lucky," he said. "You know that, don't you? The head, the spine, if there had been any complications . . ."

Mark looked into the doctor's solemn, sad eyes. He forced himself to smile. "What, you would have shot me?"

"Yes," Talzani whispered, lightly patting his shoulder. "Yes, I would have done that for you." He let his hand slide off, gazed over the valley. "Some live, some die. It's the only way to view it. Anything else is just self-torture and arrogance. Because we are not gods, none of us are gods."

He rose, started toward the waiting mullah, then suddenly turned.

"Oh, good news. I secured a place for you in one of the Jeeps to the border. It leaves at eight."

"Thank you, Ahmet," Mark said. "Thank you for everything."

The doctor shrugged, walked away.

Mark stared out at the valley and listened to Talzani's footsteps recede until they were lost on the wind. He looked to the hillside where the shepherd had been. He no longer saw the man or his black-footed animals and assumed they had reached the crest and descended the other side in their search for pasture. Reaching into his vest pocket, he took out his wallet, the photograph he had not viewed in over a month. It had developed a number of creases over the past three years, the colors losing their luster, but her smile was still radiant, her hair still black and soft, and Mark stared at her image with a tenderness and longing that was now safe for him to feel.

He looked out at the road. In his mind's eye, he saw it stretching clear across Kurdistan, over the frontier, all the way to the place where she was.

A gunshot. A soft echo that rolled back from the far mountainside. Mark leaned against the rock, his back to the cave, and waited for night to come.

TWO

Elena worked at the tack with her nails. It came free abruptly, slipped past her fingers. She heard it bounce several times on the bare floor and turned to see where it had fallen, but it was lost from sight in the great expanse of pitted wood.

Stepping from the chair, she rolled the poster and set it in the corner with the others. The white walls of the living room were bare once again. She searched the floor, paced back and forth, but the tack seemed to have disappeared.

She gathered the posters in her arms and carried them to the office closet. She turned to the plants next. The smaller ones, those that sat upon windowsills, were quickly removed to their proper locations in the apartment—the ferns to the kitchen, the miniature orange tree to the bedroom. Only the large jade posed a problem. Elena took hold of its trunk with one hand, the edge of its pot with the other, and dragged it over the floor and down the long hallway to the office.

A quick sweeping up of the bits of dirt that had spilled beneath the windowsills, and the living room was returned to barrenness. A couch, coffee table, and lamp in the corner beneath the last window, a slide projector upon a chair in the very center of the floor, a stereo system arranged along the inner wall, these and the electrical cords that ran to outlets were the room's only furnishings.

It was not what Elena had envisioned when she and Mark had moved into the converted warehouse the previous summer. The renovation had been rudimentary, the carpenters simply connecting two large storage areas, leaving one as the living room and transforming the other into living quarters—two bedrooms, a bathroom, and a kitchen—with thin partition walls. This gave the back rooms an insubstantial, temporary quality, but the living room made up for it. It was magnificent: well over forty feet long—perhaps closer to fifty—and about half as wide, with four tall windows that overlooked the street, and Elena had imagined Oriental carpets and light furniture, great plants bending to the light. On the day they moved in, though, Mark had set the couch in the corner, hooked up the stereo, and declared the room complete.

"I'd like to keep it simple," he had said.

"But this isn't simple," Elena had replied, "this is monastic. It's just empty space."

"In New York, empty space is a luxury."

They had compromised. The living room to his aesthetic, everything else to hers. So, the bathroom had seashell-shaped soaps and linen towels. The bedroom walls were adorned with photographs of her family, posters of Spain, and impressionist art. The spare bedroom—their joint office—was covered with more photographs, more posters, funny cartoons from the New Yorker, and, in return, Mark had his cavernous living room.

And, in truth, there were times when returning home from her day in the city, after being jostled on sidewalks, crammed into elevators and subway cars, Elena found the vacantness of this room soothing. Slipping off her shoes and jacket, she would lie on the couch, watch the play of sunlight on the wood floor, the patches of lighter white on the bare white walls, and feel rejuvenated. But this feeling was not constant. More frequently, she felt as if she were in an abandoned hall, the walls as dreary as those of a prison cell, and this feeling became unbearable when Mark was away. For days before he left, Elena would study the room speculatively, deciding which poster should go where, which plants on the windowsills might cast the most interesting shadows, and Mark was no sooner on his airplane than the transformation began.

She went to the bathroom, slipped out of her shorts and T-shirt, and into the shower. The water pressure in this area of Brooklyn fluctuated dramatically, and Elena had learned to simply move out of the stream during the cold stretches, the near-scalding stretches, that to fiddle with the faucets only made matters worse.

Mark had called from Istanbul at seven that morning to say he was catching the next flight to New York. They had only talked for a moment—he was rushing to catch the plane—but he had sounded good, happy to be out of Kurdistan, to be coming home. She asked how the trip had gone, and he had said, "Good, I'll tell you all about it when I get there," but Elena knew he wouldn't. He never did. "It was a good trip, it was a bad trip, it was so-so," that was about all Mark ever said, and it was only through hearing secondhand snippets from his photographer friends, or through studying the photos he published in magazines and newspapers and imagining him at the other end of the image, that Elena could divine what he meant by good, what he meant by bad. He kept the details of his work to himself, as if it were all some desperate secret.

She wondered how he would be this time. Probably much like every other time. Thin. Tired. He would be quiet for a few days, waiting for his mind to adjust to peacefulness the same way eyes had to adjust to the dark.

He came in late afternoon. Elena heard the door creak open, his footsteps on the buckled floor, and went out to the living room and there he was, standing in the day's last light.

She went to him, kissed his neck and face, ran her fingers along the sharp line of his jaw.

"Mark," she said, "I thought you'd never come home."

He smoothed her hair away from her face, looked into her deep brown eyes, and he was so grateful to see her again, to feel his fingers gliding through the softness of her hair, that he felt a clamping on his throat, as if he might cry.

"I missed you so much," he whispered, his voice thick and hoarse.

"The leaves are going to bud soon," he said. "It's spring."

They stood by one of the living room windows, looking out at the ginkgo trees that lined the sidewalk. He had one arm around her middle and pointed with the other, and Elena looked at his raised hand, its tremble, its crosshatched pattern of narrow red cuts. She touched the knuckles.

"What happened?"

"Meadow grass." Mark lowered his arm, pushed the hand into his trouser pocket. "It's like razor blades."

She turned to him and his other hand fell away.

It was an unusual face, a combination of exaggerated features—full, almost feminine lips, a long straight nose, green eyes—that somehow worked in combination to make him attractive. Not handsome in any traditional sense but a face made compelling by its energy, the stare and light of the eyes.

But something odd about the face as well. Elena could never precisely remember what Mark looked like when he went away. It had disturbed her at the beginning. When he had left for an assignment just two months after their meeting, Elena had lain in her bed that first night alone and tried to conjure his image. She could not. The mouth, the jawline—the eyes, certainly—one by one, she recalled each of his features, but she could not place them together to make his face. She had risen from the bed and dug through her desk drawer for the few photographs she had of him, but even in these the face seemed different from the one she knew.

But Elena had grown accustomed to this. Now, each time Mark went away, she accepted that she would lose her memory of him, that each reunion would bring with it a sense of startled recognition.

This time, the sensation did not come. In the tautness of his jaw, in the hard prominence of his ribs as she embraced him, in the tentative hand around her waist, Elena struggled to find something familiar. Now, standing before the window and looking into Mark's exhausted green eyes, Elena could well imagine that if she had passed him on the street that afternoon, she might have seen nothing to spark her memory and would have continued on her way.

Even with the door closed, Elena's song carried into the bathroom. It was a melodramatic Spanish pop tune, full of impassioned trills and sudden pauses. Mark couldn't tell if the pauses were part of the song or lapses in Elena's concentration as she moved through the kitchen, opening the refrigerator, taking down glasses from the cupboard.

He ran the bathwater. A great billow of steam rose to dampen and obscure the air. Elena's song could no longer be heard.

He had fled. There was no other way to describe it. Whenever there had been moments of difficulty in the past, Mark had gone to a neutral place for a few days, a quiet hotel in some foreign city where he could live off room service, listen to music, stare for hours at television shows he didn't understand, where he could find sanctuary until the fear or tension or anger dissipated enough for him to return home. But this time, he had not waited. Reaching Van at daybreak, he had taken the first flight to Istanbul, flown directly on to New York, and as soon as he stepped into the apartment, Mark knew he had made a mistake. This time, of all times, he should have waited. In the misting bathroom of his home, he felt helpless and besieged, gripped by a loneliness deeper than any he had ever known.

Waiting for the tub to fill, he lowered the toilet lid and sat. Small linen towels hung on a rack at the far end of the room. On the sink beside him a basket was filled with little soaps in the shapes of seashells. The steam grew thicker, and Mark watched the linen towels slowly lose their shape, then their color, in the dense air.

He rose and paced the small room. The mist swirled around him, breaking to let him pass. The tiles were cool under his toes, becoming slick.

He went to the sink. The mirror was clouded over, and Mark saw nothing but a faint shadow of himself on its surface. He opened the door of the medicine cabinet. The shelves were filled with things of Elena, her brushes, powders, and perfumes. There was little of his there. The entire room became indistinct in the steam. Looking down, he could not see his own feet.

"Mark?"

No answer, so Elena opened the bathroom door and stepped into the hot, thick fog.

He looked dead, his head lolled back on the porcelain, one hand dangling over the edge. Elena instinctively looked into the tub, as if expecting to see red, but the water was only gray. She saw his chest expand then, saw the vein pulse on his neck, and she closed her eyes for a moment.

She took his hand and gently settled it in the water. Mark's forehead wrinkled, but his eyes didn't open. She sat on the edge of the tub and watched his sleeping face.

"Mark?"

She looked over his body. Through the murk, Elena saw its mottle of bruises. Picking up the hand she had placed in the water, she examined the cuts. They were shallow—little more than scratches, really—and she took the washcloth from the soap rack and began to bathe him. She wondered if she were rubbing too hard, but Mark never moved.

He was filthy. The dirt came off him in dark clouds, turned the water a deep brown.

"I've never seen anyone so dirty," she said. "When was the last time you bathed?" But Mark didn't awaken, and she continued to bathe him.

While washing his hair, she felt the raised, torn skin at the back of his head; in his sleep, Mark flinched, roiled the water.

Elena worked her fingers through the soapy hair until she found the cut. It was puffy and a violent purple, a thin, jagged line of blackened blood down the middle.

"Oh, Mark," she said, hearing the note of exasperation in her voice, "what did you do to yourself?"

She took a bottle of antiseptic wash from the bathroom closet and poured a capful onto the cut. With a clean washcloth, she lightly scrubbed until the dried blood fell away. Beneath was a welling of clean red blood. The cut didn't appear to be infected.

Elena pulled the stopper and watched the brown water recede, watched Mark's body emerge from the grime. Now, the bruises on his body stood out, glistened. Some were as small as coins, others bigger than her hand—blacks, purples, reds, all ringed with an ugly gray-yellow border. The sight seemed somehow too intimate for even her eyes. She took down the shower attachment, rinsed his hair and body until the water ran off him clear and clean.

"Mark?" She kissed him on the forehead. "Stand up. Let me dry you off."

Her kisses, even her light slapping of his cheek, had no effect, and Mark lay in the well of the tub like a corpse. Elena gave up trying. Taking the largest towel from their closet, she draped it over his body and dried him as best she could. She started by softly dabbing at him, but then rubbed harder. She wadded up a portion of the towel in her fist and ran it over his chest as if scouring a pot. She smiled while doing this. It reminded Elena of how her mother had dried her as a child, the way her mother would run the towel across her chest until it tickled so much Elena would wiggle out to dance around the bathroom laughing. That was not going to happen with Mark, but it did open his eyes. He looked up at her remotely, then smiled. He reached a hand to her cheek, brushed a finger below her eye.

"I missed you," he said.

When she got him into their bed, she lay beside him, watched his eyes close, listened to his breath settle into its deep, slow rhythm. She ran her fingers through his damp hair—he was so clean now, so peaceful in sleep. Elena moved closer, felt the warmth of his body beneath the comforter, and whispered words in his ear: "You're home now. You're safe now."

Mark jolted awake, instantly alert. Staring at the high ceiling of the bedroom, he listened. He thought a voice had aroused him, but the apartment was deathly quiet. He waited to hear Elena's footfall in the hallway, but no sound came.

He became aware of a regular dripping sound behind his head.

Looking out the bedroom window, he saw a soft rain falling from a leaden sky. It appeared to be afternoon. He slid his legs out from the covers and stared down at his feet.

He had once asked a soldier in Nicaragua about his worst experience on the battlefield, and the man had told a story of being awoken by a dawn mortar attack, of how panicked he had felt being caught barefoot in the jungle and how, even as the shells had dropped through the trees around him, he had taken the time to put on his socks and boots. The soldier had meant it as a funny anecdote, and Mark had laughed along with him, but afterward he discovered he had inherited the man's fear. Ever since, whenever he was in the field, Mark kept his hiking boots on, even when he slept, if there was the slightest chance something might happen. In Kurdistan, he had gone many days and nights without taking them off.

Now, he gazed down at his feet as if seeing them in a new way. How soft and fragile they looked. He flexed them, watched the thin bones, thin as straws, stretch against the white skin. The design of them—joined at the top of his foot, radiating out to his toes—reminded him of a fan, or perhaps an exotic flute. He remembered that he and Elena had made love that morning, or maybe sometime during the night.

He rose and went down the hallway to the kitchen. Waiting for the kettle to boil, he flipped through the mail Elena had stacked on the foyer table. A couple of postcards from friends, some royalty checks from the agency, but Mark didn't read or open anything. The kettle whistled.

She had placed her note on the kitchen counter next to the stove. "Running some errands; be back around 2:00. I love you, E." Mark looked at the clock on the wall; it was a little after three.

With his coffee, he went to the bathroom to shave. Once the week-old beard was gone, he saw that his face had become drawn. He pressed at the hollows beneath his eyes, the pronounced knobs of his cheekbones. It felt like someone else's face. He checked his throat. In places, he had shaved off the scab over the chafing wound, revealing a long, narrow line of bright pink skin. He studied the cut in the mirror, turning his head from side to side, decided it was barely noticeable.

He went to the bedroom to dress. The clothes he chose—black trousers, a beige shirt—were baggy on him now. He went out into the living room, slid a Beethoven symphony into the CD player, and moved the volume knob up high. A popping of static, and then violins filled the empty air. He looked about the room.

His place. A great expanse of white walls, wood floors, and sunlight. Four huge windows that mirrored the four windows of the identical warehouse—unrenovated and unoccupied—on the other side of the street. Symmetry and starkness, a vista free of clutter, a view onto an unpeopled world of rooftops and sky.

He tried to remember if he had ever paced off the room. Not that he could recall. Calculating now, he believed he could cross its length in fourteen or fifteen long strides. Setting down the coffee mug, he stood against the wall and moved his heel back until it touched the baseboard. He started across.

He watched the scarred wood pass beneath his feet. The base of the far wall entered his field of vision, came closer, and then his toe touched. Eighteen steps. He turned, set his heel against the wall, and walked back. His toe touched the wall. Eighteen steps. He picked up his coffee. It had gone lukewarm, tasted bitter on his tongue.

Eighteen. Not bad. Not bad for someone who, seven days earlier, had felt the earth beneath him turn to powder.

A single sob escaped from his throat. It came without warning, as spontaneous as a hiccup, and then it was gone. It was so quick, so unconnected to any feeling, that afterward Mark could almost believe he had imagined it.

Elena checked over her shopping list. She had decided against the strawberries—small and misshapen—but had found everything else. She thought of the first time she had done this: Mark had phoned from London to say he was coming home, and Elena had gone to the grocery store, to the wine shop and florist, to celebrate his return with tulips and champagne and imported chocolates. It had been an excitement, spending money without care, buying whatever caught her eye.

Back then, the longing had seemed romantic. The danger he was in, the chances he took, Elena was able to live with the worry by telling herself that what Mark did was important, even noble. Asleep in their bed, nothing but cold pillows beside her, or sitting on the couch with a book, and then the harsh ring of the telephone and it would be him. A scratchy line, usually, with a maddening echo that kept them from hearing each other until they settled into a pattern of speaking and listening, and he was calling from Colombo or Luanda or Phnom Penh, he was calling at midnight or five in the morning, at any horrible hour of the day or night because he had been waiting hours for the operator to patch him through, and the inconvenience of it all, the image of him pacing in some shabby room all those hours, wondering if his call would ever go through, the growing urgency he must have felt as time passed filled Elena with a thrilling sadness, and long after the calls ended—after they had said "I love you" over and over again on lines crackling or fading into silence—she would lie in their bed, stare at the dark ceiling, and think of him; walk through the living room and try to recover every word they had spoken. She would fall back to sleep or go off to work buoyed by the knowledge that, for that brief moment, she had known everything about Mark that was important, that he was safe, that he loved her, and Elena tried to hold that moment until the next call that might come in five days or three weeks, might come at any time of the day or night.

But that had been at the beginning, three years ago. Now it was different, and on this day, as she joined the long queue at the check-out line, Elena felt a certain, unshakable detachment.

This sensation was not new or mysterious to her. It had started to take hold nearly a year earlier, in the hallway of a hotel room in Chicago, on the day they buried Stewart Kunath.

Elena hadn't known Stewart well. A fairly heavyset midwesterner in his late twenties with a quick, high-pitched laugh, he had been a member of Mark's fraternity of New York–based war photographers, the boys who went out drinking together when they were in town, who traveled with one another on the world's battlefields. Stewart had gone over a land mine in the Helmand desert of southern Afghanistan. Mark was in West Africa at the time, but had come back for the funeral in Chicago.

During the graveside eulogies, Mark and the other photographers had gathered a little apart from the rest of the mourners. Elena noticed how they fidgeted, how uncomfortable they all seemed, when David Richardson, the British photographer who had been with Stewart in Afghanistan, stood by the coffin and spoke of how Stewart had always sought beauty and essential truth in his photographs, of how his family might find some small comfort in knowing he died a quick and painless death. David's words, delivered in an elegant public school accent, had floated on the light wind and Stewart's family appeared grateful for them.

That night, they held a photographer's wake for Stewart in a hotel suite near O'Hare. Someone had rented or brought along a slide projector, and the separation of the sexes that always occurred at these events soon set in, the men crowding into one room to cast Stewart's photos on a wall, the women gathering on the veranda with Susan, Stewart's girlfriend. Occasionally, sounds from the men came to where they sat—whistles of appreciation, even laughter—and it had seemed bizarre to Elena, even cruel. Susan seemed not to notice. She stared past the hands that stroked her hair, her arms, to the lights of the city.

Later, Elena had come upon Mark and David and a couple of other photographers in the suite hallway, talking softly and clutching beer bottles. They went quiet when they saw her. Mark grinned, reached out an arm for her, but Elena stepped past him to face David. He leaned against the wall, his head lolling slightly from side to side, his eyes bloodshot and half-lidded.

"What was it really like?" she asked.

David stared at her, blinking slowly as if he were about to fall asleep. When he spoke, the elegant accent was gone. "He begged for his Mum and morphine. I held him. He died for nine hours."

And the other men all nervously raised the bottles to their lips and drank. Back in their own hotel room, Mark had tried to comfort her but instead only made things worse. "Why do you think I don't tell you what happens out there?" he asked gently, rubbing her back. "Why do you think none of us talk about this?"

That weekend in Chicago altered Elena in a way she would not have predicted. After that, she stopped suspending her life when

Mark went away. The longing held no thrill, the worry she resented, the belief that his work was noble had left her. She understood then that two lies had been spoken over Stewart's grave, that what compelled Mark and the other photographers had nothing to do with a search for beauty or truth, that this was simply something they told themselves to avoid thinking any further. After that, Elena had stopped waiting for Mark's calls, had started meeting friends for dinner again. It was a healthy change, she realized. The form of Mark's life meant she could not expect the usual things, that distance was required. Now, Mark was only important to her when he was home.

But this was not the way she wanted it. Now, after three years of this, she wanted a life free of fear, free of the strategies she devised to make it all bearable.

She placed her groceries on the conveyor belt and watched the cashier run them over the laser reader. The three heads of cellophane-wrapped iceberg lettuce tumbled their way along the belt. Lettuce was what Mark always missed most, and Elena now envisioned him sitting at the kitchen table, eating one bowl of it after another. The thought made her smile.

"So, how was it?"

At the opposite end of the kitchen table, Mark nodded. "Good. I got a lot of good pictures."

"Just good?"

He nodded again, and Elena smiled.

"On the phone, you said you'd tell me all about it when you got home, remember?"

Mark smiled back at her, but there was a trace of challenge in his eyes. "What do you want to know?"

"Well, for one thing, what happened to you? You're all bruised, you're limping, and you have a cut on your head."

He slowly set the fork onto his plate. "Nothing, really. I got lost in the dark and fell in a river, got dragged over some rocks." He gave a quick shrug. "That's all."

Elena looked down at her own hands, picked at a fingernail. "You must have been dragged for a while—you're black and blue."

"Yeah. I guess I'm getting kind of old for this. Can't get bounced around like I used to."

She glanced up to see he was watching her, still smiling but his face conveying very little. "Why didn't Colin come back with you?"

"I don't know," Mark sighed. "He said he wanted to stay a few more days, see what was going on down in the lowlands. I didn't really see the point to it, but . . ."

"Diane isn't happy about it. She's almost due, you know."

He nodded. He reached out for a spoon on the tabletop, began turning it over and over with his fingers. "What is she, eight months?"

"Eight and a half. She'll kill him if he isn't back in time."

Mark's nod became more emphatic as he stared at the twisting spoon. "He'll get back. He won't miss that. Just a few more days is all."

"But the plan was you two would stay together, come back together."

Mark set the spoon flat on the table. "You know Colin. This has happened a dozen times before. He wanted more material, and what was I supposed to say? It's not like I'm his protector out there."

But, of course, he was. That was why they traveled together, to watch over one another, to help each other in and out of bad places. And, yes, they'd split up in the past, come home weeks, even months, apart, but back then neither was about to be a father.

"Do you wish I'd stayed there with him?" he asked, and he said this in such a soft, earnest way that Elena felt her slight annoyance evaporate. She rose from her chair, went and settled on his lap, took his arm to wrap it around her middle.

"No." She kissed him on the forehead. "I don't wish that." She rested her head against his, stared down at his half-eaten salad. "I just don't understand what happens to you guys out there, the way you think." She sat up, looked into his face. "Do you even think about us when you're out there?"

His eyes were sad and faraway. He tightened his embrace of her but slowly shook his head. "No. On the way out and coming back, but while I'm there, I try not to think of you at all. When I do, it makes it unbearable."

She rose and took his hand, led him to the bedroom. Naked, her skin shivered by the afternoon chill, Elena lay on the bedspread and watched him undress. When he came to her, she placed her hands on his chest, traced the curve of a rib, felt the desperate beating of his heart.

When they lay in bed that night, Mark moved beside her and held her close.

"I should probably go back to work tomorrow," she said. "I have to finish a field report."

He kissed her neck. "Okay."

She wanted to roll over, to face him, but his arm kept her in place. "Unless you really want me to stay home another day."

He kissed her neck again. "Of course I want you to stay another day."

Elena stared at the hand that lay heavy on her shoulder. "I mean, unless you need me to."

A quick twitching in his fingers, a brief tension in his body, and then it was gone and the fingers were caressing her arm, trailing her shoulder blade. "No, I don't need you to. I'll be fine."

She tried to turn to him again, to explain or maybe just look into his eyes in the dark, but his arm still held her. Then the next kiss on her neck, longer, with an air of finality that meant no offense had been taken, that she should just close her eyes and sleep. And when Elena awoke in the middle of the night, she was pleasantly surprised to find his arm was still there. Mark had rarely held her in his sleep. He usually lay flat on his back at the far edge of the bed.

It was a harmless lie. No field report was due—nothing at all was due—but the work Elena did on Thursday afternoons was what mitigated all the sadness that passed over her desk during the rest of the week. For those Thursday afternoons, she had dragged herself out of bed, sick with flu, had walked through subzero weather—once even trekked the four miles from home to office when a broken water main had closed down the subway—because missing those hours, letting the task fall to other hands, would make everything else seem meaningless. Mark knew what she did on Thursday afternoons, but Elena didn't think he knew how important it was to her.

The New York office of the United Nations High Commissioner for Refugees was located on the twenty-sixth floor of the main UN building, the famous landmark beside the East River where delegates debated and tourists took photographs. From her office window, Elena had a view only of other office towers and—if she stood close to the glass and peered straight down—a small strip of East Forty-fourth Street.

On her wall, a world map was stuck with over one hundred pins, a visual record of the UN-assisted refugee camps on five continents. In the four years she had occupied the office, Elena had added dozens of pins and removed three.

The map pins followed a pattern. The clusters of green—in Malawi and Angola, in Thailand, a lone pin stuck into Hong Kong—marked camps with which Elena had worked as a program officer in the past. The five white pins bunched together in Pakistan were her current concern. The reds—the most common color—were camps she had yet to be involved with. Other coordinators had developed more sophisticated systems for their maps, used different colored pins to indicate outbreaks of disease or famine, colored thread to show transnational migrations—Ugandans in Kenya, Tibetans in Nepal—but for Elena the simple record of her own role was enough. In slow moments of a day, she would sit at her desk, gaze at the red pins, and ponder which camps she might request during the next rotation. At other times, the pins reminded her of the liquidity of populations, the ease with which people became dispossessed in the world.

She had come into the job almost by chance. Just out of Madrid's Complutense University with a degree in public administration, she had hoped to find something with UNESCO. In Geneva, the personnel officer—a middle-aged woman with a beautiful, silver-threaded sari and an unpronounceable last name—had told her sadly that it was impossible, their Spanish quota was already exceeded. Impressed with Elena's grades and four languages, she recommended her to Refugees.

"An excellent career path, a growing field," the woman had said, and her face remained so serene and kindly that Elena didn't immediately realize this was intended as black humor.

The Spanish quota at the High Commissioner for Refugees was also filled, but they were willing to make room for Elena; even better, they offered her a posting in New York, a city she had always dreamed of visiting. Elena, who had imagined a career organizing cultural exchanges, of accompanying Spanish flamenco dancers on goodwill tours to mainland China, immediately accepted. Just two weeks after her twenty-third birthday, she had said goodbye to her mother and aunts and uncles and cousins at Barajas airport and set off, leaving her own homeland to help people who had lost theirs.

One week in New York and she knew she had made the right choice. She loved the city, loved the job. After a year of working under others, she had been given her own project to manage, coordinating the UN programs for a refugee camp in the Guatemalan highlands for Indians displaced by the civil war.

When first introducing Elena to his parents, Mark had told an elaborate joke that had them meeting there, at that camp. That Mark, down in Guatemala on a photo assignment, had seen Elena among the army-issue tents and barrels of chlorinated water and—with her long, wavy black hair and olive skin—mistaken her for an unusually tall refugee until she had finally introduced herself. Their actual meeting had been far less dramatic—an awards ceremony for a prominent Spanish photographer in a ballroom of the main UN building—but the refugee camp story had Mark's parents quite convinced until Elena good-naturedly pointed out its implausibility.

As a program officer, Elena rarely went into the field. Her work was seeing to the administrative needs of the camps from the comfortable vantage point of the New York liaison office, filing requisition forms for blankets and cots, making sure there were sufficient stocks of penicillin and toilet paper. In truth, she had made only two visits out to the refugee camps, both times as a member of a larger delegation and both times somewhat reluctantly.

It was not something she advertised around the office, but Elena had no desire to become a camp administrator, the open ambition of most of the other New York staffers. She had heard enough of the disasters—the flash flood that had swept away hundreds of Cambodian refugees on a Thai riverbank in the '70s, the kerosene-contaminated rice that had killed dozens in Ethiopia—to want never to stand face-to-face with those suffering and tell them there was nothing she could do, that she had made a mistake.

The horror that passed over her desk—muted by its reduction onto paper, sanitized into the language of bureaucrats—was enough for her. In those reports and eyewitness accounts, she could feel the despair, hear the sounds of a family or a village dying, smell the awful stench of it, and had no wish to get any closer.

Instead, she collected the dry testimonials of miracle. Pregnant women stepping through the gates of a camp and immediately giving birth, having carried their unborn for ten, eleven—once even thirteen—months, nature refusing to deliver up a child to peril. Old men, hobbled and battered with age, hiking over mountain trails for weeks, snow their only nourishment. Families separated in a night of fleeing, finding each other again in a place of sanctuary. Elena savored these miracles, made photocopies of them, had a file drawer filled with them.

And on Thursday afternoons she became one of those who made miracles happen. Every Thursday, the UN field officers throughout the world filed roster addendums with New York, lists of any new refugees who had arrived at their camps during the previous week. Along with the rosters came search requests—hundreds of them sometimes—as the new arrivals looked for any relatives already living in the camps. It was still just paper and numbers and names, but as she methodically worked through the search requests, Elena could see in her mind the faces of those she touched, those who might rediscover their place in the world. In her office on this Thursday morning, Elena sat beneath the map and waited for afternoon to come.

Mark's slides would be ready by noon. Out the living room windows he saw a brilliant blue sky. It was nearly three miles to the development lab, and he anticipated the refreshment of air and sunlight the long walk would give him.

The side streets of Brooklyn were settled into the quiet of midmorning. He looked for the sprouting of bulbs in the tiny front gardens, for small green leaves on the trees he passed, but it was still early for that. He listened to his feet scuffing over the sand that remained on the sidewalks, the last sound of a New York winter. The day was a bit cool for the thin windbreaker he wore and he found he could not help walking briskly. His legs felt strong—the exercise made them tingle in a pleasing way.

Despite all his deliberate tarrying—looking at the window displays of the antique shops on Atlantic Avenue, detouring to the Promenade in Brooklyn Heights—he reached Purcell Street an hour early. On the sidewalk outside Aperture Studio, he was at a loss as to how to pass the time—he didn't want to talk photography with the technicians—until he saw the familiar yellow awning of Chung's China-China Restaurant a few storefronts down. He and the other photographers who used Aperture often went to Chung's when they found themselves waiting out a last-minute delay or the filling of a specialized order. He bought a copy of the *Times* and strolled down to the restaurant. The little bell above the door tinkled when he stepped inside.

The dining room, a dozen plastic-covered tables beneath gaudy Chinese lanterns and red brocaded wallpaper, stood empty in the lull before lunch. Chung peered out from the kitchen, his face pinched with annoyance. He was a cadaverous man in his late sixties, tall and bald, so thin his bones seemed ready to burst through the skin. Recognizing Mark, his irritation vanished, and he hurried out to the dining room.

"Ah, Mr. Walsh! Welcome, welcome."

He stopped with a few feet between them and scrutinized Mark, the clothes that hung off his body, the stretched skin around his jaw and eyes. He broke into a wide grin.

"You lose weight." Chung gave a thumbs-up sign. "Looking sharp!"

He led Mark to his usual table by the window.

"Someone to join you?"

"No," Mark said. "I'm alone."

Chung cleared away the extra place setting. "You are gone for long time. Vacation?"

"My job," Mark said.

"Good job for you." Chung patted his own sunken middle. "Give you lots of exercise."

Mark ordered his standard meal—Szechuan chicken—the only palatable item he had found on the China-China menu. To the sound of Chung chopping and banging pots in the kitchen, he glanced over the front page of the newspaper. In the bottom right corner was a two-column headline: "Iraq Widens Kurdish Offensive; White House Voices Concern." He skimmed the first three paragraphs, then set the paper aside.

Mark no longer read about war zones where he had been; now these places only interested him before he went and while he was there. Because if he had learned one thing over the past nine years, it was that most modern wars did not end. They continued for generations, heating up at times, cooling down at others, but the flames never went out. How many articles about the latest Mideast peace talks or Belfast bombing or Kashmiri uprising could a person be asked to read in the course of a lifetime? Who had the strength of heart to stay passionate about the struggle for a free Tibet or an independent Sahrawi or a score of other causes around the globe, causes that were lost now and would still be so in fifty years?

For Mark, war had become a job, and when stripped of its grim romanticism, what this job seemed to most closely resemble was speculating on the stock market. To prosper, one had to guess which wars would rise in public interest, which would wane. Which war was headed for a spike, a crisis that would draw American diplomatic involvement or, even better, armed intervention? The war industry even had its blue chips and its penny stocks, the bush wars no one cared about that ground on in anonymity until the day one side perpetrated a particularly grand atrocity. The photographer or journalist who saw it coming and went in at the right moment could make a fortune. The key to picking wars, as with picking stocks, was in reading the trends, knowing when to buy in and when to bail out.

If all this sounded cynical, it was a cynicism Mark had learned from the marketplace. Kurdistan, a perpetual second-tier conflict, was a textbook case.

He glanced at the *Times* headline again. A strong White House reaction to the Iraqi offensive, one that raised the specter of American retaliation, would have placed the story in the top right corner of the front page, made it the lead on the network news, and would have increased both the market for and shelf life of Mark's photos. White House "concern" meant the administration was going to do nothing, that the *Times* story went below the fold, that his photos were worth less, and that he had less time—a week, perhaps—to move them before Kurdistan dropped out of the news completely.

Still, Mark reminded himself, he had not gone to Kurdistan expecting American intervention, only on the hunch that the Iraqis would launch a spring offensive, one large enough to briefly float the war back into public awareness—and he had been right about that. If he had been wrong, the trip and all his photos would be worth close to nothing.

Colin had been smart enough to escape the hard-news scramble. Having long since turned to doing "industrials" to pay his bills—shooting modern factories or smiling employees for companys' annual reports, assignments that could earn a photographer $10,000 or $15,000 for a couple weeks' work—Colin had been able to undertake his periodic sojourns into war zones without concern for deadlines or topicality. To approach them with an artist's eye. For him, the place was largely incidental to the broader subject matter, his photographs of draftees or petty bureaucrats or funerals from one war added to the portfolios he had compiled from others. It was only when Colin felt he had amassed enough images along a theme that he would finally do something with them—an extended photo-essay or an exhibit in a gallery—and there was a sense of coherence to these collections, of thoughtfulness and depth, with which hard-news photos could not compete.

In truth, there were times when Mark had been a bit envious of Colin's situation. Not of his success in doing industrials, certainly, but at least of his lack of urgency when they were in the field. But, of course, it was the very difference in their approaches to war, the absence of direct competition between them, that made them such well-suited traveling companions.

Mark stared out the restaurant window. Few people passed, and he wondered if Purcell Street was always so empty at this time of day.

He remembered the last time he had eaten at the China-China. It had been with Colin, the day before they left, biding time while the Aperture clerks gathered their purchases from the storeroom. They had been excited, eager to escape the New York winter, to be in the field once more, and they toasted their good fortune with Chinese beer. It had been only seven weeks ago, but felt much longer.

Above all else, Mark needed time. It was what he had told himself upon first wakening in the Harir cave, what he had intoned a thousand times in the eternal days since. He would tell Elena what had happened on the mountain, in the river, in the cave, he would tell her all of it, but first he needed to make sense of it himself.

Because the best part of Mark had ended on that hilltop. He had known it instantly, even before stumbling down the hill, even before looking over his limbs to see they all were still there. At that very first moment of gazing into the gray sky, his body trembling and numb, Mark had seen the future that awaited him, both the future of the next hour and of ten years, and he had understood that when he rose from the rock and started down the hill, he would be walking into a new life, that never again would he be the easy, confident man he had been. And perhaps this was what he needed time for most of all, to reconcile himself to his new fate.

But sitting in the front window of the China-China, a question slowly formed in his mind. What if he never reconciled himself to it? And then another. What happened to scars that were never acknowledged? Did they just go away? It was a thought, the beginning of an idea, that made his heart race, but Mark couldn't be sure if this racing stemmed from fear or from hope.

His gaze fell on the headline in the bottom right corner of the *Times*. He drew the paper to him and slowly read the article leader, turned to the inside page and read the rest of it.

The Iraqi offensive, spearheaded by tanks and artillery, was sweeping over the desert plains, quickly crushing whatever resistance the Pesh Merga offered. Apparently, the Kurds now planned to form a new defensive line in the mountains, where the terrain would hamper the Iraqis' mobility.

Mark had witnessed armored assaults in the desert before, and there were few things more terrifying. With the sound of artillery carrying over the flat ground for fifty miles, with the fine earth kicked high into the sky, what approached you was not tanks or soldiers, but a colossal wall of noise and powdered dirt, a slowly advancing avalanche that turned day into twilight, that gradually closed your range of vision to a few feet, that finally gave you the sensation of being buried alive. How many men in how many wars had vanished in those storms, their remains forever lost beneath the settling dust?

Mark lowered the newspaper and gazed out the window, but what he saw in his mind was Colin. He was in the lowlands, standing alone on the desert plain, and the wall of earth and thunder was rolling toward him, closing on him, and then it was upon him and he was gone in its brown mist. The image made Mark's throat go dry.

The China-China's awning was an egg-yolk yellow, and on this sunny morning it cast the window tables of the restaurant in a garish gold tinge. Each time someone came along the sidewalk, Mark glanced quickly, hoping he would recognize a fellow photographer, disappointed by each unfamiliar face that passed.

"Ah, Miss Morales, good afternoon. Welcome!" Sem, in his shirt-sleeves and tie askew, looked up from his computer, a great smile already on his face. He held up a sheaf of papers and laughed. "There are very many this week!"

Upon being assigned the Pakistani camps five months earlier, Elena had enlisted Sem's help in processing the search requests, both because the camp populations continued to grow at a rate she found difficult to keep pace with, and because she knew the middle-aged Cambodian man enjoyed the task. Every Thursday after lunch, they met in a drab, windowless records room on the eighteenth floor, took over the two vacant computer consoles at the far end.

"Any luck?" she asked.

"Not so far, but I've only done six." He was still smiling.

She took the seat beside his and turned on the console. Sem lifted about half the papers from his pile and presented them to her with both hands, as if offering a gift.

"Amazing," Elena said, riffling the papers. "There must be over three hundred this week."

"Four hundred and twelve," Sem said. "I counted."

"Because of that assault on Kandahar?"

He nodded. "I'm thinking so. A very big storm."

Sem had a habit of referring to war in terms of weather. At first, Elena had attributed it to his incomplete command of English, but she had gradually realized he meant it as metaphor and had begun using it herself. When a battle engulfed a town, it was like a storm overwhelming a ship at sea, smashing it, ripping it apart, and a few days later, the remnants, the survivors, drifted in to safety as if on a slow tide.

She scanned the add-roster pages of the report from Loralai Camp—281 new names—and turned to the first request.

"Farida Wahed Rabbani, DOB 3/14/47, POB Helmand, Afghanistan, seeking whereabouts of son Mahmoud Ali Rabbani (DOB 11/2/66; POB Kandahar, Afghanistan), daughter Anahita Wahed Rabbani (DOB 4/24/71; POB Kandahar, Afghanistan), brother Hamid Shah Khalis (DOB 3/14/47; POB Helmand, Afghanistan)."

"Twins."

Sem looked over, puzzled. Elena held up the page for him to see, pointing out the two birthdates. "She's looking for her twin brother."

Sem's frown cleared and he nodded quickly. "Mixed twins. Very unusual in Cambodia."

Elena entered the name of Mahmoud Ali Rabbani, watched the small red light as the machine scanned the database. The red light went off and a message appeared on the screen: "No Record Found." She tried Anahita Wahed Rabbani and then Hamid Shah. "No Record Found," both times. Elena took the request and placed it face down to the left of the computer.

"Ah," Sem cried, clapping his hands together, "got one!"

Elena smiled, watched Sem rapidly click letters on his keyboard.

"Mr. Sayed Khan Aziz of Gulistan Camp II," he said to the screen, "your mother, nephew, and two sisters are waiting for you at Darbak Camp in Peshawar. Good news for you, my friend!"

After putting the thirty-four boxes of slides in chronological order, Mark was ready. He drew the blinds on the living room windows and pushed the couch and coffee table across the floor until they were beside the projector, then settled on the couch with the remote control in his hand. In the glow of the white square of light cast upon the far wall, he took up his notebook and flipped through his first pages of notes.

He had tried to develop the professional's habit of keeping a frame-by-frame record of the rolls he shot in the field but always found the system impossible to maintain; scrupulous for the first three rolls, his Kurdistan notes had quickly degenerated into little more than scribblings of dates and basic subject matter. It was enough, though. A photojournalist always knew where his good frames were, remembered the long stretches of uneventfulness. Mark clicked the remote control, and the white square disappeared, replaced by the first image of Kurdistan.

He went through the first six boxes quickly. Nothing too exciting, but a few that could go to stock—Kurdish women breaking down old bolt-actions, earnest Pesh Merga cadets going through drills with stick-guns on their shoulders, a nice shot of a young boy bayoneting a sawdust dummy. Mark pulled the good ones and set them in a pile on the coffee table, wrote down their box numbers on a blank page in the notebook. He could take more time with the stock later; the important thing was to get the photo-essays together for Amy at the agency.

The ambush started on the seventh roll. Mark turned to a clean page and slowed the clicker in his hand, took time with each image.

Leading off, the Iraqi convoy—two troop transports and a Jeep—coming through the ravine, approaching so slowly that no dust kicks off the dirt road. Mark stopped on the fourth slide: the vehicles centered in the frame, empty road at either edge giving the viewer a sense of perspective and unity, nice human detail with the lead transport driver hanging his arm out the open window. He took the slide from the stack, placed it on the table, and went on.

The attack begins, spumes of dirt as bullets gouge the road, soldiers leaping from the trucks. Very quickly four Iraqi soldiers are down in the road, smoke and dust, a globe of orange flame bursting through the canopy of the lead truck. Halfway through the roll, and an Iraqi is caught in the instant of going down, his legs buckled, a hand reaching out to break his fall. The slaughter continues, recorded in three-second increments. Flame spreads through the canopy of the lead truck until it is a pyre, the second truck starts to smoke. Thirty-six, the last slide, and now the Jeep is gone—stuck fast in the ditch, pitched almost on its side.

Mark glanced at the numbers he had written in his notebook, counted the short stack he had made on the table: five keepers off one roll. He readied the eighth box of slides, clicked the remote control button.

The ambush already winding down now, no one moving below. Six Iraqis in the road, two more on the rocks, the transports burning black, the three passengers in the Jeep slumped over and still. Then, the strange moment that had caused the Pesh Merga around Mark—already out of their sniper nests and scrabbling down the rocks—to dive for cover: two Iraqi soldiers popping up from the rocks beside the road, weaponless, staring straight up at Mark, their faces white, their mouths open, shouting something. Frame six, and their hands are coming up as if to surrender. Seven, and they seem to remember this isn't a surrendering war, and they have turned to run up the road. Good legs beneath them and the element of surprise, and they are moving off, becoming just two brown-clad backs on the edge of focus. Eleven, and the one on the left stumbles, starts down. The other turns—blurred profile—watches his comrade go, but no chivalry among the dying and he keeps on, arms pumping, head bent low, feet kicking up dust with each great stride, keeps on until he is out of focus, until he is in the fifteenth frame and then he falls, too.

Down on the road then. The Pesh Merga rushing from one Iraqi to the next, still tense, still pumped, finishing off the wounded with quick bursts to the head. The twenty-fifth frame, and it's done with. The Pesh Merga in front of the burning trucks smiling into the camera, exultant, firing their guns in the air, stripping the bodies. Thirty-three, and a Pesh Merga dances in the road, his gun held aloft with both hands, an Iraqi soldier at his feet.

Mark walked to the wall to study the image more closely. He remembered now. The Iraqi's head had been completely destroyed, flattened against the earth. An extraordinary shot, the horrific scene in the foreground, the rapturous joy of the dancing Pesh Merga behind. Mark returned to the couch, took the frame from the chute, and set it to one side. Too grisly for the essay or as a stand-alone for the domestic market, but a good prospect for the Asian magazines.

The ninth box, and more of the ambush aftermath. The Pesh Merga settling down now, the adrenaline draining off fast. They walk among the dead pensively, with eyelids so heavy they seem ready to fall over and sleep right there. Picking their way back up the mountain slope, laden down with their booty—guns, boxes of grenades, gold necklaces with Koranic amulets—and they look like so many beasts of burden, their dirt-streaked faces blending into the brown rock they pass.

Mark turned off the projector, sat back, and rubbed his eyes. He counted the ambush slides he had pulled: eleven. More than enough for the photo-essay, but he was still tempted by the sequence of the two running soldiers. He retrieved the eighth box from the floor.

He now saw that the first frames were slightly blurred; the Iraqis had popped up too close, just at the forward edge of his depth-of-field. Perfect clarity in the first part of their run, but they were moving away from the ambush site, the reference point of bodies and burning trucks slipping off frame. Besides, he had too many shots for the photo-essay already. And so, Mark reluctantly put these slides back in their box, finally accepting that the story they told, of two men trying to outrun fate, would never be known to anyone else, was destined to be just one more secreted chronicle of the dying.

Another yelp of triumph from Sem. "Miss Feroza Durrani of Shagai Camp I, a fine day for you! Your husband and children are safe and waiting for you in Darbadin Camp. Many hugs and kisses for the little ones."

Elena laughed, leaned over to give Sem a playful nudge with her shoulder. "You're crazy."

Sem giggled, a high, girlish sound.

At one time, Elena had been plagued with the possibilities for error. Those possibilities existed everywhere. If a refugee was illiterate, it was up to the camp worker to decide how to spell the names in the search request, how to convert them from Arabic to English. Then those names could be garbled in transmission, entered wrong by her or Sem. How many people had remained lost to each other, Elena wondered, because a name had been mistranslated, because she had typed a wrong number in a birth date? Was there a system to catch such things? Elena didn't know. But she had finally decided she could not think of these things; Sem could not think of these things. When they went home on Thursday nights, they could only think of those they had found.

She also no longer dwelled on what lay ahead for the people in her camps. By the time of despair, when the refugees finally understood they would never go home, would never find another country to take them in, Elena would have moved on, would be working with new camps, the old ones fading to green map pins on her wall. Forgetting those people she left behind, it was the only way to bear it. But on Thursday afternoons, she was with them, helping them in their moment of renaissance, after the horror, before the hopelessness, and Elena could almost believe this moment might be stretched forever, until all the children found their mothers, all the families found new homes. She knew this could not be true—all the pins in her wall, all the papers that crossed her desk, told Elena this could not be true— but on Thursday afternoons anything seemed possible, and it was hope that sustained her.

A few more for stock, and Mark remembered the long days of boredom, of waiting around for something to happen, for something interesting to shoot. Box twenty-nine, the roll he and Colin had run off during the drink-hazed afternoon in Ranya. Colin as Third World boulevardier at the sidewalk *chaikana*, eyes hidden behind sunglasses, raising a teacup filled with whiskey in toast. Colin as Pesh Merga, turban sliding over his left ear, Kalashnikov held at-arms, teeth bared in mock menace. Reverse shots when Colin had taken the camera: Mark the boulevardier, Mark the Pesh Merga, Mark the Pied Piper, surrounded by little kids begging for chocolate and pencils. And then the two of them together, when they had found the shopkeeper who knew how to use a camera: Mark and Colin sitting before the small metal table, arms around each other, smiling out at the world.

Mark put the slides back in their box and placed it on the couch beside him. Elena would enjoy seeing them. He'd pick out the good ones to show Diane.

By six, he had finished. He rose, turned off the projector, and opened one of the window blinds. The day had remained clear, the sky over the rooftops cloudless, the blue slipping into the deeper hue of evening. He stretched, felt the stiffness in his legs.

He took in the expanse of his living room. He walked to one end, moved back until his heel touched the wall, then started across.

Twenty-one steps. This puzzled him. He couldn't remember how many paces it had taken him yesterday, but he thought it had been less. Wondering if he had lost count, he crossed again. Twenty-one steps.

Mark leaned against the wall and stared at the patch of light cast on the floor from the uncovered window. Against his will, his gaze moved across the room, to the slide boxes on the coffee table. He felt the coming of tears and turned quickly to the window. The light dazzled his eyes, made everything he saw glitter like jewels.

He stood in the middle of the living room, barefoot and disheveled. Elena set down her briefcase, draped her coat over the hall table, and went to put her arms around him. "I missed you today."

"I missed you, too," Mark said.

Past his shoulder, Elena saw the boxes of slides, the strewn papers on the coffee table and couch. "You already started going through them?"

She felt him nod. "Pretty much finished. I'm meeting with Amy tomorrow."

"How do they look?"

"Good. Two strong essays and a lot that can go into stock. It was a good trip."

Still holding him, Elena looked about the living room. It was a moment when she wished there was more furniture because she wanted to sit with him.

"I don't ever want to lose you," she said.

Mark pulled back and smiled down at her. "You won't."

"But what if you disappear?"

The smile ebbed from his face. "People don't just disappear, Elena."

"But they do. They do all the time. I look for them every day."

He gently broke their embrace, took her by the hand. "Come here; it's going to be a beautiful sunset."

They walked together to the far window of the room, the vantage point where they could see the greatest portion of sky.

THREE

"It doesn't look like we'll be having too many more of these lunches," Elena said, "just the two of us."

Diane smiled, ran a light hand over her swollen belly. "Two weeks, and then I'm done with the little monster. It'll be so nice to walk around without feeling like I'm carrying a watermelon."

They were meeting at the Land of Thai, one of their regular spots for these late Friday afternoon lunches. The hour worked well for both of them. Elena had never been able to break the Spanish habit of eating late, and these days Diane preferred avoiding the noontime crowds. At three o'clock, there were few people in the dining room, and they could take their time, relax in each other's company.

Diane leaned over the table. "But you know what's really weird? Everyone thinks I'm a tourist all of a sudden. On the cab ride up here, the driver said he'd show me all the sights of Manhattan for fifty bucks."

Elena laughed, cocked her head to the side as she appraised her friend. There *was* something different about her. Diane was large-framed, of sturdy Scandinavian stock, and had always seemed robust, but in the last stages of her pregnancy a bright blush had come into her cheeks, her blond hair become even lighter. "I can see it," she said. "You look too healthy to live in New York."

"Great. Healthy, and prime candidate for every mugger on the street." Diane smiled, shook her head in mock disgust. "So, how's Mark?"

"Okay," Elena said. "Still a bit tired from the trip, I think. He's meeting with his agent today."

"Still black and blue?"

Elena nodded. "Still limping a little, too, but there doesn't appear to be any permanent damage."

Diane grinned. "I swear it's just arrested development with those two. How many grown men go around falling in rivers? Well, I guess it gives him another story to tell the lads."

Elena had first met Diane shortly after she started seeing Mark, at an engagement party for another photojournalist. Mark was collared by one of the men, led into a discussion, and Elena slowly strolled through the room, smiling pleasantly to everyone who met her eye, staying to the periphery of conversations. She felt out of place. The men talked about guerrilla groups and photography, their exploits in the field. Their wives and girlfriends—all of them too pretty, too glamorous—formed their own circles to talk about restaurants and children and movies.

There was a tap on her shoulder, and Elena turned to find a blond woman in her midthirties—older and not as thin as the others—smiling at her, her hand extended. "You're Elena. I'm Diane, Colin's wife. Mark told us you were coming."

Elena had met Colin, Mark's best friend, a few weeks before. It had been at another function where she felt out of place, a photo-gallery opening, and Colin had been solicitous, had even asked her questions about what she did.

Diane stood with Elena and gazed around the room at the clusters of men talking with each other. "Pretty weird, isn't it? Photojournalists think they're so fascinating, but get a bunch of them together and they're as boring as doctors or lawyers—stand around and talk shop, let the women go off and do their women things. But that's better than actually getting caught in one of their conversations—endless horror stories about F-stops and shutter speeds." She leaned close to Elena's ear. "Want some advice? I love Mark—he's a sweetheart—but he's still a photographer, and they're all alike under the surface. Don't ever ask his advice on taking pictures. Buy your own camera, something completely automatic, and don't ever let him touch it."

Diane caught herself then. "Oops. You're not a photographer, are you?"

"No." Elena shook her head, smiled.

Diane looked relieved. "Good. I mean, I didn't think so. There are a lot of female photojournalists out there, some really amazing ones, but you rarely see them at something like this; I suspect they have a broader range of interests." She motioned toward one of the circles of talking women. "Male photographers tend to choose women who are beautiful and dull and adoring. Impossible to talk with most of them. I go crazy at these things."

Diane caught herself again, seeming to notice for the first time how pretty Elena was, how easily she might fit her description. She sipped her drink. "I think I'll stop talking now."

Elena laughed. "The dull part I can do, but I'm not very good at adoration."

She and Diane had stayed together for the rest of the party, and afterward the four of them went out to dinner. Elena admired Diane's playful, gently teasing manner with Colin. They seemed to have struck a balance in their lives, Diane proud of Colin and his work but not in awe, not about to let her own career—she was a curator at the Metropolitan Museum of Art—become secondary to his. After that night, Elena found she was grateful for Diane's presence at parties and dinners, saw her as another woman who understood the anxiety of being with a war photographer but who carried on her own life in spite of it. And eventually theirs became a friendship in its own right, independent of the men, a friendship cemented by late lunches on Friday afternoons.

"I'm worried about Colin."

Elena glanced up to see that Diane had pushed her salad away.

All her attention seemed directed at the napkin wadded in her hand. "You haven't heard from him?"

Diane kneaded the napkin. "No. It's been nearly two weeks. I know that's not so unusual, but . . ."

"Mark said he wanted to see what was happening in the lowlands, that he was just taking a few more days."

"I know, I know." Diane nodded wearily. "But why now? I mean, here I am, two weeks away from delivery, and my husband's off gallivanting around Kurdistan. He's such an asshole." They both laughed, but then Diane gazed out the window to the street, and Elena saw the worry lines in her face. "The lowlands . . ." She turned to Elena. "That's where the Iraqis are attacking, isn't it? I saw it in the paper yesterday."

Elena nodded. "But I'm sure he's fine, Diane. He's been doing this a long time. He knows when to get out."

Diane gave a weak smile. "I'm sure he's fine, too, but he won't be if he doesn't get back here pretty quick."

Elena sipped from her water glass. "How about I send a cable to the Kurdish camps?"

"Kurdish camps?"

"The refugee camps," Elena said. "They're run by the Red Cross, but there's a lot of UN people over there."

Diane appeared dubious. "What would that do?"

"They could ask around for him. I'll put a priority code on it. A blond, six-foot-four American, he's certainly going to stand out in a crowd."

"But it's a huge area we're talking about, Elena. I don't even know where he was headed."

"Mark probably does, and he's coming by the office after work tonight. I can get the details from him and just send a cable. What could it hurt?"

Diane considered, slowly shook her head. "I don't know. The idea of some UN guy running up to Colin and telling him he has to call his wife, he'd be so pissed." She shrugged. "On the other hand, fuck him. Yeah, let's do it. If it's not too much trouble."

"No trouble at all." Elena took a pen from her jacket pocket, tore off a section of her paper napkin. "What do you want to say?"

• • •

Amy Mavroules exhaled smoke, looked Mark up and down. "You look like hell."

"Thanks," Mark said. "I feel like hell." He sank into the leather armchair across from her desk. The desktop was strewn with papers, enlargements, manila folders. To one side, a large glass ashtray filled to overflowing with the white filters of Virginia Slim cigarettes doubled as a paperweight.

"Good trip?" she asked.

"I think so." Mark undid the clasp of his manila envelope and slid the contents onto his lap. He handed across the first glassine sheet, the seventeen frames he had selected for stock, together with his typed page of captions. Amy stabbed her cigarette out, put on bifocals, and placed the sheet on her desk viewer.

Amy was a tall, painfully thin Englishwoman of Greek ancestry, with wild black hair and spidery fingers. She had a weakness for indigenous clothing—the excessive colors of Guatemala, the mirror-studded fabrics of Nepal—which didn't suit her; on first meeting, Mark had thought her appearance somewhat clownish. It was deceiving. In her early fifties, Amy Mavroules was one of the best independent photo agents in New York, and it had taken considerable effort on Mark's part to become one of her clients. Now she spent several silent minutes studying his work, reading the captions, peering at the slides.

She took the sheet from the viewer and held her hand out for the next one. "Nice shots, but a bit too human interest. I'll send them around, but don't count on much unless Kurdistan goes gold."

Amy had found her analogy for the business of war in the music industry. For her, wars that made headlines had "gone gold," only the most dramatic among them able to "hit platinum."

Mark gave her the second sheet. It contained the slide of the head-shattered Iraqi soldier in the road, five other splatter-shots. Amy glanced over them quickly, set the sheet to one side. "Ouch. I'll get those out to the Asians."

He gave her the next sheet. "It's an ambush of an Iraqi convoy. They killed nineteen soldiers, knocked out two transport trucks and a Jeep."

Amy read Mark's paragraph caption, then looked at each slide closely. "Good sequence. Too bad *Life* only does pap now, but I'll run it by them anyway. We should be able to find something in Europe. There's a lot of Kurds in Germany, aren't there? Or am I confusing them with the Turks?"

Mark nodded. "Both. Kurds and Turks."

"Okay," she said, "I'll try *Stern*."

He handed over the last glassine sheet. Amy read the label he had placed on top, peered at him over her bifocals. "The worst hospital in the world?"

Mark shrugged. "A working title."

Amy shook her head. "Something else; they'll think it's some new Medicare scandal." She set the slides on the viewer, picked up Mark's last page of notes.

Mark watched her face settle into a rapt grimness as she read through his captions. She took time with these slides, examined each one. After the last frame, she slumped back, gazed at him. "Jesus," she whispered, "that's an incredible piece of work, Mark."

"Yeah?" He smiled.

She looked at her watch, came forward quickly. "I'm going to put it up for auction. I'll photofax to all the national weeklies, tell them I need an answer by Tuesday afternoon." She sifted through her papers, found a pen, and started scribbling notes on the back of an envelope. She stopped abruptly, glanced up. "The *Times* magazine is sending a reporter to Burma, and they need a photographer. Interested?"

"Burma? Sure."

Amy pointed at the viewer where the triage slides were still propped, still backlit. "They see those, they'll take you in a second." She went back to writing.

Mark watched her with satisfaction. Amy had never recommended him to the *Times*.

She lit another cigarette, squinted at him through the haze. "Anything else?"

"No, that's it."

"Okay, I'll ring you."

Mark rose to leave, but halfway to the door she called after him. Turning, he saw that Amy already had the telephone receiver to her ear, but she was frowning, staring at his legs. She looked at his face. "You're limping. Are you all right?"

"Just got a bit banged up," he said. "I'll be fine."

Amy's frown cleared. She tapped the sheet of triage slides with a long fingernail and smiled. "Very nice work, Mark."

He smiled back.

He arrived bearing champagne and a dozen roses. As he described his meeting with Amy, Elena tried to shift out of her somberness, to join in his excitement.

"She's auctioning them? That's wonderful," she said, but heard the lack of enthusiasm in her voice.

Mark appeared not to notice. When he had finished, he rubbed his hands on his knees. "So, let's drink champagne." He scanned the office shelves, as if expecting to find glasses there, then looked to Elena. It was only then he seemed to realize their moods were divergent. "Something wrong?"

She shook her head. "Not really. I had lunch with Diane today. She hasn't heard from Colin and she's worried."

Mark sat back and stared at the wall above her. He began to slowly nod. "Yeah. Yeah, I know . . . But it's just been a few days."

"But it hasn't been just a few days, Mark." She pointed to the calendar on her side wall. March 9 was circled in blue ink. "You were supposed to come back on the ninth. What day was your accident?"

Mark glanced at the calendar for a moment. "It must have been the seventh."

"The seventh. And that was the day Colin left for the lowlands?"

He nodded.

"It's now the sixteenth. That's nine days."

Mark turned from the wall. "Okay, but nine days doesn't mean much in Kurdistan. It's easy to lose nine days in a place like that."

"I know, but Diane is worried. I offered to send a cable."

"A cable?" He frowned. "To who?"

"To the UN people over there, to ask if they've seen him."

Mark's gaze flitted about her office, as if searching for something to focus on, but nothing seemed to satisfy. Finally, he sighed. "Look,

I think it's a very nice gesture on your part, but I also think it's premature. Nine days doesn't mean anything in Kurdistan. Wait a bit. If he shows up and the UN are running all over Kurdistan looking for him, it's going to be embarrassing. And I really doubt the camp workers over there would appreciate being—"

"Embarrassing?" Elena felt her temper rising, the red moving up her neck and cheeks. "Is that the most important thing to you guys? Diane is about to have a baby, Mark. Her husband is in a war zone, she hasn't heard from him in two weeks, and you're worried about embarrassment?"

He stared at the desk. Condensation from the champagne bottle had created a pool of water. The pool had spread to the edge of the desk, and at regular intervals a small drop broke free to fall to the carpet. The roses lay beside the champagne. "Okay," he said. "You're right."

"Thank you." Elena flipped to a clean sheet in her legal pad. "Now, where did you last see Colin, and where was he going?"

Mark looked at the flowers. "Let's see . . . it was in Rawanduz, that last morning, the seventh. He said he wanted to go to the lowlands for a few days, just see what was happening down there. I told him I was going home, that I had all I needed."

"But did he say where he was going exactly?"

He thought for a moment. "No, I don't think he had any particular place in mind. I mean, there's a road straight down from there, but once you're out of the mountains, there's a hundred little villages, different roads. He could've gone anywhere."

"And when did the Iraqi offensive start?"

Mark turned to the calendar. "I'm not sure. I first heard about it around the eleventh, maybe the twelfth, so probably a day or so before that."

Elena finished writing, set the pen down. She stared across the desk at him. "Should we be worried, Mark?"

He looked directly into her eyes, saw her apprehension. He shook his head. "No. Colin's very careful. He doesn't do stupid things."

The concern left her face, replaced by a bemused smile. "That's your department, isn't it?"

Mark frowned, didn't understand what she meant.

[64]

"Colin told Diane that you're the one who always comes up with the bad ideas out there, nearly getting you two killed."

He looked down at his hands, folded in his lap. For some reason he couldn't quite identify, Mark found the comment wounding, as if a confidence had been betrayed. "I suppose that's true," he whispered. He tried to think of something else to say, but couldn't. "I suppose that's true."

Elena took up the legal pad and came around the table, leaned over to kiss him on the cheek. "I'm sorry. I meant it as a joke. Kind of." She kissed him again, then straightened. "I'll take this down to the telex operators, then we can go celebrate, okay?" She lightly scratched her fingers across his back. "I'm glad your meeting with Amy went so well. I really am very proud of you, you know."

Mark looked up, gave her a fragile smile.

Above them, tree branches chafed each other in a strong breeze. They climbed the winding path arm-in-arm, and Elena felt the pressure of him with every step.

"Are you okay? Do you want to go slower?"

"No, I'm fine. The knees are just a little stiff."

They passed through the arched doorway and entered the Cloisters. Mark was surprised at how empty it was; they had the place practically to themselves on this Saturday morning. But it was still early, he remembered, and the museum at the northwestern edge of Manhattan was difficult to get to.

He had not wanted to come to the Cloisters. The day was sunny, the warmest since he had returned, and he would have preferred a walk through Central Park or along the waterfront, but the museum was Elena's favorite place on the island and he had relented. He feigned interest in the exhibition rooms and naves, at the columns and arches and tapestries she led him to, but the light slanting through the stained glass windows beckoned him outside. When they neared the treasury room, with its glass cases of jewel boxes and gold figurines, he put a hand on her back.

"I think I'll walk in the courtyard. Take your time, okay?"

He pecked her cheek and moved away, out the great oak door and into the Bonnefont Cloister. The sun shone, the wind did not reach the sheltered garden, and Mark felt grateful for having left the silence and musty chill of the building. Breathing in the day, he strolled the perimeter of the small courtyard several times.

He stayed on the walkway, beneath the arches, noticed the simple pattern of the terra-cotta tiles he passed over, the way the sunlight bathed his face each time he reached the west side of the court.

He stopped before a small plaque and learned he stood in an herb garden, that the small plot of land he had been circling contained over 250 varieties of herbs cultivated during the Middle Ages. Mark stepped out into the garden. He bent to study the stems of a wintered bush, the serrated edge of a brown leaf, with no idea of what he was looking at.

He had always felt a certain impatience in the last weeks of winter for some sign of spring, of regeneration, but, now, gazing over the barren garden and finding no encouragement filled him with a hard, almost angry, sadness.

He left the cloister and went out to the promontory that overlooked the Hudson River. Here the wind struck him at full force, combed his hair straight back on his head. A painful glare came off the water, off the steel spires of the George Washington Bridge, and he squinted against the brilliance of the morning. As he stood there, he felt his mood suddenly lift, as abrupt and transforming as a light ray piercing fog. Now, in the clean, cold air that buffeted him, in the sunstruck water and steel that burned his eyes, in all the wintered plants he could never identify, Mark saw beauty, endless possibility. The joy he felt just then was as expanding as the turquoise sky.

Elena stood beside the small window and watched him. Again and again, he paced the courtyard, his head bent, his legs dragging over the bricks. From behind, he looked like an old man, hunched and shuffling with age. When he turned, she saw the pain lines on his face.

He was getting worse. The limp, the pain, despite everything he said, it was getting worse. It occurred to her then, and then a moment later she realized why she hadn't seen it before. He was keeping it from her, letting out the pain only when he thought he was alone.

She saw him step down from the walkway, into the courtyard garden. He moved among the plants with terrible deliberation, stooping over a leafless shrub, a stubble of dried stalks, like some ruined gardener.

She watched him leave the garden, walk to the promontory over the river. He was alone there and he stopped, stood up straight, turned his face to the sky, and Elena wondered if he was crying.

The sound of her footsteps surprised him. He turned quickly, and Elena saw that his eyes glittered with the glare coming off the water far below. In that first instant, he seemed to search her face as if he had never seen her before. Then he reached out, ran the back of his fingers on her cheek. He let his hand drop, looked back out at the river.

"I've decided something," he said. "I'm not going to do the Burma trip. I'm telling Amy to pull my name."

Elena watched his profile. She wanted to see his eyes, but he didn't turn. "Are you serious? But you've always talked about working with the *Times*. What—"

"Not right now," he whispered. "There'll be other wars. God knows, I'll always find another war."

Elena didn't know what to feel. She didn't want him to go to Burma—she didn't want him to go to any more wars—but she wanted to know why he was doing this. But how to ask? "Are you ill?" "Are you frightened?" How to ask why her unspoken wish of the past three years had so suddenly, so improbably, seemed to take root in him?

"Mark, did something happen in Kurdistan?"

At that moment, he thought of telling her some of it. Maybe about the artillery shell on the hillside, or about the doctor who had stood over him, shuffling his little plastic tags, deciding whether he should live or die. Or maybe about that first night in the recovery bay, when he had lain on his back and gazed up through a roof of reeds at desert stars that did not sparkle but shone like tiny, steady moons, how there had been times in that endless night when he had wondered if he would ever see her again, if he would ever walk again, how when he finally gave in and cried he had been too helpless to even hide his face from the others.

But how did you ever tell anyone any of this? Because once you started telling, there was no place to stop. One story, one pain, bled into the next, and they spilled out until there was nothing left to hold. Mark couldn't do it. He felt so delicate, so precarious, there above the river, as if with one word, one step, the avalanche would start and he would be lost. He needed time—every morning when he opened his eyes, every quiet moment of a day, he saw that he needed more time—to feel the earth beneath him and trust it would hold. He turned to Elena and smiled.

"Yes. I had a revelation. It was revealed to me that I should not lose you. It was revealed to me that I should have a baby with you."

They arrived late to Michael Barnard's party. The SoHo loft was overflowing with guests, and Michael had transformed his living room into a great dance floor, all the furniture pushed against the walls. In the center of the room was a video projector, and it cast one of Michael's documentaries—the one on the war in Burundi from the looks of it—onto the wall. The sound, if there was any sound, was lost to the waltz, playing so loud Mark felt the vibrations in the floorboards. Dancing couples passed back and forth in the projector's light, cast their shadows on soldiers at roadblocks, street battles in downtown Bujumbura, and the African colors that splashed over their bodies made the dancers appear elegant and graceful.

Diane waved to them from a couch set against the wall. They crossed to her, knelt down to hear over the soaring violins.

"Do you think all this noise is bad for the baby?" Diane shouted.

"No," Mark shouted back, "babies love classical music."

He grabbed Diane's hand, propelled her up from the couch, and led her onto the dance floor.

It was a comical sight, the enormously pregnant woman, the gaunt man with legs that seemed wooden, and the other couples stopped to watch and laugh, to shout encouragement. Standing beside the couch, Elena joined in the laughter, the sound coming from her mouth overwhelmed by the music.

But, like any joke, it was funny only for so long, and Elena began to feel a touch of discomfort as the dance went on. She glanced around at the others. Some were still watching and laughing, but most had resumed dancing, leaving a wide circle for this strange couple maneuvering across the floor, feet shuffling out of time to the music, their improbable shapes thrown onto the wall in black silhouette. Finally, Elena couldn't watch any longer. She left the room, went in search of someone familiar to talk to.

She was in the front hall, looking at Michael's framed photographs, when a hand clutched her arm and spun her around. It was Diane, her face flushed with excitement.

"You little creep, you didn't tell me you were pregnant!"

"What?"

"Mark told me just now. How long have you known?"

Elena searched Diane's face, uncomprehending, then looked past her into the living room. She couldn't see Mark.

"I don't know what you're talking about, Diane."

"But Mark said you're going to have a baby."

Elena understood now. She smiled, shook her head. "No, Mark was in some weird mood yesterday. He said he wanted to have a baby, but I certainly didn't agree to it."

"Oh, come on." Diane punched her arm lightly. "Make the guy happy. We can trade colic stories."

Elena laughed, shook her head more forcefully. "Maybe someday, not now. I'm afraid you're on your own."

Diane pretended to pout. Elena looked into the living room again, and now she saw Mark. He had his arm around Michael, was laughing at some shared story, appeared to be having the time of his life.

Elena poured herself a mug of coffee, carried it to the table, and slid into the chair beside his. Mark remained staring out the small window as if he heard nothing. She waved a hand before his face.

"Hello? Good morning."

He turned to her then, but his eyes seemed unfocused. "Hi."

"What do you see out there?"

"Just looking at the trees." He took up his coffee mug and drank from it. "I think they're about to bud."

Elena saw the ginkgo trees along the sidewalk. They were still weeks away from budding. "Why did you tell Diane we're going to have a baby?"

"Because I want to have a baby," he said quietly, staring out the window again.

"Well, I want to have one, too. But not now. We've talked about this. I thought we decided we'd wait at least a couple more years."

Mark shrugged. "Okay."

Elena was tempted to reach for the window shade and pull it down, anything to break his trance. "Mark, look at me."

He blinked slowly, turned to face her.

"I'm worried about you."

He smiled. "Worried? About me?"

"Yes. I think you should see Harold."

Harold Feinbaum was an elderly general practitioner on the Upper West Side whom Mark and most of his colleagues had gone to for years. Harold charged very little because he found the photographers an interesting bunch, and the exotic maladies they picked up on their travels—tropical infections, blood parasites—were a welcome change from the mundane medical problems of his other patients. "Why should I see Harold?"

Elena thought of his behavior of the past two days, his odd mood at the Cloisters, his uncharacteristic exuberance at Michael's party, but she knew starting there would only make Mark defensive, that it was best to keep it on the physical. She reached over, ran a hand through his hair, felt the cut beneath her fingers.

"Your cut isn't healing. And your limp is getting worse. You need to see a doctor."

He pulled away from her hand, suddenly angry. "What is it with you, Elena? I tell you I want to spend more time with you, that I want us to have a kid, and you decide there's something wrong with me?"

"That's not what we're talking about."

"That is what we're talking about. The cut, the limp, that's bull-shit, and we both know it."

And just as quickly, the anger vanished. In its place, a pleading look. "Let me see how it goes for a couple more days, okay?" he said, his voice higher-pitched, almost begging. "Because I'm feeling fine. Really."

All at once, he seemed so forlorn Elena didn't know what more to say. She reached out and laid her hand over his. "Do you still want to meet everyone for dinner?"

Mark had arranged it at the party last night, a chance to get together with his friends in a place where they could hear each other, carry on a normal conversation. He smiled brightly. "Of course. Why wouldn't we?"

Elena glanced at her watch and stood, took up her shoulder bag from the kitchen counter. "I'll probably go straight to the restaurant from work. Will you be okay to—" She caught herself. "Just give Harold a call, Mark, just to see what he says."

He nodded, smiled up at her. "All right. I'll think about it. I'll see you tonight."

When he heard the front door close, Mark rose from the kitchen table and went out into the living room. It was bright in the morning light, so silent and still as to be almost eerie, as if the room had been sealed off for some months. He set his heel against one wall and crossed the floor.

Twenty-four steps. Was it more steps than last time, or the same? He couldn't remember. He took a pen from the foyer table and with a small hand, so small Elena would never notice, wrote "24" on the wall.

He went to their bedroom. A mirror was fastened to the inside of the door, and Mark stood before it, straightened his hair, checked the closeness of his shave. He saw that the clothes he wore—blue jeans, a dark olive cotton shirt—were a bit loose on him.

It was not a full-length mirror. It stood about four feet high with a thin wood border, and Mark had to stand back by the bed to see the lower part of his body. He noticed he was stooped and made an effort to straighten. With his shoulders thrown back, he walked toward the mirror. After three steps he stopped, startled by the sight.

His right leg dragged on the carpet. His left was only marginally better. He stepped back and tried again.

Better this time, the legs still stiff but with a bit more spring to them. He tried again. Much better. An easy gait, fluid, the limp barely noticeable.

He came close to the mirror and studied his reflection. His skin was taut, flexed, and his eyes were too sharp. He concentrated on relaxing his face, calming his eyes. He smoothed his shirt collar, practiced an easy smile. He stuck his right hand out, as if to shake his reflection's hand.

"Hello," he said. "Mark Walsh."

He was a dark-complected man, still lean in middle age—Elena guessed around fifty—and he had no sooner shaken her hand than he seemed to frown slightly, to sniff at the air. It was then she remembered the roses, and laughed.

"Oh, I'm sorry, I've gotten used to the smell." She pointed to the inside of her office door; the bouquet of roses Mark had given her on Friday hung upside down from the coat hook, wilted to black. "I forgot and left them on my desk over the weekend, and it seemed a shame to throw them away so soon. My mother used to dry flowers by hanging them like that, but I'm not sure it's going to work with these."

Lewis Perez looked at the bouquet, at the scattering of petals that had fallen to the carpet, then to Elena with a wry smile.

"No. I'm afraid it won't."

She found herself scrutinizing him. With the silver traces in his hair and expensive dark suit, he had the air of a successful businessman, maybe a lawyer, but there was something in his comment, an odd familiarity, that made her uncomfortable. It was compounded by the fact that she had no idea who he was or why he was there; he had simply appeared at the office midmorning and asked to speak with her, without an appointment, without even calling ahead. She sat down, motioned to the chair across from her desk. "Please."

He slid into the chair and crossed his legs, absently pinched at the fabric above his knee. "I'm sorry for popping in on you like this. I should have at least phoned, but I was afraid if I explained ahead of time, maybe you wouldn't agree to see me." He fixed her with the same smooth smile. "I wanted to talk with you about your grandfather, Joaquin Morales. About his institute."

Elena leaned back in her chair, her gaze narrowing on the man. Instinctively, she glanced at the door, wishing now she had left it open. "What's this about, Mr. Perez? And how did you . . . ?"

"Find you?" He reached down for his soft briefcase and set it on his lap, undid the clasp, and brought out a thin sheaf of photocopied papers. He held them up. "The article you wrote for the student newspaper at Complutense. In your byline, it mentioned you were about to start working for the United Nations in New York. To be honest, I didn't expect I'd find you here so many years later—I figured you'd be out in the field somewhere by now—but a stroke of good luck for me; I live up in Hartford and come into the city all the time." He glanced at the title on the first page. " 'Granddaughter of a war criminal.' A bit harsh, I felt. Was that your choice or the editor's?"

Elena felt more composed now, her initial surprise giving way to a growing irritation. "Mr. Perez, I don't know who you are or what you want, but I don't want to talk about my grandfather. I haven't spoken to him, or about him, in years, and I'd like to keep it that way. And, yes, I chose the title, because to me what he did was a crime, a horrible crime. Treating those scum, helping them recover so they could murder more innocent people, it made him as guilty as them, and that's really all I have to say on it." She quickly got to her feet. "So, you have the article, you know how I feel, and—"

"I'm sorry. Please." Lewis Perez quickly returned the papers to his briefcase, as if they were the cause of offense. "Please, just listen to me for a couple of minutes. My father. My father was at the institute. I'm trying to find out what happened to him."

Elena stared at him. Perez's easy, assured manner was gone, and the look in his eyes now was obsequious, almost desperate. "What do you mean, what happened to him?"

"He vanished. He was committed to the institute in 1939—late spring of 1939—and he was there for three or four months, and then he disappeared. He never came home. I was just a baby, but my mother spent years looking for him. She never found a trace."

Almost against her will, Elena sat back down. In confusion, she scanned her desktop, the various piles of papers there, then looked to Perez. "I'm sorry, I don't understand."

He nodded quickly, raised the palms of both hands, as if pleading for more time. "I'll explain. He was an officer in the Spanish army, my father, a captain. From what my mother said, he had a break-down, a mental breakdown, shortly after the war ended, in the spring of 1939. He was taken to your grandfather's institute. He was released at the end of that summer, but he never came home. My mother spent eight years trying to find him, but nothing. Finally, she gave up. In 1947, we—she and I—emigrated to the United States, to Connecticut. She remarried, never talked about my father or what had happened, never wanted me to look for him, to go through what she had." He gave a weak smile. "Very deep wounds, I guess."

Elena nodded. Perez tentatively reached into his briefcase again, began pulling out more papers.

"Well, my mother died three years ago, and with the liberalization in Spain, I thought maybe now I could find out something." He chuckled. "Of course, liberalization doesn't necessarily mean greater efficiency."

He set the briefcase on the floor and spread his papers in a fan on the corner of her desk. Elena saw that most were photocopies of letters Perez had written to various agencies in the Spanish government. She couldn't make out the words—the pages were upside down to her—but she also didn't reach for them.

Perez stared down at the papers. "If it's any consolation, your grandfather's institute was not unique. The government set up a whole network of psychiatric clinics for its soldiers just after the civil war—six or seven, at least—all in out-of-the-way places, all kept very quiet. Apparently, Franco saw it as a great embarrassment, and I suppose from his vantage point it was. The very idea that the patriotic defenders of the Fatherland, the upholders of the faith, should be traumatized by what they had seen, what they had done, well, it implied guilty consciences—at least a breakdown of moral fiber—and it was very important to the fascists that they admit to none of that."

Perez looked up at her then, tapped his papers with a finger.

"But within this, your grandfather's clinic was especially sensitive. It was reserved for officers, you see. One thing to have the peasants and rabble fall apart, but the true sons of the Fatherland? Well, impossible, a contradiction, so, like so many other things, Franco simply erased the problem. The records of the officers who went to your grandfather's institute were guarded like a state secret. Those who were judged to be cured—'purified,' in your grandfather's words—were released, with no mention of their stay entered in their military record. And those who could not be purified, the incurables, they were simply discarded—stripped of their uniforms, discharged from the army, thrown out of the gates to fend for themselves. That's what happened to my father. Cast out, a nonperson, no record of him anywhere." He gave a quick, unexpected laugh. "And it has taken me three years to learn that much."

Elena gazed at the world map on her far wall, the different-colored pins there. "But the fascists loved to keep records," she said softly. "If your father was an officer, there has to be records of him somewhere—his pension, his postings . . ."

With a kind of smug amusement, Perez wagged a finger at her. He reached into his pile to extract a thick sheaf of papers stapled together, flipped it around so that it faced her. It was a report from the Spanish Ministry of Health, written in 1986, entitled, *The Unmentionables: The Treatment of Nationalist War-Trauma Victims in the Post-War Era.*

"It's where I've gotten most of my information," Perez said. "The beauty of this whole system was that once these men were deemed incurable, they were simply erased, their official records destroyed. For them, there was no pension, no medical care, no record they had ever been in the military. That way, if one of them went mad and killed half his village and people said, 'Oh, he was crazy ever since he fought for Franco in the war,' the government could say, 'But he was never a soldier, we have no record of him, to do something like that he must have been a Republican.' That's the way it worked under Franco." He pointed to the report. "They talk about two cases of men this happened to. They're now in their seventies and are going through the courts trying to get their benefits. They have photographs of themselves in uniform, affidavits from old comrades, they have given precise accountings of where they were posted and with which units, but the government cannot find official record of them anywhere. As for my father, the only reason I know anything is through my mother. From all my letters to the Spanish government"—he made a series of nodding motions at his spread of papers—"and some of these agencies have been very sympathetic, absolutely nothing."

Elena gazed over his papers, the long, detailed letters from him asking for information, the much shorter official replies saying there was none. It reminded her of so many other stacks of papers that had passed over her desk.

"I'm sorry, Mr. Perez, but—"

"Lewis. Please, call me Lewis."

Elena nodded. "But I'm not sure what you want of me, what I can do . . ."

Perez nodded energetically. "Simply this. I obtained your grandfather's address some time ago and have been writing him . . ." He sifted through his papers again, pulled out another thin sheaf held together with a paper clip. He held them up for Elena to see. "That is his correct address?"

She looked at the address on the first letter: Casa de los Queridos, Peñuelas, Spain. She nodded.

With a sigh, Perez set the papers down. "You know, at this point, I really don't have any illusions about actually finding my father, whether he's dead or alive. All I want to do is find out a little about him, what he was like, what happened to him. I've often thought I should go over there, to my parents' home village, but . . ."

He seemed to suddenly grow troubled, stared down at the thin sheaf of letters. When he spoke again, his voice was much softer, barely a whisper. "But I am especially interested in what he was like at the institute, and the only person I can think of who knows that is your grandfather. I must have written him seven or eight times, but I've never received a response." He searched Elena's face. "That's why I came here. I'm hoping that perhaps you could make an introduction to your grandfather for me, a note, maybe a phone call. You mentioned in your article that you were once very close."

Elena stared into a middistance. She was moved by Perez's story and, for a moment, tempted. But then she saw where it would lead, that any word from her would be just the opening her grandfather had been waiting for.

"I'm sorry, Mr. Perez," she said quietly. "I really would like to help you, but what happened with my grandfather . . ." She scanned the walls of her office, trying to find the words. "When I learned about all this, I vowed never to speak to him again. I'd like to keep it that way. I'm sorry."

Perez dolefully nodded his understanding.

"I have his telephone number, though." She opened her top desk drawer and drew out her address book, flipped to the first page. "Perhaps you'd have better luck in calling him. He speaks perfect English."

"Thank you," he said, reaching into his coat pocket for a pen. "And let me give you my business card, in case you think of something else — or maybe change your mind."

While he took down her grandfather's number, Elena read Perez's card; he was an investment banker, a vice-president for a firm based in Hartford. When she looked up, she saw that he was studying the photographs and artifacts she had mounted on the walls.

"It's ironic, isn't it?" he said. "You working with war refugees, trying to reunite families, and here I come to you . . ." He focused on a photograph Mark had taken in El Salvador, of a young girl in a tattered red dress, eating an orange and smiling sweetly into the camera. "Tell me, the ones who go missing, do you find many of them?"

Elena slowly shook her head. "No. We find very few."

Perez nodded somberly. In the silence, Elena gazed over his fan of papers. He had not brought out her article again, but she remembered what she had said, her indignance, the scorn she had heaped on her grandfather's patients.

"I'm sorry for what I said before," she said, "about those sent to the institute. I'm sure they weren't all war criminals. I'm sure some were simply too gentle for what they had to endure, traumatized by what they had seen. Perhaps your father was one of those."

Perez gave her a tender smile, and in his eyes was a deep and sad gratefulness. "Thank you, Elena. Thank you very much. But my father had a nickname. He was called the 'Beast of Olía.' That's the name of my parents' village. So, you see, that's why I've never gone back myself. I know it's cowardly of me, but to learn about all that he did . . . It's the institute, what happened there, why he was taken there, if it was because he was tormented by what he had done, that's all that interests me now. But that is very kind of you to say."

He began gathering up his papers, sliding them back into his briefcase. "If I do succeed in talking with your grandfather, is there any message you would like me to pass on?"

She considered for a moment. Again, she was tempted. Again, she saw where it would lead. "No. No, thank you."

"And then I lost my balance, and away I went. It felt like I was underwater for twenty minutes, getting bounced from one rock to the next. And then when I finally get to the hospital, the doctor takes one look at me and says, 'Who beat you up?' "

Scattered laughter at the table, mostly from the other photographers. Elena smiled, sipped her club soda.

The waiters at Francesca's had joined three tables to accommodate the eleven of them, and the overlapping tablecloths were littered with wicker baskets of bread rolls, short red straws discarded from drinks. Sitting at the far end, Elena watched Mark with a certain critical detachment, listened to the way he repackaged his ordeal as a humorous anecdote for his friends.

"And then he comes and sits next to me and says, 'Well, I trust you've had an enjoyable visit.' "

More amused chuckles, and Mark, shaking his head in mock disbelief, took up his drink and raised it to his lips.

Michael Barnard leaned far out over the table, craning to see past the others. "Where was Colin during all this?"

Mark's face fell, and he set his glass down without drinking from it. "I don't know. He'd left for the lowlands right before. We lost contact." He played with his glass, turning it again and again on the table. "No one's heard from him in almost two weeks." He gazed down the expanse of tablecloth to Elena. "We're kind of worried about him, aren't we?"

All looked to Elena. She felt under scrutiny. "Yes," she stammered. "Yes, we are."

The conversation grew serious. Some of the men offered theories to explain Colin's lateness, while the women pointed out how nerve-wracking it must be for Diane, so close to her due date. The fretful mood wasn't dispelled until Warren Parkham, a photographer in his early forties and the father of two, leaned over the table.

"Well, if he's smart, he'll stay away until the kid's third birthday."

An eruption of laughter, and Elena looked down at Mark. He was laughing louder than anyone else, but it sounded strange—mechanical and forced—and he scanned the faces of the others as he did so. And then Elena saw the change in him, so fast, so dramatic, that she wondered if she had really witnessed it or if it had been a trick of the light. Just as the laughter began to taper off, Mark's mouth—open wide in unrestrained mirth—snapped shut. The laugh lines creasing his cheeks were instantly gone, his face instantly composed, became a mask from which two eyes peered out, searching the faces of the others. It was as if he were hearing things at a different speed from everyone else, his reactions a split second ahead or behind. And then Elena realized what it meant and felt the hair on her arms bristle. Mark's reactions were out of sync with the others because he was copying them. He wasn't having any of his own.

It was not yet eight, long before most of her coworkers would arrive to work, and Elena sat at her desk, listened to the unfamiliar silence of the building.

She had lain awake most of the night, it seemed, battling with herself over what to do. Many times she had been tempted to rouse Mark, to confront him with what she'd seen at the restaurant. Each time, though, she decided against it. And in the very first light of morning, she awoke again. She looked at him sleeping close beside her, at the pallid blue sky out the window, and had suddenly been anxious to escape. She dressed quickly, made barely a sound as she moved through the apartment, and as she walked toward the subway the sun came over the rooftops to give the deserted street a golden shine. Elena had not seen that in a long time, and it comforted her.

Now she stared at her office telephone and tried to think of who to call. Under normal circumstances, Diane, but there was no way she could burden Diane with this right now. She thought of coworkers, her other girlfriends, even considered some of Mark's friends, but it was still early and no one seemed right.

She gazed over her desk, noticed the business card Lewis Perez had placed there the afternoon before. She picked it up, distractedly scratched at the raised company logo in the top right corner, thought of his sad search, wondered why her grandfather had never even bothered to answer him.

Elena set the card down, glanced at her watch again: just before eight, almost two in the afternoon in Madrid. Almost instinctively, she picked up the receiver and dialed.

"*Diga?*" It was her mother's voice, distant and scratchy—another bad connection.

"*Hola, Mama.*"

"*Elena?! Mi querida! Dónde está?*"

Elena laughed. "*En Nueva York, Mama. Yo vivo aquí, recuerdas?*"

"*Ah, Nueva York,*" her mother said. "*Estupendo.*"

It was a routine they went through with every conversation. Her mother was still old-fashioned enough to view transatlantic phone calls as lesser miracles, and all Elena's calls over the past four years had done nothing to dispel her sense of wonder. She rattled off the family news in rapid-fire Spanish, gripped—as always—by her two fears: that the line would soon fail, that Elena was spending a small fortune by calling. Barely pausing to breathe, she told of the ballet she had seen at the Royal Opera House the previous weekend, the academic progress and romantic complications of Elena's cousins, the comings and goings of neighborhood friends.

"But that is enough," she said all at once, "we're about to be cut off. What of you? When are you coming home for a visit?"

"Oh, I don't know." Elena sighed. "Soon, I hope."

"What's wrong?"

"Nothing." Elena smiled. "Nothing is wrong. I'm fine."

"Don't tell me there's nothing wrong when I know there is. I can hear it in your voice."

"Really, Mama, nothing is wrong."

"You're a bad liar, Elena. You never could hide anything."

The words spilled out in a torrent. She told her mother everything, how Mark seemed to be deteriorating before her eyes, the fear she had felt watching his face at the restaurant the night before. "I don't know what's happening," she said, her voice stretched. "I think he's having some kind of breakdown."

"You have to get him to a doctor, Elena." Her mother was steady, controlled. "Get him to a doctor right away."

"I've tried. He won't go."

"He has to. Just take him."

"I can't just take him," Elena said, managing a smile. "He's bigger than me."

"Do you want me to come over? I'll come over. I'll help you."

"No, Mama, no. Thank you, but it'll be okay." Now, as she began to feel better, Elena wished she had shown some restraint. "Really, it will be fine. I'll insist he go to a doctor."

"Immediately," her mother said. "Make him go immediately."

"Okay. I promise."

"And call me, okay? Call me tomorrow night. I'll wait for your call."

"Okay."

Another silence, a soft clicking on the international line. "You're always in my thoughts, Elena."

"Thank you, Mama," Elena said, feeling her throat tighten again.

Mark lay on his back and listened for a sound—a footstep, a door closing, her soft humming as she went about her morning routine. There was nothing, and he decided he was alone. He threw back the covers, slid his feet to the edge of the bed and over the side. Using his arms as support, he tried to stand. His knees shook, his feet felt leaden, but the legs held beneath him. Not trusting his balance, he sat back on the bed to dress.

He undid the clasps, lifted the mirror from its mount, and carried it to the living room. He propped it against the far wall. Walking to the other end, he turned and saw he was a small distant object in the center of the mirror. He started across, watched himself grow larger in the reflection. He concentrated on lifting his knees, stretching his legs out until he felt on the verge of falling. Twenty-seven steps.

He went to the stereo, put on a recording of Mahler's second symphony. Back and forth he went, violins and French horns drowning out the sound of his footfalls, of his toes touching the walls. Twenty-eight, and he turned off the symphony that had run through and gone back to the overture. Thirty, and he heard his watch beep the tenth hour. The soles of his feet became sore, so Mark put on slippers.

Thirty-three steps and he stood before the mirror, extended his hand.

"Hello. Mark Walsh."

Too stiff, the words clipped. He tried again.

"Hi. Mark Walsh."

Better, but still tentative.

"Hello. I'm Mark Walsh."

Nice. Confident. But the shoulders were hunched, the legs trembling.

"Hi, how are you? Mark Walsh."

Assuredness in the posture, the trace of a friendly smile on his lips. He saw the number he had written on the wall—24—and tried to remember when he had made it. Yesterday? Could it really have been only yesterday?

A moment that turned on him. A quick clamping in his chest, and Mark was held by the thought that none of it was true, that he hadn't survived, that he had vanished back there on the hilltop, out in the meadow grass, or in the blue-dark river. Or maybe long before, in Afghanistan or Lebanon, in a remote valley or outside a village whose name he didn't know. How could it be that after nine years of this, after all he had done, all he had seen, with all the memories that filled his mind, he was still alive to stand in this room, before this mirror, to feel the sun of another day come through the window?

In a desperate last effort, he turned to the mirror. He stood straight, his shoulders thrown back, a broad smile of welcome and pleasure, his hand extended in a hearty way—"Mark Walsh. Glad to meet you"—and in that instant he knew it was true, that he had not vanished, that he was still there, that in spite of all that had happened and all he had seen, he was still there and doing just *fine*.

•　•　•

Elena leaned against the kitchen counter and watched him pick at the dinner she had made. "You have to see Harold."

Mark looked up, wary. "Well, sure. In a couple of days, if I'm not still improving, I'll—"

"Tomorrow. Not in a couple of days. Tomorrow." She went to the table, took the chair beside his. He stared down at his plate. "You're not well, Mark. I don't know what's wrong with you, but I know you need to see a doctor." She squeezed his hand to make him look up, but he wouldn't. "I'll go with you if you like."

"No, that's okay," he said quietly. "I can manage."

"But you'll go. Promise?"

He nodded, blinked rapidly. She leaned over, kissed the knuckles of his hand. "I love you so much." Then she released his hand and sat back.

So that was it. There was nothing more to be done that night, nothing to be gained by pressing further. Elena glanced out the window at the twilight sky. "It's still early. What would you like to do?"

"I want to make love."

She turned to him. It was absurd. As absurd as if he had said, "I want to go waterskiing." And she knew from looking at his face—so sad, so frightened—that he didn't want to make love, at least not for any reason she might recognize. But how could she say, "No, that's not what you want, you're such a mess you don't know what you want."

She slowly nodded. "All right."

His eyes were what Elena had first noticed on that night three years before. They were too sharp, too quick, with an intensity Elena had not seen before. On that night, she had thought they were fearful eyes, or perhaps a bit possessed, and this had intrigued her, appealed to her curiosity. It was only with time, after they had become lovers, that she understood they were simply eyes that had seen too much, that maintained a permanent vigil.

He entered her, and Elena felt his body with her hands. The shoulder blades jutted out and seemed fragile. The ribs were thin and close against the skin. She cupped a hand over his hipbone, grinding down on her like a dull axe, and caressed it. Mark's body was like a collection of blunt weapons, so delicate they could snap.

After a time, his movements slowed, became erratic. Finally, he stopped altogether. Elena opened her eyes to see him gazing down at her abjectly.

"I'm sorry," he said. "It's my legs. They're tired."

She gently rolled him off her, onto the bed, felt his lifeless legs slide over hers. She got on top of him, settled into a slow, rocking rhythm. She looked into his face, into his eyes. Not vigilant or quick anymore, possessed of nothing, feeling nothing, eyes of the dead. Elena lay her head on the pillow so she wouldn't have to see them. Her fingers felt through his hair, touched the torn skin at the back of his skull. She closed her eyes, pushed down on him faster, harder, just wanting it to be over.

His back arched and Elena imagined blood spraying inside him. She imagined it rippling the sides of his rib cage, coursing down into his belly, leaving him and flooding into her until he had no more to give.

It stopped. She lay beside him on the pillow and felt his breath, shallow and hot, on her neck. She grazed a hand over his arm, felt the tickle of his hair on her fingertips. She lifted her head to see him.

"Mark, tell me what happened out there."

"Nothing, Elena." The eyes were green stones. "Nothing happened."

Elena was in the office ten minutes when her mother called. She had never telephoned before, and Elena was immediately alarmed. "What's happened, Mama?"

"Nothing, darling, nothing. Well, a little something."

Elena thought of her aunts and uncles and cousins, thought of car accidents and cancer, but then realized there was no grief in her mother's voice. Instead, it was halting, slightly hushed, the sound of contrition.

"I think maybe you are going to be upset with me."

"What have you done?"

"Me?" Her mother's voice rose in protest. "But I have done nothing."

Elena sighed. "Okay, but what do you mean?"

"Well, after our talk yesterday, I was concerned about Mark—naturally—and I tried to think of who might know what to do. Well, naturally, I thought of your grandfather, so I called him."

Elena relaxed. "Is that all? Oh, Mama, you didn't have to worry about calling me for that."

"Not my father. Your father's father. Papa Joaquin."

"Oh," Elena said.

"I knew you wouldn't want me to, Elena, but, after all, he is an expert in this field."

Her grandfather was not an expert in this field and never had been, but Elena didn't want to have this conversation with her mother again. "Well, I guess it's okay. I would have preferred you not tell him, but I suppose there's no real harm done."

Her mother gave a little, forced cough. "He's coming to New York."

"What?" Elena sprang forward in her chair.

"I told him it wasn't necessary, but he is adamant. He says he can help Mark."

"No, he can't!" Elena shouted in spite of herself. "There's nothing he can do."

"He only wants to help, Elena."

"But he can't help. He'd only make things worse. Call him back and tell him not to come."

"I tried. I told him you were handling things fine, but he insisted. Besides, he is an expert in this field."

"No, he isn't, Mama, he's a fraud! And a criminal. I'm sorry, I know he's your father-in-law and you care for him, but you have to understand that."

Her mother's voice took on a wounded inflection. "You need to learn forgiveness, Elena. What he did happened a long time ago. Dear God, it's been nearly fifty years."

Elena kneaded her temple. "I don't have time to get into all of that again, Mama. I just don't want to see him—and especially not now. Will you please call him back again and tell him not to come."

"I've tried. You know how headstrong he is."

"Okay, I'll call him."

Another nervous cough at the other end. "You should do it soon. He's leaving Granada in three hours."

"He's coming today? Mama, no!"

"He's a man of action, Elena. You have to give him that."

Mark swung open the bookstore's glass door and stepped inside. "Where's your travel section?" he asked the cashier.

The middle-aged woman gave him a puzzled stare before motioning with her head. "Upstairs."

Mark strode through the downstairs room so swiftly, with such obvious purpose, that the browsers glanced up from their reading, edged back to get out of his way. He went up the stairs.

He started with the shelf of regional guidebooks, flipping through those describing the environs of New York City. It was something he and Elena had talked about for some time, this idea of moving a little ways out of the city, but it had never gone beyond idle wishes. The biggest problem had always been Elena's job, her need to get to Forty-fourth Street every day, and Brooklyn was convenient for that.

But now it was different. Now, if they were going to have a baby, Elena would probably take a six-month leave. After that, she might not want to return to work at all—Mark had seen it with other couples who had a baby. And with Mark's career finally taking off, his photoessays going to auction, being recommended for top-line assignments, they could afford it. He could support all of them, himself and Elena and the baby.

He glanced through the books on Long Island. Not his preferred spot but the easiest commute for Elena. But then he remembered the baby, remembered that commuting distance would soon no longer be a concern, and put Long Island back on the shelf.

Connecticut? No. Not a place at all. Just a great lawn, tended to on weekends by insurance agents and bankers. Not northern New Jersey, either—still within the city's sprawl, an ugly stepchild.

He spotted a guidebook on the Hudson Valley and snatched it off the shelf. Photographs of the little river towns—poor composition,

badly reproduced, but interesting in a down-at-the-heels sort of way. Hudson Valley? The Adirondacks close by, pockets of real country still beyond the reach of exurbia, fairly good schools for when the child was of age. Yes, a possibility, a definite possibility.

Mark's eyes darted over the rows of books, came to rest on the foreign travel guides.

But first, perhaps a vacation. He hurried to that shelf and began pulling down books.

The Caribbean? Indonesia? Brazil? Somewhere exotic but not too taxing, somewhere they could lie on a beach and feel reborn by the warmth of the sun. The world was filled with such places, and the brightly colored covers of the guidebooks offered endless promise.

A series of double rings, and then Elena heard her grandfather's recorded voice come on. It startled her. Answering machines were a fairly recent innovation in Spain, and Elena certainly didn't expect her grandfather to be a trendsetter. She wasn't prepared to say what she felt into a machine, but then the beep sounded.

"Hello, Papa, this is Elena. I just learned from my mother that you are planning to come here. I think it would be a bad idea. Mark is . . ." Elena groped for a suitable lie. "He is seeing a doctor who's helping him a lot. Already, he is much better than he was even yesterday. So, please, don't feel you need to come. Please, don't come." It felt needlessly direct, even rude, as soon as it came out. "I'm sorry, but everything is very difficult right now and it wouldn't be a good time for a visit. Okay? Okay, please call me back at my office when you get this message." She gave him the number. What more to say? That she loved him, that she missed him? But Elena couldn't lie about such things. "I guess that's all. Goodbye."

She replaced the receiver and stared at her desktop. It was still three hours until his flight. Surely, he wouldn't have left for the airport yet, would still be packing, and Elena imagined her grandfather standing in the living room of his home, listening to her words on the answering machine, her first words to him in nearly six years, and stinging with hurt.

Joaquin stood over the machine, watching the tape rewind, when Carmen came into the room.

"Who was that?" she asked.

"Elena. I didn't get to the phone in time."

"Is she excited you're coming?"

" 'Excited' isn't the right word," Joaquin said. "I would describe it more as . . . overjoyed. Ecstatic, even." He turned to his housekeeper. "We're very close, you know."

"Excuse me, sir, do you need any help?"

Mark turned from the display of children's stuffed animals. A clean-cut man in his midtwenties wearing a dark tie and white shirt had appeared beside him. "No, thanks," Mark said, "I'm only looking."

The salesman moved in a little closer, lowered his voice. "I mean, are you all right? You don't look well."

Mark reached for a small figure—a panda bear, perhaps, or maybe a raccoon—and the young man caught his elbow as Mark started to lose his balance.

"Are you here with someone? Is there someone you'd like me to call?"

An entire wall of stuffed animals, row after row, climbing almost to the ceiling, and Mark suddenly felt hemmed in, as if he couldn't get oxygen. "No," he whispered, "no, I'm fine."

He left the store, went out onto the sidewalk. Making his way to the subway, Mark saw himself in a new way. Now he noticed the stares of passersby, how their expressions turned from curious to troubled as he drew nearer and, before they could meet his eyes, he looked away. He saw his reflection in a store window, the shuffling gait, the stooped back, and he looked away. He felt the back of his head, the great lump there. He expected to see blood on his fingers, but they were dry and clean.

At the subway entrance, he stopped. Gazing down the long flight of stairs, at the darkness gathered there, he was unable to move. He leaned against the stairway railing, tilted his head back, and panted for air.

"Do you need help?" A stooped elderly woman peered up into Mark's face like he was a confusing piece of modern sculpture.

"Can you get me a cab, please."

She helped him in, and as the taxi pulled away Mark leaned against the sideframe, the cold wind on his face, and was overcome with gratitude at being away from the eyes of others, at leaving behind that part of him that was crippled and grotesque.

Elena called home again, and again the answering machine clicked on after the fourth ring. She hung up and dialed Harold Feinbaum's office.

"Hi, this is Elena Morales again. Has Mark Walsh shown up yet?"

The receptionist sighed with irritation. "No, he hasn't, Ms. Morales, and he hasn't called. Why don't you give me your number, and I'll let you know as soon as we hear from him."

Elena considered. Mark would think she was checking on him. "No, that's okay. I'm sorry, I won't bother you again."

"Thank you, Ms. Morales."

Elena banged the receiver down in frustration. Where was he? She snatched up the phone again, endured the eternity of rings before the machine came on.

"Mark, I don't know where you are, but when you get in, will you call me?" She thought for a moment, saw the absurdity of trying to work anymore that day. "Actually, forget that; I'm coming home. It seems we're about to have a visitor."

He lay his head against the cool porcelain and watched the steam rise into the air. He felt the heat working its way into his flesh, deep into his knees and hips, and this soothed him.

From far off, the telephone rang. Mark heard its four rings, and then his own voice as the machine came on. He couldn't hear the message being left, and wondered if it was Amy calling with news of the auction. He closed his eyes and saw each frame, each moment, as clearly as if he were reliving it, as if he had never left it.

Mustafa Karim, thirty-one, father of three, once a farmer's son, once a line-worker at the Opel factory in Rüdesheim, Germany, now with a bullet in his stomach and lying in the Harir cave. Dr. Ahmet Talzani, thirty-four, once a shopkeeper's son, once a neurology student at the University of Michigan, now walking down the line of wounded men, his once-white coat stained to rust. Now Talzani standing over Mustafa, talking to him, his fingers playing with the tags he holds in his left hand. Now the right hand is out, the fingers extended, and the tag is a blur in midair, halfway between Talzani's open hand and Mustafa's chest. Now Mustafa stares into the camera, his eyes wider, his lips pulled back to reveal crooked stained teeth, and in the foreground, at the very bottom of the frame, the blood-colored fingers of Mustafa Karim clutch the triage tag and the tag is blue.

Outside now, and the flash is off. Three men on stretchers in the sunlight before the Harir cave, and there is Mustafa and his eyes are blue. Mustafa being carried to the cemetery, the mullah beside him reading from the Koran, Talzani at the left edge of the frame, and his head is bowed. A last prayer, Mustafa's hands folded over his chest, mouth twisted into a grimace, and he is afraid. Now Talzani kneels beside him, draws the blanket back, and the blanket is brown. Mustafa's eyes closed tight, mouth open in a cry, and the gun is coming up. Motor-drive because it will all be very quick now, and there is a bright yellow flash in Talzani's hand, a puff of red mist, and now Mustafa's head is turned to the side, his mouth is pursed, his face smoothed of pain or fear or worry, and Mustafa is at peace, his soul already halfway to Paradise, rising into a sky that is blue.

And then, against his will, another vision came into Mark's mind. It was of Colin and he was standing alone out in the desert and the wall of sand and noise was coming for him, sweeping over the flat land like a wave, and then it was upon him and he was thrashing, staggering, trying to get out, but already it had his feet, already it was too late.

Mark opened his eyes, and the vision vanished. He looked into the water. His body was splayed before him, white and indistinct. He touched his legs. They felt as if they belonged to someone else.

He tried to raise them out, but his effort only roiled the surface of the water, and the legs stayed down in the milky wash. He gripped the side of the tub, attempted to hoist himself up, but the legs lay dead before him. A stab of fear, the heat and moisture of the room suddenly suffocating, pinching the life from him. Mark crawled over the rim of the tub and the legs followed, flopped hard onto the tiles. The floor felt cold and good beneath him, but the legs felt nothing. He lay on his back and watched the steam rise off his body, ascending to join the cloud of white vapor building high above.

And then he was back on the mountain, stumbling his way toward the river, and he was saying his last prayer—"I don't want to die here, I don't want to die here"—and this time he let the tears come.

That is where she found him. A white body lying on white tiles, green eyes open, a naked body trembling with cold.

She did not panic. She brought a towel and dried him as best she could. She brought clean clothes, helped him dress for the trip to the hospital.

She did not cry. She sat beside him on the tiles, lifted his head into her lap and stroked his cheek, waited with him for the siren of an ambulance.

She did not ask if he was frightened. Instead, she told him about her grandfather.

"He's coming here to see you," she said, hearing the siren now. "I think you'll like him. He's a fascist."

A time of helplessness. Mark felt strong hands dig beneath his back to lift him from the bathroom floor onto the stretcher, straps drawn tightly across his chest and knees, felt both disoriented and intrigued by the strange low view of his own living room as he was wheeled out. Tilted upright in the too-narrow service elevator, and he felt the strong hands again, pressed against his chest, wedged into his armpits, holding him in place all the way to the lobby. Secured into the back of the ambulance, Elena on the opposite bench, Mark studied the face of the young Hispanic man who hovered above, who placed a cold, leathery hand on his neck to feel his pulse.

In the emergency room, he shivered from the chill, squinted against the brilliant light that reflected off chrome and tile and white bedsheets. Everyone mysterious beneath face masks and shower caps and surgical gloves, in baggy green clothes that resembled pajamas, and Mark felt calm, a peaceful surrendering to the quiet bloodlessness of his surroundings.

A woman with a face mask and butterfly glasses appeared above him. "How do you feel?" she asked.

"All right," Mark said, seeing the small white nameplate on her left breast that read "Patricia Swenson, Triage Nurse" in black letters.

He watched the muscular forearms of the orderly who wheeled him down a corridor, listened to the hum in the half-darkness of the X-ray room. On the journey back to the emergency room, they passed an old black man strapped to a gurney, holding his stomach and moaning, and Mark remembered the car bomb in the Karachi bazaar, how Colin had left his side and stumbled over the remnants of the dead to vomit into a ditch.

Beneath the lights, Patricia Swenson stood over him again. She held up an X ray, and Mark looked at the vaporous white image of his own skull, followed Patricia's finger as it moved across the film to stop at a small burst of light.

"You've got something in your head," Patricia said, and Mark remembered that night at the Karachi hotel, Colin drunk and raging, "Fuck this, fuck this, I can't fucking take this anymore," clutching the sides of his head as if it might burst.

Rolled onto his stomach, Mark felt the vibrations of an electric razor behind his ear. A man's voice — "This is going to sting a little" — and Mark felt the first needle go in. His hands gripped the sides of the gurney, his teeth clenched against the pain, and behind his closed eyes white lights coiled and spun like phosphorescence as he remembered the afternoon at the Blue Moon Tavern, four months after Karachi, one week before Kurdistan, when Colin had said he wasn't going:

"It leaves scars in my head. It leaves scars all the time."

Wheeled under operating lamps that were close and hot. Over

the anesthetic, Mark felt rubbery fingers spread his cut wide, the scratch of steel against his skull—not pain, only sensation—and he remembered the words he had used at the Blue Moon to make Colin change his mind:

"You have to keep it separate," he had said. "Keep it separate, and you don't feel a thing."

FOUR

The waiting room had the dreary feel of a bus terminal, rows of molded plastic chairs, a dull gray linoleum floor, overhead fluorescent tubes that threw a harsh and shadowless light. Directly across from Elena, a Hispanic family—a mother, a father, three small children—huddled close together and talked in soft whispers. The youngest boy sat on his mother's lap, and Elena watched her heavy fingers stroke his rich black hair, the way her pensive eyes studied the floor as if it were a confusing map.

The frosted glass doors to the emergency room retracted, and a white woman in glasses and green hospital scrubs stepped out. She glanced at her clipboard, scanned the waiting room. "Ms. Morales?"

Elena rose and went to her.

"Hi," the woman said. "You came in with Mark Walsh?"

Elena nodded.

"Well, we cleaned him up a bit in there." The nurse tilted her head toward the frosted doors. "He's been sent on to neurology."

"How is he?"

"Oh, he'll live." The nurse smiled cheerfully. "We only dealt with the head wound. It was just a superficial—no fracture or infection—but we did remove a foreign object."

"A foreign object? What do you mean?"

The nurse's smile eased away. "An object that is foreign to that particular area of the body, that doesn't belong."

"But what kind of object?" Elena asked.

"I really couldn't say; that's pathology." The nurse rocked slightly on her heels, ready to turn. "So . . ."

"What's wrong with his legs?"

The nurse stared at Elena for a moment. "That's neurology, I'm afraid. But I'm sure the neurologist will be able to answer all your questions." Her gaze slid away from Elena, traveled over the dismal waiting room. "It should only be a few more minutes."

Mark felt the soft, firm hands tracing along his spine, stopping at different spots to rub or poke. The hands squeezed the flesh around his hipbones, his knees, clasped his feet, and gently turned them in their ankle sockets.

"Kind of like an extremely expensive rubdown, isn't it?" Dr. Christopher said. She drew the sheet up to his shoulder blades, rolled him onto his back.

She was in her midthirties, her blond hair tied back, and for several minutes Mark watched the way her mouth silently formed words as she scanned his file, held his X rays up to the light. Earlier, while she had been bending his legs, an orderly had come into the examination room and placed a small plastic bag with a green label on the bedside table. Dr. Christopher now picked up this bag, tapped at the object inside with a fingernail. She turned to Mark and smiled brightly.

"So, Mr. Walsh, is there something else you want to tell me?"

Mark didn't understand. Dr. Christopher palmed the plastic bag and slid onto the stool beside the examination table. "What really happened? I knew the river story was bull the second I saw you."

"No, it isn't," Mark said. "It happened."

She searched his face, then shrugged. "All right, but something else happened you're not telling us. You didn't get these injuries from being dragged over some river rocks." She pointed at his covered body. "You've got swelling and hypersensitivity along the length of your spine. It's called spinal shock. It means you suffered a high-impact trauma, probably either head-first or feet-first, and the shock passed through your body and was absorbed by the spine. Around here, that usually means someone fell out a third-story window, dove into shallow water, or was struck by lightning. High-impact. You'd have to hit a river rock awfully hard to produce that kind of force, and if that'd happened, I don't think you'd be here."

Dr. Christopher took up the open manila folder from the bedside table. "Then I see in your file that you're a war photographer, that you've just come back from Kurdistan, and it reminds me there's another way you get injuries like this: bomb concussion." She looked at Mark over the top of the folder. "Any bombs go off near you in Kurdistan, Mr. Walsh?"

He didn't answer. Dr. Christopher set the folder aside and held up the plastic bag for Mark to see. Inside was a curved black object about the size of a fingernail.

"Well, to be honest, I didn't really put it together until I was given this. It's what they took out of your head. It's metal—steel, to be exact." She read from the attached green tag. "Composition: steel and cadmium alloy with powder traces of trinitrotoluene, or TNT. Characteristics: one-eighth of an inch thick, jagged edges, curled on two sides, indicating sudden and extreme metal stress. Conclusion: probable military ordnance shrapnel."

Dr. Christopher placed the bag on the table, and leaned back on the stool. "What happened, Mark?"

He looked away, to the wall at the far end of the room. "There was an artillery explosion."

"How close?"

"Maybe forty, fifty feet. I was standing on a hilltop. It hit on the slope just below me."

"So you were shielded from the direct blast," she said. "What kind of hill was it, rock?"

Mark nodded. "Mostly rock, I guess, with patches of soil."

"And were you standing on rock at the time of the explosion?"

He tried to remember. "Yes, I probably was."

Dr. Christopher nodded. "And rock is a perfect conductor of shock waves. Okay, now your story makes sense." She took a pen from her coat pocket, picked up his file, and began writing in it.

Listening to the scratch of pen on paper—a pleasing sound—Mark toyed with the plastic bracelet on his wrist. Having finally spoken of the explosion out loud, he felt vaguely relieved, a slight easing of his burden.

After a time, he noticed the sound of handwriting had stopped and looked up to see Dr. Christopher watching him. In her gaze was a tenderness—perhaps more, a curiosity—he had not sensed before.

"One mystery solved," she said softly, "but it raises a larger one, doesn't it? Why didn't you just say what really happened? Why didn't you tell your girlfriend?"

On the examination table, Mark felt stripped, defenseless. "I don't know. It just seemed . . . easiest."

"Easiest how?"

"Elena worries about me when I'm out there. If I'd told her, she would have been upset. I fell into the river after the explosion and got banged up, so I just thought, 'Say it was the river, who's to know the difference?' "

Dr. Christopher stared at him, her arms folded across her chest, her torso rocking slightly. "I'm not sure that's the whole reason," she said at last. "When she admitted you, your girlfriend said you've been acting strangely since you got back—detached, but also nervous, on edge. She said you had only a slight limp at first, but that it's become progressively worse. Would you agree with that?"

"I guess so," Mark whispered, feeling his throat go dry.

"And yet, you're healing." Dr. Christopher unfolded her arms, waved a hand over his covered body. "With MRIs, we've become quite good at charting the symptoms of spinal shock, and all indications are that you went through the worst effects of this some time ago, a week, maybe two." She reached out to absently rub the plastic-encased piece of shrapnel. "There doesn't seem to be anything organically wrong with your legs. By organic, I mean in the physical sense. No major neural destruction, no broken bones or muscular separation, no purely physical reason why you shouldn't be able to walk. Of course, we can run a bunch more tests, send you over to some specialists, but . . ." She looked into his eyes tentatively. "It seems pretty clear to me that what happened to you in Kurdistan, the physical injury, is now being complicated by some kind of psychosomatic reaction. Between examining you and reading what your girlfriend said, it's the best explanation I can come up with." She picked up the shrapnel, placed it in her coat pocket. "I'm not a psychiatrist, Mark, but I think that may be the kind of doctor you need."

She glanced at her watch and, rather abruptly, stood off the stool, took up his folder from the bedside. "So," she said, looking to him with a slight smile, "what do we tell the girlfriend?"

"What do you mean?"

"She's waiting to talk to me, but by law I can't tell her anything if you don't want me to. It's completely up to you."

Mark looked at the plastic bracelet on his wrist. "It's okay," he said finally. "You can tell her."

"Good choice." Dr. Christopher gave his arm a couple of light taps with the edge of the folder. "The orderlies will come by to take you upstairs. Take care of yourself, Mark." She walked quickly from the room.

He recognized her immediately. A beauty, a striking young woman with long black hair and delicate features, and it would only be later that Joaquin would wonder why he had so instantly spotted her amid the crowd. When he had last seen her, Elena had been twenty-two—attractive, to be sure, but awkward and gangly, still closer to a girl than a woman—and it would only be while lying in his hotel bed waiting for sleep to come that Joaquin would realize he had recognized his granddaughter because she was the only one standing at the railing of the international arrival hall who did not seem pleased, who did not scan the faces of the arriving travelers with anticipation.

"Elena, my darling," he called in Spanish. He left his baggage cart and hurried to the railing, reached across to embrace her. He kissed her forcefully on both cheeks, clutched her shoulders as he leaned back. "Let me look at you. By God, I always knew you would be a beautiful woman, but this, this is almost criminal."

Elena smiled, rolled her eyes. "Thank you, Papa." She looked past him. "Maybe you should come on through; you're holding people up."

Joaquin quickly dropped his hands. "Yes, yes, of course." He retrieved his baggage cart, rejoined the stream of passengers funneling out into the terminal.

Elena observed how nimble his step was for a man in his midseventies. From behind, sure and straight-backed, he could easily be mistaken for middle-aged, even younger if one ignored the thin white hair. She left her spot at the railing, walked down the line of greeters to join him.

Away from the others, he hugged her again. "You look wonderful, my dear. Truly wonderful." She was stiff and unyielding in his embrace, and Joaquin let go.

"How was your flight?" She took the handle of his baggage cart, began propelling it toward the terminal exit. He followed alongside.

"My flight? Unspeakable. It used to be that air travel was an event, like going to the theater. People dressed for it." Joaquin ran a finger along the lapel of his expensive wool suit. "Now"—he flipped his hand dismissively in the direction of the other passengers—"it's all shorts and T-shirts and chewing gum. Even in first class. Call it egalitarianism if you like; for me, it is barbary's last triumph. The meals were quite good, however."

It was cool and damp outside, a light rain falling, and Joaquin buttoned his overcoat as they walked to the taxi stand. He breathed in deeply, smelled the mix of auto exhaust and aviation fuel in the air. "Ah, New York. It's been twenty years since I was last here. A very exciting city as I recall, but dangerous back then, no place for a young woman alone. Mark didn't come with you?"

"No." Elena had been gazing at the line of yellow taxis, the slowly diminishing queue of passengers before them, but she turned to her grandfather then. "He wanted to, but"—Joaquin saw a flicker of uncertainty in his granddaughter's eyes—"but I thought it would be best to meet you alone."

"Absolutely right." Joaquin beamed. "A chance for us to become reacquainted." He reached out and took Elena's hand. She gave his a quick squeeze, but then let go, looked at the stream of yellow taxis.

An awful beginning, and it only became worse. In the ride to the hotel, Joaquin chattered on about family news, about his garden and painting, grasped for anything that might break the awkwardness between them. Elena listened with a stiff smile, nodded occasionally, stared out the rain-streaked window at the night. He ran out of things to say and fell to listening to the regular thump of the taxi passing over concrete slabs, the wet hiss of its tires in the rain.

"Mark is in the hospital," she said finally.

"What?" Joaquin turned, clutched her arm. "Good heavens! Elena, darling, why didn't you tell me? What has happened?"

"He collapsed this afternoon." Joaquin heard the calm steadiness in her voice. "He couldn't walk."

"Can't walk?! Dear God!"

She looked to him in the dark. "They don't think the problem is physical. It's psychological. Mark never told me, but there was an explosion in Kurdistan. He's lucky to be alive. The doctors think he is suffering a psychological trauma."

"Psychological? They're sure?"

"Fairly sure."

Joaquin slumped against the seat back with relief. "And to think I should arrive at this juncture. Remarkable, no? Surely it is fate."

Elena reached into her shoulder bag and withdrew a sheaf of papers. "The hospital is going to help me find a psychiatrist for him. I have an appointment in the morning."

"An appointment you can cancel now that I am here." He took the papers from her hand. "Cast away your cares, Elena, I will see to everything."

"He needs to see a specialist. They think he is suffering from some type of war-zone stress."

"Excellent," Joaquin said, shuffling through the papers. "War zones are my specialty."

"He needs a doctor, Papa. A real doctor."

"Is that what the hospital told you? They sound incompetent." He held the papers to the window, read in the weak light of passing streetlights. "What is this, a checklist? A checklist of symptoms? What do they take us for, goatherders?" He turned to another page, ran a finger along one column. "Ha!" he chortled. "Listen to this: 'Successful treatment may require long-term and intensive psychotherapy.' " Joaquin slapped the papers down on the car seat. "Bandits! Imagine, intensive psychotherapy! They should be reported to the authorities."

"They are the authorities," Elena said.

"Well, rest assured, I shall put a stop to this ugly scheme. One week. One week, Elena, and I will have Mark completely cured of this little trauma of his."

Elena shook her head. "I'm going to get him a real doctor."

"Don't be ridiculous, my child. You are tired, upset, and these"— he jabbed the papers with a finger—"these gypsies are trying to take advantage of that."

"I know you just want to help, but—"

"But nothing. I can help him—more than any of these doctors, as you insist on calling them."

"Like you helped the others? He's not really your type of patient, is he, Papa?"

Joaquin looked across to her then. In the sweep of passing lights, he saw the cool anger in her eyes. "That was a long time ago, Elena. You don't know what it was like."

"I'm sorry," she said, looking away. "You're right, I'm tired and upset. I don't mean to open up all that again."

He turned away from her, gazed out the window at the rainy night. He felt her hand on his knee, patting lightly, but Joaquin didn't turn.

"Let me just do what I think is best, okay?" she said. "Then maybe we can have a nice visit while you're here."

"I came to help you." He didn't look at her, and Elena didn't answer. For the rest of the ride no words were said, and Joaquin felt only an icy cold in his stomach, the patting of her hand on his knee.

In the hotel driveway, they stood a few feet from each other, silently watched the bellhop take the single suitcase from the taxi trunk.

"If you come by in the morning," he said, "we can go to the hospital together."

Elena forced a smile, glanced at her watch. "You'll want to sleep in, Papa; it's almost five in the morning for you. Why don't I call after I've talked to the doctors."

Joaquin nodded. "Maybe I can meet you there. What's the name of the hospital?"

"Brookdale. But, please, wait until I call, okay?"

Joaquin nodded again. Elena crossed to him then, kissed him lightly on the cheek. "I'm sorry for what I said. Good night, Papa. I hope you sleep well."

He stood on the sidewalk and watched her get back in the taxi, watched it pull away, wondered how he had lost his only grandchild so completely. Only when the taillights were gone from sight did he go inside.

"There you are, Mr. Morales, room 417." The clerk handed a key over the marble counter. "Is there anything else I can do for you?"

Joaquin looked at the clock above the young man's head: a few minutes before eleven. He felt shattered with fatigue, almost ill. "Yes. Can I be awakened at six o'clock?"

"Of course." The clerk busied himself with a console of buttons below the counter. He glanced up, smiled perkily. "All set, Mr. Morales."

"Thank you." Joaquin started away, but then wheeled around. "It's 'Doctor.'"

"I beg your pardon?"

"It's Dr. Morales."

"Oh, I'm sorry." The clerk shuffled through the papers on his desk, held up an index card. "It wasn't on the reservation slip; I'll correct it."

Joaquin grinned, gave a magnanimous shrug. "Quite all right. My granddaughter made the reservation. I'm sure she just forgot."

As he followed the bellhop toward the bank of elevators, he reached into his coat pocket for the papers Elena had shown him in the taxi, which he had forgotten to return.

It was a time when the ruthless and cunning were blessed, an age when all good things came to those quick enough to seize them. That was how Joaquin explained it to himself.

What he refused to entertain—had always refused to entertain— was the suggestion of a more complex explanation for what happened in Spain in the 1930s, that it was somehow a conflict between ideologies or empires or even armies. To Joaquin, the war had hurtled down on Spain like a meteor—unforeseeable, a bad coincidence of nature—and even before those first tremors subsided, even before that first hysteria of bloodletting had spent itself, already the brutal and the daring had found their moment, had begun creeping out from their lairs to take over the land. And because decent men never act as quickly as tyrants, the decent of both sides were soon dispensed with. And because cruelty has always been man's most awesome weapon—capable of shocking entire nations, entire peoples, into submission—the spoils of victory went to those who showed mercy the least, who knew cruelty the best.

Was this regrettable? Of course it was regrettable. But Joaquin had always understood that regrets were useless, like lamenting the weather; this was the age into which he was born, and it formed him. And if he suffered great cruelties himself, he was also quick, he was also cunning.

The manor home had been built by the seventeenth Duque de Orellana, on a small rise of land in the heart of the Vega de Granada, the broad, fertile valley that extends westward from the city of that name. It was called Casa de los Queridos—House of the Dear Ones—and this in itself should have been seen as an omen; there was no place in southern Spain, certainly not in the southern Spain of the 1930s, for such sentimentality.

The Orellana family had been masters of a vast stretch of the vega for some four hundred years, but the seventeenth duque was different from all Orellanas who had come before: more ambitious, less pious, he fancied himself a man of the modern era. Immediately upon his ascendancy in 1909, he had begun to sever the family reliance on the harvest, selling off most of the old lands, investing in the new technologies and trades that were changing the world. To reflect his modernism, he decided to build a new manor home; it was to honor his wife and four young daughters that he named it Casa de los Queridos.

In furnishing the home, the duque was profligate. Italian furniture and English dolls for his daughters' bedrooms, gilt tables and brocade draperies for the ladies' parlor, cherrywood cabinets to display the silver and crystal and china in the dining room. For the salons, there were chandeliers and tapestries, Louis XIV divans and armchairs in cordovan leather, and for his rosewood-paneled office a splendid mahogany desk, a desk so massive it had to be built within the room and could never be moved.

This last conceit might have alerted a different kind of man that fate was being tempted, for in Andalusia, as in most agrarian places, it is a sure harbinger of bad luck to imagine anything built by man as permanent. But that, of course, was the duque's intent; he had cut himself free from the chains of faith and tradition to walk boldly into the dawn of a new time.

Yet, standing as he did on the very cusp of a new era, the duque had no way of comprehending that he was only partially a modern man. Despite his progressive ideas about commerce and technology, he still viewed history much as his ancestors had, as the mere march of days and seasons. He could not possibly grasp that history was now to become like a falling object, constantly gaining momentum, could not see that in this new time everything would be exponentially greater—more grand, more terrible—than it had been before, that now a man could destroy in twenty years what others had taken four hundred to build.

Construction of Casa de los Queridos was completed in the autumn of 1913. That winter, no snow fell in the mountains. No rain came to the valley in spring. By summer, the Vega de Granada was as brown as the surrounding hills, its fields of wheat withered to useless straw. Too late the duque realized that if the land failed, all his wealth—all his shares in shipping companies and rail lines and investment banks—turned to worthless paper, that in his modernism he had not broken with the earth but merely maneuvered himself into a more desperate dependency upon it.

So began the descent of the Orellana family, a descent so rapid as to be beyond the imaginings of any Orellana who had ever lived before. The seventeenth duque offered up ever-greater sacrifices—the last of his servants in 1919, the very last parcels of land in the recession of 1923, even the eucalyptus trees for firewood in 1927—but these could never do more than forestall the day of final ruin. By the depression of 1930, all he had left to offer were the furnishings of Casa de los Queridos, and these, too, began to disappear in the same systematic manner that marked all the duque's undertakings. First to leave for the auction houses of Madrid were the fixtures of the salons, then those of the parlor and dining room, the erosion eventually spreading up the stairs and into the bedrooms. With each new loss, the family retreated deeper into their diminished home, so that by the summer of 1938, the Orellana domain, once so vast a walking man could barely cross it in a day, was reduced to a kitchen, an office, and two bedrooms, and the surrounding villagers had punned a new name for the manor house on the hill: Casa de los Caídos, House of the Fallen.

It was at this twilight moment that Joaquin had appeared, a thin, twenty-five-year-old former medical student in a borrowed Falange uniform, originally from the coastal city of Almería, now living in refuge in the city of Granada. In a fitting irony, the duque first regarded him as a kind of savior.

What Joaquin saw when he emerged from the sedan taxi that afternoon in July 1938 was a once-grand home gradually succumbing to the earth. The perimeter wall had not been painted in many years, the plaster fallen away in places to reveal the rough stones beneath. Even the entrance columns of machine-made brick were chipped and gouged, only rusted hinge mounts indicating a gate had once stood between them.

He stepped through the opening and surveyed the garden. There was the suggestion of a remarkable devotion to uniformity. Within the enclosing stone wall, the grounds appeared to form an exact square— some sixty meters on each side, Joaquin calculated—with the trees and shrubs planted to one side of the pebbled drive precisely matching those planted on the opposite. At one time, eucalyptus trees had been placed every three meters along the inner base of the wall, and their stumps still lent a scent to the air.

He looked to the house. It was a massive two-story square building with a pair of great quartered windows to either side of the front door, four identical windows on the upper floor. In Andalusian tradition, the stuccoed exterior walls had been painted ochre, the angles of the roof highlighted with glazed green ridge tiles. The place seemed abandoned; many of the windows were missing or cracked, and a number of roof tiles had slid from their moorings, great sprouts of weeds growing in their place.

Walking up the drive, past a lawn and flowerbeds long since surrendered to nature, he climbed the stone front steps to an oak door.
He was about to announce himself, reaching for a brass knocker in
the shape of a human hand, when the door swung open. On the
threshold an elderly, stooped man peered at him with that slightly
startled expression Joaquin had come to recognize in the faces of the
hungry.

"Good afternoon," Joaquin said, "I am looking for the Duque de
Orellana."

The old man slowly drew up, raised his chin to an imperious
angle. "*C'est moi*," he said in the manner of the Spanish aristocracy.

Joaquin gave a quick bow and introduced himself. "I hope I have
not come at an inconvenient moment, Your Excellency, but it has
been suggested in certain circles in Granada that you might entertain
the idea of placing this magnificent estate on the market." He gave
the duque an obsequious look. "If this is in error, please accept my
apologies, and I will leave immediately."

The duque stared for a long moment. He then opened the door
wide and, returning the slight bow, ushered Joaquin in. "Please."

Joaquin followed the duque through the downstairs. The symmetry he had noticed from the gate extended into the home. To either
side of the foyer, arched doorways let onto enormous matching
salons, which in turn led back to two more large rooms, a formal dining room, and a ladies' parlor. Discreet narrow doors connected these
last two rooms to the kitchen and the servants' quarters at the back of
the house. These rooms were now stripped bare, and the only sign
that life had ever taken place in them were the lighter patches on
walls where paintings had once hung.

"It was not always like this," the duque said softly. "At one time,
we had many things."

"But this way," Joaquin offered, "the rooms are even more spa-
cious."

The duque led the way back to the entrance foyer, up a marble
staircase to the second floor. An interior walkway girdled the staircase
opening, creating the sensation of a courtyard, and Joaquin followed
the old man along the passage.

"There are five bedrooms, two bathrooms," the duque said, flinging open doors onto large empty rooms. He paused, turned to point to the closed door they had passed at the head of the stairs. "And, of course, my study."

Only two of the bedrooms were inhabited—straw beds, crude campesino furniture, crucifixes on the walls—and in one Joaquin was introduced to the duquessa and the one daughter who remained at home, a nervous, gaunt woman in her early forties whose splayed teeth and deep color suggested the swiftness of the Orellana family's descent to peasantry. Out of politeness, he merely glanced into these rooms and saved his thoughtful lingering for those that were empty, paced the floors, gazed out windows, knocked on the masonry walls as if to gauge their soundness. Throughout, the duque stood nearby, as solicitous as a butler. Only at the end of the tour, did he open the door into his study.

"What a magnificent desk," Joaquin said, with genuine awe.

"Yes," the duque said, "made of Brazilian mahogany. It took three artisans a month to build it."

"I can well imagine." Joaquin studied the extraordinarily fine carvings adorning the front and sides of the desk: trains and ships and factories, all in operation, all releasing delicately cut billows of smoke. Leaning close, he examined the burnished top panel, wondered how the artisans had joined the sections so flawlessly, until he realized the entire vast panel had come from one tree. He turned to the duque. "A masterpiece. And you simply can't bear to part with it?"

"It was built in here," the duque said with a note of embarrassment, then gestured toward the door. "It can't be moved."

Then you brought this on yourself, Joaquin thought to himself, because you are a vain and arrogant man.

They returned to the downstairs. Leaving Joaquin in one of the grand salons, the duque went to the kitchen and brought out two plain wood chairs. He placed these in the center of the room, facing each other, and here he sat with the young man whom he had already come to view as a godsend.

"I see you are a plainspoken man, sir," Joaquin said, "so, with your permission, I will be frank." He shifted in his chair, gazed over the cavernous room. "Given my youth, it might surprise you to learn that I am something of a scholar in the field of human psychology—all modesty aside, a scholar of some consideration—and for much of the past two years, since shortly after this war began, I have worked with the military junta in Granada—on a strictly informal basis, you understand—to deal with certain problems that have arisen among the officers and troops there, very delicate problems"—he gave the duque a sly, knowing look—"ones that could be said to fall somewhere outside the powers of either the church or medicine. The degree of success I have had in these matters has led elements of the military administration—elements who, in all candor, we might call progressivists—to propose establishing a permanent facility, a clinic, if you will, specifically designed to address these problems as they become more prevalent in the near future. As an educated man yourself, you can surely appreciate the importance of such an endeavor."

Joaquin paused. In the duque's naked stare there was not the slightest hint of comprehension.

"This war is ending, sir. The Republican back has been broken. The final collapse might come next month or it may take another year, but it is coming and it is inevitable. And what will happen in Spain then? A time of celebrations and parades—yes, of course—but also one of great trials. Quietude. A terrible quiet." He gave the old man a sardonic grin. "One always imagines that war's end will be a joyous thing, but I doubt this is ever so. War, you see, is an anesthetic. When the guns are firing, we feel nothing, we are numb; it is with peace that we feel pain. And what happens then?"

The duque merely stared. Joaquin leaned toward him, spoke in a hushed, almost conspiratorial tone.

"As difficult as it may be for us to admit, it is not only the Republicans who have committed injustices in this war. We must recognize that there have been times—aberrant moments, to be sure—when our patriots have transgressed, when they have overstepped the boundaries of Christian duty and surrendered themselves to passions of a plainly excessive sort. Is it heresy to say this? But we are speaking here as one man to another." He came even closer, continued in a whisper. "And so it will come again, sir. When this war ends, when the Republicans surrender and the eastern provinces are freed, Spain will be washed in the blood of revenge. The vigilantes and tribunals will be vigorous, the poorly disciplined given over to libertine displays. Who will be safe? How far will the revenge-seekers go? You see? A most perilous time we are entering. For many of us, perhaps more perilous than that already endured."

Joaquin leaned back, never taking his eyes from the old man.

"But this, clearly, cannot become a way of life for us. We must take steps to ensure the Fatherland does not fall prey to an enduring cult of violence. It is to this end that the progressivist elements within the junta have asked me—implored me, if the truth be told—to establish a facility here at Casa de los Queridos, a clinic devoted to the treatment of those patriots who have fallen victim to their lesser instincts, so that we might cure them, ease their pain." He smiled. "In fact, arrangements could be made that might be ideal for all concerned. At present, I'm occupying very pleasant apartments near the cathedral, four rooms and a terrace from which you can see the Alhambra. I would not go so far as to call them opulent, but they are certainly sufficient for your wife and daughter and"—he cast a flitting glance about the desolate room—"your possessions. And, of course, my close relations with the provisional junta bestows certain privileges that, given the unfortunate circumstances in which many of our countrymen currently find themselves, might be looked upon with envy: a high degree of security, a variety of friendships that ensure that obtaining sufficient food or fuel is never a preoccupation. And this is to say nothing of the cultural life of Granada, an aspect I suspect your wife and daughter would find most appealing."

A silence descended in the room. The duque's gaze moved away from Joaquin, drifted along the edge of the ceiling until it came to a spot where the plaster had fallen and exposed a supporting wood beam. He cleared his throat.

"Perhaps some negotiation is possible, Don Joaquin, but I must tell you: This is a very expensive house."

Joaquin watched the old aristocrat's eyes for a long moment, as if they might yield a crucial piece of information. At last, he sighed, rose to pace the length of the room several times, as if deep in thought. He stopped to look out a window at the late afternoon sky.

"You know, sir," he said quietly, "I had a very difficult time finding Casa de los Queridos. In Granada, I was told it was twenty or thirty kilometers to the west, but there are a number of roads in this area and each time I stopped to ask a villager for directions, they could not answer me. You can imagine my confusion, I'm sure. Finally, one farmer explained it. He said, 'Oh, you mean *caídos*—not *queridos*—Casa de los Caídos.' It was only then I was able to find my way."

Joaquin turned from the window to see the old man staring at the floor.

"Surely you know this, sir. Surely you know that, throughout the vega, your home is called the House of the Fallen."

The duque did not answer.

"Forgive me for saying so, but this house is of little value to you now. You and your wife and daughter are starving, and you cannot eat this house."

Joaquin leaned against the window and waited. When the old man finally looked up, he was angry, his posture suddenly defiant. "My family has been on this land for over four hundred years. It is my birthright and I will not be pushed off it, and I will not be insulted. We have gone through hard times and we have survived, and we will continue to survive." He leapt to his feet. "I've wasted far too much time with you already, so if you will—"

"Sit."

The duque seemed almost to physically stagger. He looked to his young visitor with astonishment, as if he had just been slapped. Joaquin, still leaning against the window, pointed to the chair.

"Sit."

As obedient as a child, the duque did so. Joaquin slowly walked back, took the chair opposite. With an amused expression, he studied each feature of the stunned old man's face. He smiled. "What time do you think this is?"

The duque was baffled. "Time?" he repeated softly.

"The age we are living in. Do you have no idea of what has happened? Have you been in this house the entire time?"

The duque, his eyes blinking rapidly, didn't answer.

"Well, then, I will tell you a story," Joaquin said. "It is about Spain, about how the living and dead are chosen now." He reached into his coat pocket and withdrew a packet of cigarettes. He did not offer one to the duque but lit his own, sent a stream of smoke into the air. "I was lucky. I happened to be away from home when the mob came for us, I managed to escape. My family had no such luck. They were home. This was in Almería. Surely, even you know of what happened in Almería in the early days of the war?"

He waited until the old man nodded.

"Of my family, my parents, my brothers and sisters, my aunts and uncles and cousins, I have heard nothing in nearly two years. Given what I saw on the streets of Almería that last day, one must assume I will not hear from them in the future." Rolling the cigarette between his fingertips, he watched the duque. He smiled again. "But, of course, those were Republican mobs, communists and anarchists. Our mobs are much better behaved—Christians, after all."

Joaquin's smile crept away.

"So, you see, sir, I know what time it is. You are still talking about birthrights. I am telling you about something much simpler. What does it take now for a family to vanish? It takes nothing. It takes a word, it takes a gesture"—he gave a lazy, backward flip of his hand— "sometimes just silence." He looked appraisingly about the room. "So, a time to ponder, to imagine what our luck might be. What do you think, sir? After so many years of misfortune, are the fates now to turn in your favor? More to the point, are you prepared to match your luck up against mine—I, who have been so terribly lucky?" He turned to the duque and laughed lightly. "Difficult questions, no? So much resting on the outcome."

The old man, gone ashen, shook with rage. "My God," he whispered, "you are threatening me."

"No," Joaquin said. "I'm educating you."

The duque tried to calm his anger. Still trembling, he stared out the window, and for a long time the only sound in the room was his heavy, labored breathing. "What price?" he asked finally.

"I beg your pardon?"

Summoning a last trace of pride, he straightened, looked to Joaquin with contempt. "In addition to the apartments in Granada, what price are you offering?"

Joaquin smiled, reached into his trouser pocket, and drew out a one-peseta coin. He held it up for a moment, then tossed it at the old man's feet.

And so, the Orellana family departed from the home that had

borne witness to their ruin. In August 1938, they loaded their few remaining possessions onto a flatbed truck and set off on the pitted dirt road that led to Granada and the small apartment near the cathedral that was to be their new home. After introducing the duque to the various men who now controlled his fate—lieutenants and colonels in the military administration, the local *Guardia Civil* commander—Joaquin placed his own few possessions on the same flatbed truck and made the journey to his new home at Casa de los Queridos.

It would be seven more long months—March 1939—before the civil war finally ended, before the shattered Republican soldiers escaped into France or laid down their arms in a thousand Spanish villages to be processed, culled, and slaughtered by Franco's Nationalist militias. Until then, Joaquin would waken each morning in the barren, darkened shell of his new home, walk the three kilometers to Peñuelas when he was in need of food or companionship or rumors, occasionally hike all the way to the crests of the foothills when he desired to see a long distance, and, throughout, he would tell himself, "I'm waiting, I'm simply waiting," and he came to regard this waiting as a kind of punishment.

When it was over, no relatives came from Almería. Instead, there came beds, forty-six of them on metal frames, requisitioned from the Jaén fort and arranged barracks-style in the upstairs bedrooms. Soon after, more items—file cabinets, footlockers, an odd assortment of couches and armchairs for the downstairs rooms—and then a work crew of Republican prisoners. By June 1939, Casa de los Queridos had been transformed, its walls replastered and painted, its rotted beams and broken roof tiles replaced, all its rooms fitted with electricity. Even the grounds were put to order, the flowerbeds replanted, a new gate mounted upon the brick pillars, and—a new feature—the perimeter wall crowned with shards of green glass. Then came the staff—the nurse, the cook, the two housekeepers—then a shiny brass plaque for the entrance and, at last, the first truckload of patients.

When these sixteen men stepped down to the dirt road, their eyes tearing in the harsh Andalusian sunlight after the half-darkness of the covered truck, this is what they saw: two *guardias* in black uniforms standing at attention, a wrought-iron gate, two pillars of machine-formed brick, and upon one of these pillars a brass plaque that read: Instituto Morales para la Purificación Psicológica.

Out of their officers' uniforms, clad in civilian dress or hospital gowns, these sixteen men appeared to have little in common. The youngest was nineteen, the oldest sixty-two. Their ranks ranged from corporal to full colonel, their origins from peasant to aristocrat, but in the coming days they would discover that here, at the Morales Institute, they were among comrades who understood them, fellow patriots who had gone forth to perform their duty for the Fatherland and come instead to a place—a mountain meadow, a village street, a ravine—where the wrong decision had been made, the wrong action taken, a place where, like water beneath a wheel, the blood-wet earth had sprayed up to stain their souls.

"I am Dr. Joaquin Antonio Morales. The room number for Mr. Mark Walsh, please."

The middle-aged nurse behind the desk looked at Joaquin dubiously, then scanned a paper before her. "He's in room 1523, bed 2-R. But I'm afraid I don't have you on my attending list, Doctor . . . ?"

"Morales. Understandable. I just flew in from Spain—something of an emergency, you see—and these oversights do occur. Which way to the room?"

The nurse uneasily pointed down the corridor to her left. "But Mr. Walsh's attending physician, Dr. Christopher, has placed him on a restricted visitor list."

Joaquin nodded. "Most wise, very prudent. Please see to it that we are not disturbed." He left the nurses' station and strode briskly down the hall.

The hospital room was quiet and murky, the window at the far end admitting only a pale yellow light in the overcast dawn. Joaquin went to the second curtain on the right, silently slipped past it. Waiting for his eyes to adjust, he peered at the dark outline of the sleeping figure. He crept closer.

An attractive young man. A bit thin in the face, perhaps, but with a nice facial structure, a strong jaw. Joaquin was relieved to see there were no tubes attached to him, not even a glucose drip.

A reading lamp sat on a table at the top of the bed. Joaquin stepped past an armchair, angled the lamp so that it was directed at the sleeping man's face.

A brilliant light and Mark recoiled, raised a hand to shield his eyes. Squinting, he looked past the beam to see an elderly man in a business suit watching him.

"Ah, so you're awake then. Good sleep?" He spoke with a heavy accent, but Mark couldn't immediately place it—not French, perhaps Spanish or Italian. The old man turned the lamp to the wall and smiled, displayed two perfectly straight rows of white teeth. "And how are you feeling this fine morning?"

Mark shifted in the hospital bed. He gazed down the expanse of white sheet and saw the motion around his knees and feet. "Okay," he said.

"Marvelous." The old man brought the armchair closer and quickly sat. Crossing his legs, he folded back the cover of a legal pad, took a silver pen from his coat pocket. He smiled at Mark again.

"If I may be candid for a moment, I must say I find all this quite remarkable. Just yesterday I was at my home in Granada when Isabela told me of your difficulty and asked if I might help in some way. I was reluctant, of course, as I've been retired from the field for many years, but the woman was anxious—distraught, if the truth be told—so, naturally, I agreed and flew right over. The least one can do for family. Little did I imagine, however, that I should arrive at such a decisive moment." The old man suddenly caught himself, wagged a finger at Mark. "But, please, do not take from this that I came only out of some sense of familial obligation. No! I was intrigued by the prospect, flattered, frankly, to be called upon after so many years. You see, my technique was rather revolutionary for the time—all modesty aside, it made me famous in certain European circles—but then everything became contentious, politicized, and I always felt that if I had the opportunity to perform on a wider array of patients—civilians such as yourself, for example, rather than combatants exclusively—I might finally defeat my critics and prove to the world that the technique is of great benefit. And now, here you are, here I am, and the opportunity has presented itself. Well, call it fate, I suppose. Perhaps we should get started."

Mark stared at the old man. His suit was ancient, probably from the 1950s, but expensive and well cared for. His thinning white hair was combed straight back, long enough to reach his shirt collar. He had sharp brown eyes beneath bushy eyebrows and a large, aquiline nose over a thin-lipped mouth, still curved into a smile. "I'm sorry, but . . . who are you?"

The old man chuckled, shook his head in self-rebuke. "Oh, how silly of me, I forgot to introduce myself." He leaned forward and took Mark's hand in both of his. "I'm Joaquin Morales, Elena's grandfather—paternal, of course. I've heard so much about you, I feel we're already old friends." He eased back into the armchair. "Elena and her mother—that is Isabela—are always telling me of your adventures, your travels. A very exciting life you lead, no? And now, I finally have the chance to meet you face to face after all this time. Pity that it is under these circumstances." He gazed at Mark expectantly. "And I imagine you've heard a great deal about me."

Mark didn't know what to say. Elena often spoke of her maternal grandfather, but he couldn't recall even the mention of her paternal one before last night. But Mark didn't want to hurt the old man's feelings. He bunched a pillow under his head, settled into a more comfortable position. "Well, not that much, actually."

"Hmm, curious." Joaquin nodded. "But that is Elena. A very private girl. Even as a child, very self-contained, very quiet, never one to reveal too much of herself. But I'm sure you have no need to be told this, knowing her as well as you do. I always suspected it had a lot to do with her father dying when she was so young, that it made her cautious about attachment, careful who she confided in. A traumatic experience for a young child, of course, and I suppose it was only natural that as she grew up she saw me as something of a surrogate father. But now, I'm old—close to death, one might imagine—so she must minimize the importance of that bond—quite unconscious, to be sure, and let me assure you I have never taken it personally, but self-protection, you see? It's all rather basic human psychology. Basic but complex. A very complex young woman, as I'm sure you've discovered. But sweet, at her essence a very sweet and loving girl. Perhaps a bit too sheltered in her upbringing, being an only child with no father, the sort of childhood that can foster a certain rigidity, a certain tendency toward orthodoxy and harsh assessment that a wider range of relationships, a large familial unit, might counteract, but there you have it. Perhaps she has even told you things about me of this nature?"

Mark looked around the room, confused. "She told me you were a fascist."

"Ah, precisely my point." Joaquin threw his head back and laughed. "A fascist, that's rich! She always was a humorist, Elena, but I don't recall her previous tastes running to the political—testament to your sophisticating influence, no doubt. Fascist, what a wit!"

He sighed with pleasure, but then quickly straightened as if with dismay. "All this pleasant conversation is straying me from our task, and time is vital. Regrettable, I know, but we simply must get to work."

Suddenly brisk and businesslike, he propped his legal pad against one of the chair arms. "First, I would like to compile a patient history, if that is all right?"

Mark nodded.

"Age?"

"Thirty-one."

Joaquin scribbled this down. "Brothers and sisters?"

"Two sisters, one brother."

"Younger, older?"

"All older."

"And childhood, fairly normal?"

"Yes, fairly normal."

"A religious family?"

"No, we never went to church."

Joaquin looked up. "And what of you? Would you consider yourself religious?"

"No, not really."

Joaquin clicked his teeth. "A pity. Belief in God would make things much easier. Well, we'll just make do, won't we?" He turned the page. "Very good. Let's get started."

"That's it?" Mark asked.

The old man seemed puzzled. "I beg your pardon?"

"That's all the background you want?"

Joaquin returned to the first page and glanced over his scant notes. "Yes, I believe so. Unless there is something you wish to add."

"I just thought psychiatrists asked all sorts of questions about childhood experiences, relationships."

Joaquin shook his head. "Quite unnecessary. Exotic."

"What about dreams? Aren't you supposed to ask about my dreams?"

Joaquin frowned. "A personal failing, no doubt, but I've always found listening to other people's dreams somewhat . . . tedious."

Mark stared at the old man. "You're not really a psychiatrist, are you?"

Joaquin gazed thoughtfully at the ceiling. "I suppose the answer might depend on one's definition. If by 'psychiatrist,' you mean someone who studied psychiatry at university, who received a degree and has carried on a recognized practice, then, no, I am not a psychiatrist." His gaze slid down until it rested on Mark. He smiled serenely. "I prefer to think of myself as a scholar of the human spirit."

"Terrific," Mark said.

Joaquin grinned. "Tell me a war story."

"What?"

"A war story. Tell me your first one."

Elena set her coffee on the hall table, rewound the answering machine, and relived the day before. Her voice on one message after another—"Mark, where are you?"—becoming increasingly frustrated and strained. One from Diane, sounding tired, a bit on edge, just calling to chat. Mark's agent, Amy Mavroules, in a throaty cigarette voice announcing that his triage essay had been picked up by *Stern* for $10,000, that she was still waiting for bids from several American outlets.

Welcome news, Elena thought. Mark's insurance didn't cover psychiatric care; ten thousand dollars just might cover his therapy bills for the first few months.

After the last message, she wandered about the living room, sipping her coffee, thinking of all she had to do that morning. Tell the office she wouldn't be in. Call Mark's parents: "He's in the hospital, but he's fine, just suffering from . . . exhaustion"—something mild and unalarming. Then the appointment at the hospital referral office. Choosing a doctor. Convincing Mark. Papa.

At the thought of her grandfather, Elena felt a blush of remorse. She had been harsh with him the night before. It was the tension of the moment, she told herself, that he would arrive uninvited at this worst possible time, that he was again trying to insinuate himself into her life.

She went down the hall to the study. Sitting at the desk, she slid open her file drawer, took out the folder filled with his letters. Dozens of letters over the years, most never opened, all of them unanswered. Her remorse deepened into shame. She put the folder back in the drawer, returned to the living room.

She would call him, she decided, apologize again for her brusqueness last night. But it was only eight in the morning. Papa would still be fast asleep after his long and exhausting trip.

"What kind of war story?" Mark asked. "I have quite a repertoire."

Joaquin bowed his head slightly. "Imprecision; it's a curse. I mean an experience that affected you deeply. Not necessarily the most dangerous one, the personal effect is the important element. Your first experience of this nature."

"What's the purpose of this?"

"Please." Joaquin raised his hands. "We are voyagers into a mysterious science, and it is not always possible to have a clear destination at the outset. For the moment, just imagine you are satisfying the indulgence of an old man."

Mark looked to the curtain and thought. "First time, I guess, would have been Beirut."

"Beirut!" Joaquin beamed. "Magnificent city. The 'Paris of the Middle East,' they called it. Before the hostilities, of course, before your time." He shook his head wistfully. "But, please, go on."

"It was in the summer of 1980. At that time, the city was just in complete chaos—probably a dozen different sides alternately fighting each other, forming alliances, falling out again—absolutely no way to predict who would be fighting who on any given day. Total madness." He shook his head, scratched at his jaw.

"Yes, a most lamentable history," Joaquin said. "Go on."

"Well, on this particular day, it was the Lebanese army—what was left of it—and one of the Shiite militias going at it, down in the old city center, just west of the Green Line. They'd been battling down there most of the morning, and when I got there—it was early afternoon—the army was mopping up. They were collecting the Shiite teenagers in the neighborhood, the boys, to take them down to the barracks for questioning, and they had set up a kind of forward processing center at this intersection. There were three or four transport trucks lined up on one side and, every couple of minutes, a Jeep loaded with boys would come out from one of the side streets, stop in the middle of the intersection, and the boys—their hands were tied behind their backs—would be ordered to jump out one by one. They had to run this gauntlet of soldiers to the transport trucks and were then hauled up inside. There was still a lot of firing going on—you could tell it was close, just a couple of blocks away—and the soldiers were jumpy. They weren't taking it out on the boys—not hitting or kicking them—but you could see they were trying to get them loaded up quick, that they wanted to get the hell out of there."

"Of course," Joaquin said, "quite natural. And then you arrived."

"And I arrived. I looked around for the best vantage point to shoot from and went over and stood in the doorway of one of these burnt-out buildings. It gave me a perfect side view of the boys running the gauntlet. And, you know, there's smoke and dust in the air, and I get these kids—they're scared, eyes wide, hands tied behind them—running past, running left to right, and you just see the soldiers from behind—no faces, just uniforms, guns raised in the air."

"Very nice," Joaquin said. "Cinematic. But then, misfortune."

Mark nodded. "It was maybe the tenth or twelfth Jeep that came in. I spotted him right off—I mean, my attention was naturally drawn to him. All the other boys were huddled down in the bed, waiting for their turn to run the gauntlet, but this one kid, he was standing straight up, staring around with these huge, frightened eyes. And the other boys were looking up at him, probably telling him to get down, but it was like he couldn't hear them."

"And this boy, do you remember what he looked like?"

"He was young. Maybe fourteen. He had short black hair, dark skin. He was thin—I remember his arms were very thin—and he wore a white T-shirt."

Joaquin made some quick notes on his pad, nodded for Mark to continue.

"He just stood there, trembling, looking around at all the soldiers. And then he saw me standing in the doorway. He stared at me for a long time—well, it seemed a long time, probably only three or four seconds. But it was an intent stare, you know? You could tell it meant something. And then he jumped."

Joaquin looked up from his note-taking. "He jumped?"

"Jumped out of the Jeep and started running toward me."

"Why would he do that?"

Mark shrugged. "I have no idea. Maybe he saw me—obviously a foreigner, not a soldier—as someone who could help him, protect him, but I really don't know why he did it. I'm not a psychiatrist either."

Joaquin grinned. "Touché. Please, go on."

"Well, the soldiers were caught off guard. Just for a second, but he manages to get past them, past the gauntlet, and he's coming toward me. And then the soldiers scramble. They're swinging their guns around, yelling at him to stop, but the kid just keeps coming, across the street, right for me. I get my camera up, get off one shot, and by the time I bring the camera down, he's standing there, maybe five feet in front of me, standing there, staring at me. He doesn't speak, just stands there. I can hear him breathing—panting—he's so close, but he doesn't say anything. And it's like I want to say, 'What the fuck are you doing?' Because I can see behind him, I can see the soldiers coming on. They're maybe twenty feet away, and they've got their guns up and I know they're about to shoot him, and I'm thinking the bullets are going to go through him and into me. So, I duck. I duck down in the doorway, cover my head. And I'm crouched there, waiting, but nothing happens. It feels like ten minutes go by and nothing happens. So I look up, and he's still fucking standing there. But it's different. He's looking down at me, but his eyes are different. Not frightened anymore, not crazy. Calm. Relaxed. And then he sighs. I swear to God, he just closes his eyes and sighs. It's the strangest thing. No scream. No cry. Just one very deep, long sigh. I'll never forget it. And then . . . well, that's the end of it."

"That's the end of it?" Joaquin cocked an eyebrow.

Mark nodded.

Joaquin sat back a little. "I'm not sure I understand what you mean by 'that's the end of it.'"

"Well, a soldier had swung out to the side—to get me out of the fire line, I guess—and he came in on the kid from an angle. He comes in from the side, has his gun up—he's maybe ten feet away— and then he fires."

"He shoots the boy?"

"He shoots the boy."

"And the boy is dead?"

"The boy is dead," Mark said. He paused for a moment. "I don't even know if his family got the body back."

Joaquin finished writing, placed his notepad on the floor, and returned the pen to his coat pocket. "An intriguing story. Sad, but intriguing. Why do you think this incident affected you?"

Mark stared at the old man somewhat incredulously. "Wouldn't it affect anyone?"

Joaquin shrugged. "Not necessarily. It's always been a fascination to me how very differently people react to troublesome situations." He folded his hands in his lap. "I once worked with a man who had witnessed and participated in many terrible things during the war—the Spanish Civil War—and, by all appearances, none of it had upset him in the slightest. He returned to his family, his profession, all appeared to be going well until one day he happened to see an old woman carrying a basket of oranges to the marketplace. The basket broke. The oranges spilled everywhere. For some reason, the sight of this old woman running after her oranges, it shattered this man. When he was brought to me, he was a ruin. For days, all he talked of was the woman with her oranges, and he would cry and cry at the thought of her. I've often wondered, what would have happened to this man if he hadn't seen the old lady? Or if the incident had occurred a day earlier or a day later. What if she had lost eggs instead of oranges? Could he have gone through the remainder of his life untouched? Perhaps, perhaps. The heart is an unpredictable beast." He smiled at Mark. "But you. Why do you think this boy in Beirut affected you so?"

Mark scanned the hospital room. "I guess I felt responsible somehow."

"Because if you hadn't been there, maybe the boy wouldn't have jumped? If you had grabbed him instead of protecting yourself, maybe the soldier wouldn't have fired?"

"I suppose so," Mark whispered, still staring off.

Joaquin nodded. "Well, this makes perfect sense. You feel responsible because, to a large measure, you were."

Mark turned to him, stunned.

"You think I'm too harsh? Tell me, Mark, how many people have you told this story to? Three? Four? Twenty?"

Mark didn't answer.

"And they all told you it wasn't your fault, didn't they? They all said, 'Don't blame yourself, there was nothing you could do, it was out of your hands.' Is that correct?"

Almost against his will, Mark nodded.

"But you've never been convinced," Joaquin said. "You're still haunted by it. Everyone who has heard the story has absolved you of all guilt, but still you feel it. So now you tell me the story and expect to be told the same thing. Do you think this time will make the difference? Do you think that if I—a person you have just met, who you view as something of a charlatan—said, 'Forget it, your conscience is clear,' you would finally be convinced?"

He smiled, waited for a response that didn't come.

"You are faced with a problem, Mark. You are looking to others for forgiveness, but, as you yourself have discovered, that is something no person can give you. Only God can grant the forgiveness you seek. Yet you don't truly believe in God. This means you are searching for something you have no hope of finding. This is what we call a dilemma."

"What are you, some kind of wandering Catholic proselytizer?"

Joaquin threw his head back and laughed. "Oh good heavens, no. I've been an atheist for many years now. A proselytizer—that's splendid!" He reached down for the legal pad, retrieved the sheaf of papers he had taken from Elena and tucked in back. He fluttered the papers in Mark's direction. "So, instead of God, we have Western medicine." Taking a pair of bifocals from his coat pocket, he placed them low on his nose and read aloud from the first page.

"Post-traumatic stress disorder. The person has experienced an event that is outside the range of usual human experience and that would be markedly distressing to almost anyone." He peered indulgently at Mark over the top of his glasses. "Well, how shall we proceed? Was the artillery explosion in Kurdistan a markedly distressing event?"

Mark didn't answer, just stared at the old man. Joaquin flipped pages until he found the next passage. "Successful treatment may require long-term and intensive psychotherapy." He tossed the papers onto the bed, fixed Mark with a grin. "God would be so much cheaper, no?"

Joaquin sat back in the armchair, returned the bifocals to his pocket. "They have very big plans for you, my boy. Intensive psychotherapy. They are going to match you up with an expert, and he is going to delve into your mind until he finds the problem and tears it out like a weed. They are going to stand you up in front of therapy groups and ask all about your markedly distressing events. They will psychoanalyze your childhood, your sibling rivalries—and, yes, you will even have the opportunity to talk about your dreams. And all that time, Elena will wait for you to recover, for the real Mark to come back to her." He folded his hands. "But I would like to hear what you think. Is intensive psychotherapy going to cure you? I would like you to imagine five years into the future. You have been through a thousand therapy sessions, you have laid your soul bare. Are you better? Are you cured? Is the boy in Beirut gone? Is the artillery explosion gone?"

Mark looked away. "I don't know," he whispered.

"I think you do know," Joaquin said. "There is no salvation, Mark. There is no God to forgive you and there is no psychiatrist who can cure you. This Western idea that we can pass over our pains, how absurd! You never pass over them. You carry them with you forever. That is what it means to live."

Joaquin rose to stand over Mark. He reached out and took his hand. "But I can help you, my boy. In one week—two at most—I can do more for you than these so-called doctors will do in ten years. I can show you how to carry the pain. Look at me. I'm seventy-six years old. I lost my entire family: my parents, my brothers, my sisters. I lost my wife and my only son. I've lost everyone I ever loved, and I've carried all of it with me forever. But look at me: I'm still here. I'm still smiling, I'm still light on my feet, and the world is still a wonderful place."

He smiled down at Mark for a long time, then lightly patted his hand. "Well, something to think about, perhaps, something to think about." He let go of Mark's hand, took up the notepad and photocopied pages from the bedside. "Elena will be here soon. I suspect she won't be pleased that I came—this was all my idea, you see—but you might tell her I've gone down to the cafeteria."

"I will," Mark said. "Thank you."

The old man shrugged. "Not at all. The least one can do for family." He went to the curtain, started to step through, but then turned. "I'm curious. That last photo you took of the boy, did it come out?"

Mark nodded.

"And how did it look?"

Mark's gaze fell to the white sheet covering his body. "It was good. I got him in center frame, running toward the camera. His eyes were lit up, hair blown back. The background was slightly blurred, but you could see the soldiers pivoting in, their guns coming up."

"A powerful image," Joaquin said. "And you sold it?"

Mark looked up. "No. No, I didn't."

"But you tried to."

Mark studied the old man, his vaguely amused expression. "Yes. They said it lacked context."

"Ah, context," Joaquin said, "always a problem." He turned toward the curtain.

"You think badly of me?" Mark called. "You think I shouldn't have tried to sell it?"

Joaquin slowly swung back around. With an indulgent smile, he watched Mark, his old brown eyes shifting from the bedsheet to his face. The smile widened until Mark saw the two rows of perfect white teeth again. "You're the moralist, Mark, not I."

There was color in his cheeks and he was calm, not at all the trembling, white figure she had found on the bathroom floor the afternoon before. Elena sat on the edge of the bed, brushed his hair back.

"I told your parents it was just fatigue," she said, "that maybe you picked up some parasite over there. It seemed best for the time being. They want to talk to you, of course."

Mark nodded. "I'll call them."

"And there was a message from Amy. *Stern* bought the triage essay for ten thousand dollars."

He looked up at her quickly. "European or just German rights?"

"She didn't say."

He stared off. "Probably just German. I hope it's just German. I'll find out."

Elena turned on the bed, ran a hand along his covered leg. "How do they feel?"

"All right." He shifted his legs so she could see the movement beneath the sheet. "A physical therapist is coming up in a little while. He's going to work up an exercise plan I can do at home."

Elena watched his legs, nodding, then looked to him. "Why didn't you tell me about the explosion, Mark?"

He averted his gaze, methodically rotated the plastic bracelet on his left wrist. "I don't know."

"Were you frightened? Worried what I would say?"

No answer. She reached for his face, caressed his cheek. "You're being released from the hospital tomorrow. A doctor is going to come by the apartment in the evening. His name is Robert Hershbach. He's a Vietnam veteran who specializes in war-stress cases. I talked with him on the phone and he sounds nice. I think you'll get along well with him."

"What about your grandfather?"

Elena's hand flinched away from his cheek. "What?"

"Your grandfather. He's offered to help. I think he might work fine."

Elena stared at him, dumbfounded. She shook her head, as if trying to make sense of what he had said. "Wait a minute. When did you talk to my grandfather?"

"He came by this morning. We talked for two or three hours."

"What? Two or three hours!?"

"He's a fascinating man. Why haven't you ever told me about him?"

Elena gazed at the wall above Mark's head. She thought back on the previous night, the taxi ride with Papa. She had told him everything. And then, standing in the hotel driveway, when he had asked the name of the hospital, already he was planning. And this morning, while she made her phone calls and went to her appointments, while she felt bad about hurting the old man's feelings—the old man sleeping off his exhaustion in a hotel room—he was there, at the hospital, working on Mark.

She looked down at him. "My grandfather can't help you."

"Why? He says he's an expert."

"He is not an expert, Mark. He's a fraud." She slid off the bed, felt the old anger surging. "You want to know why I've never talked about him? I'll tell you. After the Spanish Civil War, my grandfather ran a phony psychiatric institute. His patients were war criminals, fascist officers who had committed atrocities during the war—the 'Fascist Father Confessor,' they called him. If you had wiped out a village, if you had tortured people to death, all you had to do was go see Dr. Joaquin Morales at the Morales Institute for Psychological Purification, and he absolved you of all guilt. Of course, he wasn't really a doctor, he wasn't really a psychiatrist, but that didn't matter in Franco's Spain."

"But he has some interesting ideas, Elena. He . . ." Mark tried to find the words, to offer some logical reason, but he couldn't. At that moment, he couldn't even be sure why he wanted Joaquin, if it was because he really thought the old man would help him, or because he was quite certain he would not. "Anyway, you're talking about

[126]

what happened in the Spanish Civil War. Do you know how long ago that was?"

"Yes, Mark, I know how long ago it was. And I also know that there has never been any justice for the dead. Hundreds of thousands of innocent people, and when the murderers felt pangs of conscience they went to my grandfather and he told them, 'Don't worry about it, you did the right thing, get on with your life.' "

"That's not what he does," Mark said. "I've seen his technique."

"His technique? He has no technique; he's a fake. A fake, and a war criminal. Maybe he didn't kill people directly, but he did worse, he erased them. All those innocent people, and they were reduced to ghosts. At least as ghosts they could live on, haunting their killers, but my grandfather took those ghosts and he killed them again, banished them from memory. Purification he called it."

"I think he can help me."

"No, he can't, Mark. Please. For me, please don't do this. Papa has tried to find some way back into my life ever since I learned the truth about him. Now he's trying to use you. Please, don't let him. For me. Don't do this."

Mark reached out and brushed Elena's hair from her face. "He's your family, Elena. You need to learn forgiveness."

She pushed his hand away. "Don't tell me what I need to do." She pointedly glanced over his covered body. "Don't you dare."

He stared down the length of the bed, to the metal railing there, his shrouded feet. He nodded. "Just for a few days. That's all." He turned to her, reached a hand for her cheek again. "A few days, and if it doesn't help . . ."

She sighed, slowly shook her head, but it was a gesture of exhaustion, resignation, and this time she let his fingers rest on her skin.

As she approached his table in the cafeteria, Joaquin rose, extended his arms as if to embrace her. "Ah, my darling, you are even more beautiful in daylight."

But Elena didn't go to him. She stopped at the far side of the table, took the seat opposite his. She was angry and stared at her intertwined hands when she spoke. "I didn't expect to see you here this morning, Papa."

"A surprise to me, as well," Joaquin said. "Six o'clock and I popped right up—the disorientation of travel, I suppose."

"I thought you were going to wait at the hotel until I called."

"Exactly so. But then I thought, 'Since I'm awake, why not go over to the hospital and meet Mark, get acquainted?' A whim, if you will. So, I came over, we had a nice visit, and it all seems to have worked out splendidly. A fine young man, by the way. I can well understand your affection for him."

Elena still stared at her hands. "It's not going to work."

"Of course it will, darling. One week—perhaps a bit longer, considering he's a civilian."

She looked up. "I'm not talking about Mark, I'm talking about me. I know why you came here, Papa. It's not going to work."

Joaquin gazed at the ruins of his cafeteria lunch, at the cup of weak coffee that had long since gone cold. "You are all I have left, Elena," he said.

Mark was released from the hospital the following morning. As soon as Joaquin stepped into the apartment living room, he set down his suitcase and cast his arms wide.

"Marvelous!" He looked to Mark sitting in the rented wheelchair being propelled by Elena. "I presume you decorated it yourself?"

FIVE

His family had scattered, formed its own small constellation across the land, but no matter where he happened to be Mark could instantly conjure an image of each of their homes. His parents' condominium in Ft. Lauderdale, the veranda with its view of the marina and the ocean. In San Diego, Jessica's stucco three-bedroom, halfway up a burnished brown hill. Robert's vaulting creation on the Seattle waterfront, cathedral ceilings and great windows, the sound of foghorns at night. On a tree-lined street in suburban Chicago, Laura's split-level with the pool in back for the girls. Florida, California, Washington, and Illinois: four homes, four tiny orbits, each separated from the next by at least a thousand miles. Like a sailor charting a course across night seas, these distant points served as Mark's compass when he found himself in the black reaches of the world.

He called his parents first.

"It's really nothing," he told them, "just some blood infection that gradually wore me down. I'm supposed to rest for a couple of weeks, take antibiotics."

"Well, thank God," his mother said. "We've been worrying about you ever since Elena called." She laughed lightly. "I have, anyway—your father won't admit to worrying about anything."

"Oh, hell, I knew it wasn't anything serious," his father said. His father was on the veranda with the portable; in the background, Mark heard the steady clank of winches against aluminum masts. "But, overall, how was the trip? Worthwhile?"

Yes, Mark said, it had been worthwhile, and he told them about the sale to *Stern*, the other magazines that were interested. They didn't ask him for details on the photo-essay, and he didn't give them.

"Say, I've got an idea," his mother said, "why don't you rest up down here? The sun would do you good, and I imagine Elena wouldn't mind getting out of the cold for a few days."

It held an appeal. It had been nearly six months—late September—since he and Elena had last visited. Mark remembered walking the marina with his father, his father admiring the yachts, scowling at the cigarette boats—"trash boats for trash people"—thrilled by the sight of a passing windjammer under sail. His mother had been more vibrant than Mark had seen her in years. Since their move to Florida, she had fallen in with a crowd of feisty Unitarian women and was forever involved in some letter-writing campaign to draw attention to the plight of Vietnamese boat-people or to save a Louisiana wetlands from development.

"I realized it was time to give something back to the world," she had explained.

"Great," his father had said in mock annoyance, "and she's decided to give it back to the post office."

His parents seemed to have drawn closer together in Florida, as if the sun itself had softened them, as if the unfettered sweep of their days had allowed them to regain what was truly important. For Mark, the visit had been relaxing, and he now imagined walking the beach, the feel of cool March water on his feet.

"It sounds nice," he told them. "Let me ask Elena about her schedule."

But when he hung up, Mark remembered his legs, the wheelchair, Joaquin. He also remembered his father's words from that last night in September. The women had gone to bed, and they were playing gin rummy on the veranda table, drinking cheap beer and smoking the Cuban cigars Mark had brought back from Europe. His father was squinting at his cards, working the cigar around his mouth like a '30s gangster.

"You know," he had said, "you were always a sensitive kid. Of all the kids, you were the most sensitive. Very inquisitive, too. The other kids, they didn't give a damn what was going on in the world, but every night you'd come into the den to watch the evening news with me. Remember that? You'd get up on my lap, ask all these questions about what was going on, where that place was, why that man said that—just annoying as hell."

They had laughed together, his father clenching the cigar with his teeth.

"But this one time—you must have been seven or eight—something came on—I can't even recall what it was, maybe a plane crash or something out of Vietnam—but it was pretty ugly, pretty graphic. You started crying your eyes out. You jumped off my lap, went up to your room, and locked the door. Your mother and I must have knocked on that door for fifteen minutes, but you wouldn't let us in. We could hear you in there crying, but you wouldn't open the door. One of the most frustrating moments of my life, so I finally went down, got my toolbox, and just took that goddamned door off its hinges. You remember that?"

Mark shook his head.

"Oh, yeah," his father said, "you were real broken up about that, broken up for days." He had studied the fan of cards in his hand, finally dropped one onto the discard pile. "And that's what's always baffled me. I mean, now Robert, Robert was a little bastard, nothing bothered him, and if someone had told me twenty years ago that one of my sons was going to be an architect and the other was going to be a war photographer, I never would've guessed right." His father had folded his cards, set them on the table. "I know your mother is always on you about the danger, how she worries about you, but I'm not talking about that here. I figure it's your life and you're smart enough to not take any crazy chances. I'm talking about something else. You forget, I know what it's like out there."

Mark hadn't forgotten; it was simply never part of the way he saw his father. Even with the ramrod-straight back, even with the fading blue tattoo on his left bicep, Mark had never thought of his father—a softhearted, gentle man—as a former Marine, a veteran of Pacific beachheads.

"Hell, Tarawa was forty-five years ago," his father said, "and I still relive it. I can be walking down this boardwalk"—he had waved the cigar out over the veranda, toward the beach—"and all of a sudden I'll get a snapshot—a picture snapshot—of a buddy I haven't thought of in years, remember exactly what he looked like, how he talked, what happened to him. I don't care what anyone says, it affects you, it never stops affecting you. You don't just come home and pick up your life again." His father had looked across at him. "You've been doing this now, what, seven, eight years?"

"Nine."

"Nine years. You've got a name for yourself now, a reputation, you can branch out into another area. Why keep doing this?"

"Because I'm good at it."

"So be good at something else. This shit takes a toll."

Mark had smiled at his father. "You were nineteen at Tarawa, Dad, just a hick kid out of Fresno. Of course it affected you."

"Oh, and you're so much tougher and wiser, right? A regular hep-cat. Look me in the eye and tell me it doesn't affect you."

Mark had looked him in the eye and said, "It doesn't affect me."

His father had squinted at him, through the cigar smoke, through the half-dark, for a long time. Then, he had looked down at their card game and shaken his head.

"Then I feel sorry for you, son. I think that's the saddest god-damned thing I've ever heard."

Remembering that conversation, Mark knew he couldn't go to Florida, not yet, not until he felt stronger about what had happened in Kurdistan. His father would see the truth in his eyes, and at some point—maybe while prowling the marina, maybe while smoking Cuban cigars on the veranda—Mark would no longer be able to hold it in.

He called Jessica next.

"Hello?" Jessica's voice, and in that instant Mark saw what would have taken place in four living rooms in America if he had not come back from Kurdistan. In their initial shock, his family—his mother, his sisters, his brother—would have paced their living rooms or stared at windows or muted televisions or porcelain figurines and nothing would have made sense, nothing would have seemed real, but at some point they would have remembered the atlases on their bookshelves. They would have taken these down, flipped the pages until they found Kurdistan, and they would have stared at that word, trying to imbue it with some significance until the letters ran together before their eyes, but already they would be thinking: "What a stupid thing, to die so far from home."

Only his father would have been different. Only his father could have drawn some solace from a thought so terrible he would never share it with the others: "Mark died a long time ago, Mark stopped coming home a long time ago."

"I suppose it was the flowers that first inspired me," Joaquin said, "the poppies, to be precise. In spring, the fields around Granada are filled with them. Just a few in the lower fields at first, but very quickly they multiply, move up the hillsides, up, up, until finally the mountains are ablaze. I follow them. In the early days, I stay to the lower fields, but as they begin to die off there, I follow them into the mountains, all the way to the snowline and, yes, a rather silly conceit, I admit, but I think it was my desire to capture them, to hold them as one would a bouquet—never wilting, never dying, a touch of spring even in the depths of winter—that first led me to painting."

They ate at the kitchen table, Joaquin and Elena at either end, Mark in the wheelchair between them. Joaquin lowered his knife and smiled at his granddaughter.

"But, of course, Elena remembers the poppies from her childhood. Do you remember how you loved them, how you would gather them in the fields by the house? Your mother and I would stand in the garden and watch you come so proudly through the gate, holding your dress up with your two little hands, a basket for all your poppies."

Elena smiled thinly. "Yes. I remember." She sipped from her wineglass, turned to Mark. "Papa is quite famous in Granada for his landscapes."

"Please." Joaquin raised his hand. "Van Gogh is famous, I am merely noteworthy. Yes, all modesty aside, I have a certain gift, a certain mastery of aesthetics that sets me above the hobbyist, but I can hardly take full credit for this, for I have the advantage of the land that surrounds me." He looked to Mark. "There are places in the world, you see, that naturally inspire fine art—Arles, Venice, Granada . . ." He sighed. "Well, I suppose to fully understand, you must see for yourself."

Mark nodded. "I'd like to. I've always wanted to see Spain."

"A noble aspiration, my boy." Joaquin looked to Elena. "You know, already the poppies are beginning to bud. On the morning I left, I saw the first of them in the fields. In another week, they will be in full bloom." He turned back to Mark. "Yes, an excellent idea. It would be wonderful for your therapy, and, of course, we have plenty of room. The house, as Elena will remember, is enormous, and it would give Carmen something to do."

Elena pushed her fork around her plate. "How is Carmen?"

"Please." Joaquin raised his hand again. "Let us talk about something pleasant. Carmen is my housekeeper," he explained to Mark. "A completely useless woman, but unfortunately she has become a fixture over the years, quite impossible to be rid of now. Her cataracts are so bad she can't even clean properly anymore, but still she refuses to see a doctor. A true primitive: hot-tempered, superstitious, and mulish. She is from Galicia, of course."

Elena laughed in spite of herself. "You are terrible, Papa. Carmen is a wonderful woman."

"Precisely my point. And she always adored you, Elena. She would be so pleased to hear you are coming for a visit."

"That's a bit unrealistic, don't you think?" She nodded toward Mark's wheelchair.

"Not at all," Joaquin said. "Two or three days and that device will be of no use to us, a relic."

Elena stared down the table at her grandfather, felt her annoyance with him rising again. "I'm surprised you can be so sure."

Joaquin gave a smug little chuckle. "Well, my dear, I am something of an expert in this field, after all."

She continued to watch him, the way he grandly raised the wineglass to his lips. "But not such an expert, really," she said, "not without your failures. Isn't that so?"

With a certain satisfaction, she saw the change come over him, confusion mixed with consternation.

"I had a visitor to my office the other day, the son of one of your old patients. The father's name was Carlos Perez. Do you remember him?"

Joaquin slowly set his glass on the table, searched the tablecloth. "Perez . . . Carlos Perez . . ." He shook his head. "*Pues*, it's a very common name."

"He had a nickname from his home village," Elena said. "Olía, I believe it was. They called him, the Beast of Olía."

Joaquin gave a thin laugh. "Oh, such dramatic nicknames back then. I remember the Beast of Gijón, the Beast of Segovia. Not too creative, perhaps, but dramatic!" He grinned at Mark but then seemed to wither under Elena's icy stare. "But, no. Beast of Olía? I'm sorry, I don't remember. Anyway, that was—"

"He was one of the incurables," Elena persisted. "Isn't that what you called them, the ones who were thrown out of the institute gates, left to fend for themselves? He never made it home, his family never saw him again. His son has been writing you letters, asking for information."

Joaquin sat back in the chair and, as if in relief, began to nod vigorously. "Of course, the letters. Yes, now I remember. He started writing me about a year ago." He glanced quickly between Mark and Elena. "Absolutely shameful on my part—I should have written back long ago—but, you see, I have no memory of his father and his file was sent on to the authorities. That was all so long ago, so many patients, so many men who . . . but still, I should have written him, disgraceful that I haven't." He leaned toward Mark. "You know how it goes? You plan to do something and then a little time passes and you forget and—but, no, really, there is no excuse."

"I have his number," Elena said. "You can call him while you're here."

At this, Joaquin visibly brightened. "Excellent! Much better to talk directly, anyway. Of course, better still if I had something to tell him, if I remembered something, but, yes, that would be perfect."

"I have to say, I'm a bit surprised, Papa," Elena said, picking at her plate. "With him being such a difficult patient, I'd have thought you'd have some memory of him." She looked up. "But maybe there were a lot of incurables."

They stared into each other's eyes for a long moment, a duel of wills.

"Not so many," Joaquin said at last. "Not so many." He turned to Mark. "Yes, it happened sometimes. Terrible. A terrible necessity but, you see, always more patients were coming, more waiting, so, after a time, those who couldn't be helped, those who didn't respond fast enough, well, what could be done? We had to make room for the others. When all else failed, we had to release them. What else could we do?" He turned back to Elena, a sudden cool defiance in his manner. "But never were they simply dumped. Always I tried to return them to their families. A point of honor with me. What went wrong in this particular case, with this Perez fellow, I don't know, I can't even imagine." He sighed, shook his head. After a brief silence, he looked to Mark. "You play chess?"

"No," Mark said, "I've never learned."

"I will teach you."

The apartment had been transformed into an exotic place. Gazing about the kitchen, Elena saw things she hadn't noticed before—paint cracks along the ceiling, a buckling linoleum tile in one corner. Even those things she had put there—the Gauguin print above the sink, the dried rosemary on the windowsill—seemed foreign, as if seen for the first time. It was not a momentary sensation. Elena realized she had felt it all day, from the moment she had unlocked the apartment door and her grandfather had stepped across the threshold.

She leaned against the kitchen doorframe and watched them at the far end of the living room, Mark in his wheelchair, Papa on the couch, both their heads bowed as they studied the tiny chessboard on the coffee table, the overhead lamp casting them in a pyramid of yellow light. For long minutes, they did not look up, remained oblivious to her presence.

It was her grandfather's arrogance, his breezy insistence that Mark would soon be fine, Elena had told herself, that led her to bring up the matter of his lost patient at the dinner table. As the evening wore on, though, she realized her irritation had a deeper source. Like a nimble spirit, her grandfather was slipping his way back into her life, and Elena felt powerless—outmaneuvered at every turn—to prevent it. At least now he knew she wasn't going to acquiesce in silence.

At the end of the night, when she had helped Mark out of his wheelchair, out of his clothes, she lay close beside him on the bed. "Do you think Papa is helping you?"

"I can't tell yet. But chess seems interesting."

"We're not going to Spain, Mark. No matter what he says or promises, we're not going back with him."

A few minutes later, as she hovered on the verge of sleep, Elena was brought back by his soft words.

"Where do you think he went?"

She raised her head from the pillow, not understanding. Mark was on his side, facing away from her, toward the window. "Who?"

"Joaquin's old patient, the incurable. What do you think happened to him?"

She laid her head back down, reached out a hand to stroke his neck. "I don't know. If he was lucky, maybe he wandered into some village where the people took him in, watched over him. That happens sometimes in Spain. If not, I suppose he just roamed around until he died—starved or froze or . . . I really don't know, Mark."

"Do you think he was trying to go home?"

She found a small curl of his hair, twirled it around her finger. "Probably. He had a wife, a young son. He was probably trying to find his way home."

He was quiet for a long time, but Elena heard the soft brush of his eyelashes against the pillow, knew he was still looking out at the night.

"That would be terrible, wouldn't it?" he said at last, and his voice was very thick, pained. "To die like that. Out there, lost, no one to find you. That would be so terrible."

She wondered if he was actually thinking of Colin at that moment. It had been five days since she had sent the cable to Kurdistan, and there had been no reply. Diane had heard nothing, and each day her stolid cheeriness had sounded more forced. Elena knew Mark was concerned now about Colin—everyone was growing concerned—but this wasn't the time to talk about it. Instead, she moved to his side, pressed her body against his. She kissed his neck, the small bandage on the back of his head, the soft, cool tip of his ear. "You never have to go back, Mark," she whispered. "I'll never let you go back."

Elena awoke to a regular thumping sound coming from the living room and was puzzled until she remembered her grandfather's regimen of exercise. She put on a nightgown, went out to make coffee.

"Good morning, my dear." Clad in a baggy blue sweatsuit, Joaquin was performing jumping jacks. His old arms barely rose above his head, his feet only shuffled a few inches on the floor, but he did not stop. "I've made coffee in the machine."

She helped Mark dress, helped him into the wheelchair, wondered how long this would be part of their daily ritual. She walked behind him down the long hall, straightening the wheelchair each time he veered close to the walls.

"Ah, the patient arrives!" Joaquin roared, his face still florid from his calisthenics. "Out of the chair, my boy, out of the chair. Your first set of exercises, a light breakfast, and then, perhaps, a game of chess."

He strode across the floor, his new white tennis shoes squeaking with each step, gripped Mark tightly by the arm, and hoisted him to his feet.

"Wait," Elena said, "he's supposed to stretch first."

"Stretch? A waste of time, my child, a luxury we cannot afford. The important thing is to walk."

She watched her grandfather lead Mark across the floor, propping him up as his legs trembled, as his bare feet took tiny steps.

"Remarkable," Joaquin managed amid his exertions, "already your rate of recovery astounds me."

Elena went into the study and closed the door. She spent the morning writing postcards to friends, updating her address book, cleaning out files, inventing tasks to keep herself occupied. Through the thin wall, she occasionally heard them talking, Papa laughing, his heavy step and squeaking shoes as he crossed the floor. She felt marooned in her own home, wished she had gone to the office.

"The photographs in the hallway are exquisite," Joaquin said, "especially the ones of the mountains. You took them?"

Mark looked up from the chessboard and nodded. "Years ago, up in Alaska. I first started out doing nature photography."

"But you stopped? Why, with such an obvious talent?"

Mark shrugged. "There's not a lot of money in it. It's kind of like being a poet."

"And so you turned to war instead." Joaquin shook his head sadly. "Terrible, isn't it, the economic imperatives imposed on the artist? One would wish for a world where the creative mind could be freed of such base concerns and allowed to simply roam with abandon." He let out a quick laugh. "Good heavens, I sound like one of those awful little socialists!"

Mark smiled. The telephone rang. Through the wall, Mark heard Elena answer it.

"So where did you learn to speak English so well?"

"Oh, please!" Joaquin chuckled, raised a hand in protest. "I butcher the language. Very kind of you to say, but there is no need for false flattery between us. No, perhaps once I was quite proficient, back in the days of the institute, but now it's mostly lost to me."

Mark was puzzled. "You learned at the institute?"

"Yes, there was a British nurse there, a volunteer. Erica Humphries was her name. She stayed for over a year and, when there was time, she would teach me a few words. A delightful girl, very well educated."

Mark was even more puzzled. "What was a British nurse doing at the institute?"

Joaquin grinned, wagged a finger at Mark. "Ah, you see? You've read too many history books. You think all of Europe, all the civilized world, was against Franco. Not true, not true at all. That came later, after the world war, when everyone wanted to say they had been antifascist all along. As in France—everyone was in the Resistance, no one was Vichy—the same way with Spain, everyone had to hate Franco. The truth is, hundreds, maybe thousands, of volunteers came to Spain from all over Europe at the end of the civil war—teachers, engineers, nurses—people who thought Franco was a hero and wanted to help rebuild the country. Erica Humphries was one of these. Maybe not too sophisticated politically but a very sweet girl, very capable at the institute."

Mark gave him a sly look. "And more than just a nurse?"

Joaquin frowned, not sure what he was asking. "Well, she was British, as I said . . ." It dawned on him then. "Oh, heavens, no. We practiced a very strict morality back then. Fraternization with a nurse, especially a foreign one, it would have been unthinkable. A very strict morality under Franco!" He stopped, seemed to realize the irony of his words. "Well, morality of a type, of course, the morality of *La Cruzada*. Killing, one could find excuses for, but adultery? Even in a *cruzada*, there is no excuse for sex."

They both laughed. Mark looked back at the chessboard, tried to reorient himself to the game. The moves of the king, queen, bishops, and rooks he had figured out quickly—there was a clean logic to them—but the pawns and knights were a bit trickier. Without any clear plan in mind, he brought the queen back a couple of squares. Joaquin immediately hunched over the board to study the move.

"But I must say I find your photographs of the mountains quite exceptional. Perhaps it's because I sense in them the hand of a kindred spirit, being a landscapist myself. Oh, I've tried portraits, to be sure, but I'm afraid people don't interest me very much. Nature, that is what fascinates." Joaquin wagged a crooked finger at Mark. "No, this is imprecise. The rebellion of nature against man's design—the flowering weed along the planted furrow, the unruly limbs of the olive tree in its plotted field—that is what compels. Yes, call me a neoclassicist if you must—although I prefer the antimodernist label—but it's for this reason, a reason you can no doubt appreciate, that all my work is in oils."

He lunged forward, leaned over the table until his face was just inches from Mark's.

"Would you believe that a few years ago, a gallery owner in Granada—an odious man spawned in some Barcelona coffeehouse—actually suggested I try my hand at watercolors? Yes, it's true! How to account for such barbarism? How can the artist not despair when his world is controlled by these vandals? If I'd been a younger man, I should have thrashed that little pimp right there in the doorway of his souvenir shop."

He retreated, slumped wearily against the couch.

"Ambition, that is what they don't understand. They talk about inspiration and aesthetics and discipline, but these are all tiny components of art. Without ambition, they mean nothing. Worse, they are affectations. After all, what is a landscape, but an attempt to render the world in all its complexity, its difference in hues and depths and textures. Impossible, of course, but it is the attempt—the ambition—that is important. Oils. Only oils can convey the ambition necessary for true art." He smiled across at Mark. "But, of course, I have no need to tell you these things. Surely, you encounter much the same perversions in your field."

Mark was confused.

"In photography," Joaquin said, "you attempt to seize a particular instant in time, no? It might be of a mountain or a person or a soccer game, but the ambition is to preserve that image exactly as it appeared at that moment, correct? To artificially enhance that image, to use filters or dyes that make the skies bluer, the clouds darker, it is a corruption of the artistic process, I would imagine." He caught himself, looked stricken. "Dear me, I hope I haven't offended . . ."

Mark grinned. "No, no offense taken. I think you're just a bit conservative."

Joaquin nodded. "An accusation that has been made in the past."

"In my business, I use filters all the time. If there isn't enough contrast or the light is too hard, I have to use filters."

"Yes, of course, but as you say, it is your business." Joaquin motioned toward the hallway. "I am thinking here of your photographs of the mountains. For those, did you use filters? Did you change the color of the sky?"

Mark shook his head.

Joaquin was triumphant. "You see? I knew it. I know nothing about photography, but looking at those mountains I saw your ambition. War photography, it is your job—one that you are very good at—but it is not your art. But if you were to return to nature photography—if, for example, you were to come to Spain to photograph the mountains—you would throw away your filters. I know this about you. I see in you the purist. You would walk the mountains until you found the precise image you wanted, you would be prepared to wait hours for just the right moment, the perfect blend of sunlight and shadow, because that is what your artistic standards would demand and anything less would be beneath you."

Mark smiled at the old man. "Maybe so," he said. "Maybe so." He turned back to the chessboard and moved a rook up three squares.

"Ah," Joaquin said, "bold move. Already I see you are a keen strategist."

Her first thought, inexplicably, was not of Diane, but of Sem. It was Thursday afternoon and although she had called the office to say she wouldn't be in, Elena could envision Sem sitting there, in the records room on the eighteenth floor, the stack of search requests beside him, glancing up each time someone passed in the hallway, hoping it was her, come to share the burden and joy of their work.

Elena hung up the telephone and rose from the desk. They looked up from their game when she approached.

"I have bad news," she said to Mark. "It's about Colin."

He seemed to shrink, to literally become a more compact person, and she heard his back press against the soft vinyl of his wheelchair.

"My office called. The UN team in northern Kurdistan just answered my cable. They found Colin's things in the hotel room at Rawanduz. He never made it to the lowlands."

She watched Mark's gaze slowly slide away from her, away from the room, to the sky outside the window. She watched the muscles beneath his cheekbone flex like a pulse. "But he was only going for a few days," he said. "He would've left most of his things—"

"All his things were there," Elena said, "his clothes, his cameras, his passport, everything. He never got out of Rawanduz, Mark."

Joaquin cleared his throat. "Surely, there might be a simple explanation. Perhaps he has been detained somehow, taken prisoner by the other side . . . ?"

Elena nodded. "Maybe. It seems we should have heard by now, but I suppose it's possible. Mark?" She waited until he turned to her. His eyes were remote. "You were both staying at the Rawanduz hotel; on the day you split up, did you see Colin leave?"

"No," he said, "I left in the morning. He was leaving in the afternoon."

"And what about after your accident? Didn't you go back to the hotel?"

Mark shook his head. "I sent someone for my stuff. I left straight from Harir."

She watched him, waited for more, but Mark's gaze fell away, to his fingers that rubbed the padded armrest of the wheelchair.

"Can you think of anyone there we should contact," she asked, "anyone who might know something?"

He slowly shook his head, didn't look up. "I don't know. I don't know."

"There must be someone, Mark. Please, think."

Joaquin rose from the couch and moved to Elena's side. He touched her arm. "I don't think this is helpful," he said, "not just now."

Elena nodded and rubbed her eyes with trembling fingers. "Diane. My God, what do I tell Diane?" She dropped her hands from her face, saw that Mark still stared at his kneading fingers. "What do I tell her, Mark?"

He didn't look up, continued to shake his head as if in shock.

"You tell her exactly what you know," Joaquin said. "I think you are taking too grim a view of this, Elena. Even in the worst of times, even in war, most of those who go missing turn up safe in the end. Besides, if the very worst had happened, someone surely would have found his body by now. Without a body, there is always room for hope. Isn't that so, my boy? Isn't that your experience?"

Finally, Mark looked up. He seemed close to tears. "I don't know," he whispered. "Maybe so."

Elena touched her grandfather's hand, resting on her elbow. For the first time, she was glad for his presence. She didn't believe his words, but for the moment they were a comfort.

It was like viewing a movie. He watched Elena move through the apartment as she prepared to leave, felt her kiss his cheek, heard the front door close behind her, but it was all at a distance, vicarious, as if he was not there at all. Even Joaquin sitting across from him, even the chessboard before him, seemed abstract. And finally Mark realized it was because he had slipped, he was back in Kurdistan, and the images of that afternoon on the hilltop, of that night on the river, had risen up between him and the world. He blinked, looked to Joaquin.

"You're concerned for your friend," the old man said gently. "Do you wish to talk about it?"

Mark shook his head. "I don't know what there is to say."

Joaquin nodded. "For the best, perhaps; you are in no position to take on another's problems just now. Anyway, he'll show up. I'm sure of it." He looked at his watch. "Come. It's time for your exercises. After that, maybe another of your stories."

"Beth and I flew in this morning," Sylvia explained, "just to help out with the pregnancy and, you know, wait for some word . . ." She turned to Diane, sitting beside her on the couch, and grinned. "The meddling mother, right?"

Sylvia was a lean woman with a vigorous air and a golfer's tan. Her words and movements were quick, slightly clipped, and Elena was reminded of the brisk, determined women she passed on the sidewalks of Manhattan. Beth, Diane's younger sister, was very different. A soft, sweet-faced girl in her early twenties, she sat on the arm of the couch, watching over her mother and sister with a mixture of bemusement and quiet concern.

"You haven't heard anything from the UN people?" Diane asked.

Elena felt Sylvia's sharp gaze upon her, and looked down at her hands. She wasn't ready yet, had struggled all the way over in the taxi to find some way to tell it with at least a trace of optimism. "No," she lied, "not yet."

Diane sighed, lightly punched at a small pillow beside her.

"I'm sure there's nothing to worry about." Sylvia smiled. "We've contacted the State Department and our congressman—and, of course, Colin's folks are doing all they can." She spun to Diane. "You know, Colin's father told me that some of his coworkers have asked if they can start up some kind of fund, a reward for information. Isn't that something? It really restores your faith in people, doesn't it?"

Diane nodded, looked to Elena. "How's Mark?"

"Okay. He and my grandfather have become inseparable. I don't know if you can call it therapy, but at least he's learning to play chess."

Sylvia threw her head back and laughed. "That's priceless!"

"Does he have any suggestions," Diane asked, "anyone we should contact?"

Elena shook her head.

"Well, I'm sure something will come to him when he's had more time to think about it." Sylvia leapt to her feet. "You girls visit; I'll go rustle up something in the kitchen."

She strode swiftly out of the living room and left silence in her wake. Beth slid off her perch to sit beside Diane, and the three of them listened to Sylvia in the kitchen, humming softly to herself as she opened cupboards, took things from the refrigerator.

Elena didn't know how to begin. She wished Mark were there, wished he was in any condition to be there with her. But if she still couldn't bring herself to tell Diane, she also couldn't carry out a charade of idle conversation. She rose from the chair. "Maybe I'll go help your mother."

Sylvia cast her a quick glance and smile when Elena stepped into the tiny kitchen but immediately returned to her task. "Honestly, her kitchen is so disorganized, I can't find a thing. Where do you imagine she keeps the mustard?"

Elena reached into the cupboard beside the stove and took down the jar.

"How strange," Sylvia said, taking it from her hand, "I always keep mine in the fridge." She surveyed the things she had placed on the counter: bread, lettuce, cheese, luncheon meat. "Let's see, what else . . . ? I guess that's everything."

Elena watched Sylvia's thin, nimble hands as she set out the four paper plates, the bread, spread the mustard. She moved like a very efficient automaton, and Elena found watching her reassuring, a diversion from the grim stillness she had left in the living room.

"May I help you with anything?" she asked.

Sylvia's hands suddenly stopped. She looked up, and Elena was quite startled to see that her eyes shimmered with tears. "You know something, don't you?"

Instantly, Elena felt her own tears coming. She nodded.

Sylvia leaned against the counter. "Oh, no," she said. "Oh, no."

"Uganda?" Joaquin glanced up from his notepad excitedly. "Ah, the land of Idi Amin. A very colorful figure. Quite mad, but one could not help but be amused by his flamboyance." He chuckled. "I remember when he scolded the Queen of England about how to run her country. And do you remember when he was carried about on that throne chair by a group of white men? Very entertaining. Well, I suppose not so entertaining if you happened to be one of his victims." He tapped his pen against the notepad. "But I'm sorry, I interrupted your story."

Mark smiled. "That's okay. But this took place in 1986. Amin was long out of the picture by then."

Joaquin seemed disappointed. Mark sipped his beer, gazed out a window at the late afternoon sky.

"Not many people know this—and the media was never around to report it—but Uganda actually got much worse after Amin. As insane as he was, at least Amin kept the country together. With him gone, the place just tore apart. Civil war. Every once in a while in the early eighties, I'd come across some small bit in a newspaper about it—just a paragraph, usually. The main battlefield was an area called the Luwero Triangle, just north of the capital, and there were stories about the army going in there and carrying out massacres, but it wasn't much more than rumors because the area was sealed off and no one was getting in. Then, in early 1986, the government finally fell, the rebels took over, and I decided to go and find out what had really happened. So I went there, into the triangle. I guess I was one of the first outsiders to go in."

Mark stared at the beer bottle in his hand, scratched at the label with a fingernail.

"I don't know how to describe it. How do you describe the triangle? Shock. I suppose that comes the closest. It was so much worse than I'd expected—than I think anyone had expected. For two years, the army had worked their way through and killed anyone they could find. No one knows how many died—maybe three hundred thousand, maybe a half-million — but it went beyond that. They hadn't just tried to exterminate the people, they'd tried to exterminate the place itself. They'd bulldozed hospitals, dynamited wells, smashed irrigation systems, they'd brought in trucks and loaded up anything they could steal — windows, doorknobs, lightbulbs — and hauled it back to Kampala, and what they couldn't carry, they smashed. They'd gone into the triangle and tried to erase it.

"But that wasn't the worst part. It was the survivors. You know, they'd spent the past two years hiding in the bush, living on roots and bugs, and they were just starting to come back — their villages destroyed, their families gone. Shock, a state of suspended shock. And what they were doing — they weren't doing the things you'd expect after a disaster, not clearing the fields or rebuilding their houses — they were harvesting the dead, the bones of the dead. You'd drive down a road and see them out in the fields gathering the bones, walking along the road carrying a bundle of them on their heads, and what they were doing was taking them to a central place, a communal place, and separating them out by parts — the skulls in one pile, over here the ribs, the hipbones, and so forth. In every village you came to, that is what they were doing. And the survivors were coming to these places and looking through the piles. It was like they were imitating normal life, like they were going to market, but what they were doing was looking for their families, trying to find the bones that belonged to them, and I think that was the hardest part, because there was no way to tell — you know, one rib, one skull, is pretty much the same as the next, no way to tell if it's your father or your mother or your next door neighbor — but they seemed to have this faith that if they were very methodical about it, if they just concentrated enough, eventually they would find the ones that belonged to them."

Mark set the empty bottle on the coffee table. Its label had been reduced to tiny balls of paper by his feet.

"It was the most ghoulish thing I've ever seen. Everywhere I looked, there was a photograph more horrific than the last. I must have run off thirty rolls that day."

Joaquin smiled slightly. "I would imagine so. And there was a particular moment that was notable for you?"

Mark nodded. "It was late afternoon, good light, and I came into this village that had an especially big display—three or four hundred skulls—and I started shooting when this woman came up to me. She was maybe thirty, thirty-five. I don't know why she chose me, except that I was white—you know, this is a pretty primitive area, and the only whites most of them have seen are relief workers or priests, so they have this idea that white people are there to help them—or maybe it was my cameras or, who knows? Anyway, she had this picture, just an old snapshot of her and her husband and their four children, small children, maybe from five to about eleven, and she wants me to help find them. She keeps pointing at the photo, pointing at the skulls.

"I try to explain to her that it's impossible, that you can't tell one skull from another, but she doesn't speak English, and I can't make her understand. She just stands there with the photograph, looking at me, waiting, very patient, and I know she isn't going to leave, that even if I find someone who can translate she isn't going to believe what I'm saying." Mark picked at a small tear in the vinyl of the wheelchair armrest. "So, finally, I give in. I pretend to help her. I go over to where the adult skulls are and I make a show of looking them over, like I'm really studying and analyzing, and then I choose one and bring it back to her. She unwraps this cloth from around her waist, spreads it on the ground, and puts the skull on it. Then she shows me the picture again, points to her oldest child—I remember it was a girl, a girl wearing a white blouse and a little skirt, maybe like a Catholic school skirt—and so I go over to the children's skulls and do the same thing again, walk around, study one, frown, go to another, come back to the first, you know, put on this act that I know what I'm doing, before I very confidently decide on one and bring it to her. And we go through her whole family that way until I've picked out five skulls, and then she arranges them all on the piece of cloth, ties it up into a bundle, and lifts it onto her back."

Mark stopped picking at the armrest, rubbed his hand against his jaw. "And I think what struck me the most, the thing that kind of bothered me, was that she tried to pay me. She had this pocket in her dress and she brought out this old purse and she tried to give me her money, and it was just very . . ." Mark gazed at the ceiling, trying to think of the words. "I don't know. I don't know. There was just something so sad and dignified, proud, in that. Well, I told her I wouldn't take the money, of course, that I'd done it as a gift, but she was very insistent and I kept refusing, saying it was a gift. It took a long time, but finally she gave up. She smiled at me, thanked me, and turned away, started down the road with her bundle, and . . . and that's all there was to it." He looked to Joaquin. "Sorry. It's not a very good story, is it?"

"In this business," Joaquin said, "there is no such thing as good or bad stories." He set his pen on the table, gently massaged his writing hand as he read over his notes. He glanced up. "No photographs this time? No pictures of the woman?"

Mark shook his head.

"Hmm, curious."

"Is that significant?"

Joaquin shrugged. "Who's to say?" He placed the notepad on the cushion beside him, folded his hands in his lap. "But I think you're wrong about one thing. I think the woman understood very well that this was a hopeless exercise, that you were simply pretending. What she was grateful for, why she tried to pay you, was for the charade, your performance for her benefit. It's a very complicated matter to be a survivor. Sometimes we must place our faith in magic, believe in answers we know are not true, in order to continue. Sometimes we must envy the dead."

A pained look came into Joaquin's eyes, and Mark realized the old man had wounded himself, that his words had cast a reflection back. Joaquin turned quickly away, gazed at the far wall of the living room. "Such sadness in this world," he whispered.

He took a deep, shuddering breath, opened his mouth as if to speak. Mark watched him, waited, but the moment dissolved. Joaquin turned back with a grin, patted his stomach.

"I'm famished. How about a sandwich?"

An evening that passed with interminable slowness, the four women moving through the apartment on delicate feet, speaking in muted voices, as if any loud sound might make their worst thoughts come true. It reminded Elena of the night at the Chicago hotel, after they had buried Stewart Kunath, a chamber of quiet, grieving women. She felt choked by the sadness, wanted to flee, but she knew this was what women did—they waited together, they grieved together—and to leave Diane at that moment was unthinkable. She called Mark to say she was staying the night.

As she hung up, Diane came into the living room. She wore a nightgown, was pale and exhausted. She sat beside Elena and patted the couch cushion. "You're sure you'll be okay here?"

"I'll be fine," Elena said. "I can sleep anywhere."

Diane nodded and looked to the far wall, at the display of African masks and Hmong headdresses, the pre-Columbian artifacts Colin had brought back from Central America. She smiled.

"It was so good there for a while, wasn't it? I remember the first time I flew out to meet him. It was in Bangkok. He'd just come out of Cambodia, and he met me at the airport. We got in a rental car and drove straight to the beach, this incredible, deserted beach with palm trees, white sand, a tiny hut twenty feet from the water. It was like a dream, sitting in hammocks, listening to the waves, to the fan over my head at night, and I remember thinking, 'We are so cool, this is so glamorous.'" She laughed softly, turned to Elena. "Remember how we used to joke about it, how smug we were? The perfect arrangement, the boys off doing their boy things, staying out of our hair, no meals to cook, no football games on TV. 'Better than marrying doctors.' Remember?"

Elena watched her friend, the way her smile crept away.

"He's dead, isn't he?"

"I don't know, Diane." Elena took her hand. "I don't know."

Diane rested her head on Elena's shoulder.

"God, Elena, what happened to us?"

Mark felt an intense hot light bathing him. He buried his head in the pillow, squinted out to see the reading lamp had been turned on, lowered to just inches from his face. Out the bedroom window the sky was still dark, just a few streaks of blue on the horizon.

"Ah, so you're awake," Joaquin said.

"Jesus, what time is it?"

Joaquin stood behind the lamp, already dressed, already vigorous. "A quarter to six. Almost noon in Granada."

"We're not in Granada, Joaquin."

"It's vital to get an early start on the day."

He helped Mark dress, gripped him under an arm, and lifted him to his feet.

"Where's the wheelchair?"

"Not needed," Joaquin said. "We'll walk to the living room."

"I need coffee."

"Afterward. Your first set of exercises, then coffee."

Mark turned to the old man. "Are you sure you're not still a Catholic?"

Joaquin laughed heartily. "Splendid! Sarcasm is a delicate faculty, always the last to return in cases of psychic trauma. Your progress is astonishing."

They made their way down the hallway. Occasionally, Mark bumped the wall or lost his footing beneath him, but he was surprised at how much better he moved than even the previous night. They went the length of the living room: twenty-five paces. Just yesterday it had been almost thirty.

"Remarkable," Joaquin said. "Tomorrow, you will walk without any assistance at all."

Mark smiled. The legs still felt rubbery and weak, but just as his paces had once been a gauge of his decline, they were now a measure of his recovery. Twenty-five now, by night perhaps twenty, tomorrow the crossing without anyone's help. And then, an escape from the apartment, a walk to the corner, maybe as far as the park.

After some twenty trips over the floor, Joaquin settled him into the wheelchair and went to the kitchen for their coffee. As Mark gratefully sipped from the mug, Joaquin stood over him, studying the room with curiosity.

Mark remembered that he had been dreaming when Joaquin woke him, and now, fortified by coffee, wisps of it came back to him. It had been of Joaquin's lost patient and he was walking, along a dirt road, through a forest, over hills, and that was all that had happened in the dream, just walking.

"That man Elena was talking about the other night, the patient at your institute, what do you think happened to him?"

Joaquin turned to him, drank from his mug. "That Beast fellow?" He shook his head sadly. "I can't imagine. I was so careful about those things, made sure everyone got back to their families—the incurables most of all. How he was overlooked, I haven't—"

"But I mean once he vanished, not what happened at your institute." He looked up at Joaquin. "Do you think he just wandered?"

"Hard to say. Impossible to say."

"Do you think he just went up into the hills somewhere and died, no one ever found him?"

Joaquin began to shrug, but then he saw the desperate way Mark searched his face. "No," he said. "I don't believe it happened like that." He turned, took a couple of steps away, looked at the far white wall. "Tell me, why do you keep the walls bare?"

Mark followed his gaze. "I don't know. Elena accuses me of being an ascetic."

"A discipline to be encouraged." Joaquin nodded. "Would you happen to have a pen, a felt pen?"

"There's probably one in the study."

Joaquin went down the hall and returned with a thick-tipped black marker. He handed Mark the pen and wheeled him over to the interior wall.

"I don't know the geography of Kurdistan very well. Perhaps you could draw me a map."

Mark looked to him, puzzled. "On the wall?"

"Yes. Just a rough map of the overall region. Don't worry; we can paint over it later."

Elena was awakened by a hand shaking her shoulder. She saw the clock on the fireplace mantel—a little before eight—then Beth, standing over her in a man's flannel nightshirt.

"Diane's gone into labor."

"What?" It seemed absurd somehow, an unpleasant joke. "But it's too early."

"Only by a few days," Beth said. "We've called for a taxi. It'll be here soon."

Elena threw off her blanket and went to the bathroom. Once she had splashed water on her face, changed into clothes, she felt oriented again.

When she returned to the living room, the others were by the front door, Sylvia holding a large bag of supplies, she and Beth clutching Diane by either arm. Diane was flushed, her lip trembling slightly, and she gave Elena a ragged smile. "I guess this is it."

They left the apartment and hurried along the corridor to the waiting elevator. To Elena, it did not seem they had any specific destination in mind at that moment, only that they were fleeing a place of sorrow and waiting.

Mark wheeled himself back into the living room. "That was Elena. Diane has gone into labor. They just took her to the hospital."

"How delightful," Joaquin said, "a very special day for her. It's their first child?"

Mark nodded.

"Wonderful. And what of Colin? Any word?"

"No."

Joaquin shook his head with disappointment. "A source of some concern, I should imagine. Still, I'm sure we'll hear from him soon." He smiled, returned to the notepad on his lap. "But perhaps we should get back to your story."

Mark sighed. "Do we have to do this right now, Joaquin? I'm not sure I feel up to it at the moment."

"It would be for the best, yes. Unless there is something you'd rather do?"

Mark gave a bitter laugh. "There's a whole world of things I'd rather do. I'd rather walk. I'd rather breathe real air. I'd rather get out of this damned apartment."

"That's good," Joaquin said. "I've often felt that the surest sign of recovery from psychic difficulties—and probably from many physical ones, as well—is when the afflicted become bored by the symptoms.

It is not very pleasant, is it, to constantly live inside one's mind, to always be going over the past, over memories? Far more pleasant to not think sometimes, to just live, yes?"

Mark nodded.

"Which is why I am here, my boy, to help you do that. I can promise that, very soon, the world will open up to you again, that you will have a happy life, happier than before. But we are not quite there yet. Very soon, I assure you, but not quite yet."

"And what's standing in the way?"

Joaquin glanced at his notepad, at the notes he had started. "At the moment, a picnic for some young navy cadets in Sri Lanka." He looked up at Mark and grinned. "A picnic I suspect is about to go badly awry."

And later, after Mark told of how he had arrived late to the secluded seaside picnic to see the cadets, boys really, in their little blue uniforms stretched out under the palm trees as if napping; of how it was only when he had walked into their midst, when they lay around him in every direction, that he realized they were dead; of how he had leaned against a tree and listened to the rustling palm fronds over his head, the ocean surf, the pop and hiss of the cooking fish, charring to black on the small grills the cadets had erected in the shade; of how he had breathed in the intermingled scent of brine and blood and burning fish and understood he was the only living thing on the beach; after all this, Mark had turned to look out one of the living room windows to see that a bright day had spread over the city, and he had flexed and unflexed his jaw until he felt the pain in his head, behind his eyes, as if pain itself might sear away the vision.

"This is not easy for you, is it?" Joaquin asked quietly.

"No," Mark said, not looking to him. "No, it isn't."

"But if you will just tell me one last thing. At that moment, when you understood you were the only one alive on the beach, what were your thoughts?"

"I had no thoughts."

"But what did you feel?"

"I didn't feel anything."

"Come, you must have felt something? Fear? Sorrow? Relief at having survived?"

He turned to him then. "Fuck you, Joaquin."

The old man sat back, as if shocked. "I beg your pardon?"

"Fuck you. You're not really a psychiatrist, I'm not one of your war criminals, so let's just stop all this shit."

Joaquin studied him, his mouth gradually widening into a broad smile. "But you didn't want a real psychiatrist, remember? You wanted me. And at this particular juncture, a most wise choice. A real psychiatrist would never be satisfied with your responses; for me, they are quite enough. You see? You are very lucky to have me, my boy."

He looked across the room at the wall where Mark had drawn the map of Kurdistan earlier that morning.

"They really do suffer from bad location, don't they? Iraq, Iran, Turkey, a bit of Armenia, a bit of Syria—very bad location, destined to always be pawns of their neighbors." He clucked his tongue, turned to Mark. "A peculiarity of mine, I'm sure, but maps help me visualize a place. Perhaps you can draw me another map, one on a closer scale. I'm curious about the area where the explosion occurred. Maybe you could draw for me how it looked—not in any minute detail, of course, just the location of the hill, the river, where the artillery shell landed."

Mark shrugged wearily. "Sure. Whatever."

Joaquin took up the black felt pen that lay on the coffee table. They went together toward the already defaced white wall.

Elena believed she remembered her father. She believed she remembered sitting on his lap, playing with him in the small garden of their home in Madrid, but she was not sure. He had died when she was not yet three, and Elena had never known if her memories were real or taken from photographs and family stories. This she did know: Ever since that evening precisely one month before her third birthday when her father's car left the road between Madrid and Burgos, Elena had lived in the company of women. From that evening, there had been only her mother in the house and garden in Madrid. Her classmates at school had been girls, her neighborhood friends had been girls, and during family gatherings she had played with cousins who were girls. It had continued at university, at the office on Forty-fourth Street, and so it was still, here in the waiting room of a maternity ward in central Manhattan, where Elena waited with two women for news of another.

Beside her, Sylvia leafed through an old magazine. She had a way of pinching each page she turned, of holding it an instant too long so that it produced a snapping sound. Sylvia reached the end of the magazine, tossed it onto the side table, and picked up another.

"I can't concentrate on a thing," she said. "We haven't heard anything for nearly three hours; do you think we should ask?"

Elena smiled at her. "I'm sure everything's fine. They'd tell us if there were any problems." She returned to the magazine, open on her lap, that she had been pretending to read.

Her father was an imperfect memory given shape by folklore. He could never be more than that. In all her life, Elena had only truly known two men. One, Mark, was now a shadow to her; the other, Papa, she had long ago forsaken.

They sat at the kitchen table. They were finished eating—TV dinners from the small grocery down the street—and Joaquin had opened a second bottle of red wine. He sipped from his glass as he leafed through his notepad, flipping from one page to the next, pausing occasionally to read a passage or make a quick note in a margin.

"As I'm sure you realized, I asked for your war stories to see if some psychological pattern might emerge, some common threads. In that regard, a certain degree of success. Guilt, of course. The guilt of the survivor. It is very pronounced in you. You feel guilty about the boy in Beirut, about the woman in Uganda, that dreadful picnic in Sri Lanka. Again and again, guilt at not having done enough to help or save others."

"And that's abnormal?" Mark asked.

Joaquin peered at Mark over the top of his bifocals. "Let us hope not. Let us hope that anyone placed in these situations would respond the same way. To feel guilt in war only shows you have a conscience, a quality to be admired. But not, lamentably, a quality that is helpful in your profession."

He turned to a new page in his notes.

"Something else I noticed. In your stories, you are always the outsider, the observer—logical, of course, since you are always a stranger in these places, but I'm reminded that one of the peculiar pleasures of being a stranger is that sense of the world as a moving picture that you don't truly inhabit. I imagine this sensation is heightened if one happens to be a photographer. Surely not an original thought, but it occurs to me the camera is a very convenient device for placing distance between oneself and one's surroundings. Would you agree?"

"Sure," Mark said. "We talk about that all the time. It's probably why so many more war photographers are killed than reporters. You can kind of forget you're actually there, that what's happening in front of you is real."

Joaquin nodded. "But sometimes it fails you, doesn't it? Sometimes the real world intrudes: the boy, the woman, the cadets. It's never foolproof. And when it fails, there is no one there to assist you. Naturally, I compare your situation with that of a soldier. In some ways, it is easier for you—you are not being asked to kill anyone, you do not have to suffer knowing those who die, they are not friends or comrades—but hard in other ways, I should think. When your sense of immunity leaves you, you are completely alone, no one to share the burden. And, as you well know from telling me these stories, no way to ever fully describe the effect to someone who wasn't there. A lonely existence. I imagine it's one reason why you often travel with other photographers."

He stared at Mark.

Mark stared back. "Yes," he said, "I imagine so."

Joaquin returned to his notes. "Well, that covers the more obvious points. I don't know what significance they hold, but perhaps as we proceed . . ." He flipped through the pad, humming softly to himself. Finally, he stopped at one page, tapped it with a fingernail. "Something a bit more exotic. An odd little preoccupation—I wouldn't call it an obsession, certainly—but you seem to be very concerned with what happens to the dead. I first noticed it with the boy in Beirut. At the end of your story, you said, 'I don't know if his family ever got the body back.'" He peered up at Mark. "An unusual observation to make at that moment, no? One might even call it a non sequitur." He turned to another page. "Again, in Uganda, even before you meet the woman, you describe the villagers looking through the bones, trying

[157]

to find those of their families: 'That was the hardest part, because you can't tell one skull from the next, no way to know if it's your father or your mother or your next door neighbor.' " Another page. "With the cadets. You wondered if the boys' bodies would simply be scattered by animals, their bones carried into the forest, if they would simply cease to exist." Joaquin put the notepad aside. "Intriguing, no? Why is the fate of the dead so important to you?"

Mark looked out the kitchen window at the sky slipping out of twilight and into night. "I don't know," he said. "Maybe it's superstition."

"Superstition?"

"That the dead need to be returned to their families, that they can't be left to wander alone."

"Ghosts," Joaquin said. "You're talking about ghosts now."

"Maybe."

"And you believe in ghosts?"

"I don't know."

Joaquin sat back. "You realize, of course, that the dead are just a symbol—oh, I'm sure the doctors have a grander word for it, but they are just a symbol to you. The dead, who cares what happens to the dead? What difference does it make if they are blown to thin air or their bones are scattered through a forest? The dead are not important at all. It is the survivors who are important. It is they who are lost, they who are left to wander alone. Wouldn't you agree?"

Mark didn't answer. Joaquin took up the bottle and refilled their glasses. He seemed extremely pleased with himself, almost preening.

"You know, when we first started, I had great doubts about my ability to help you. Yes, it's true. I know that my professional demeanor suggested the utmost confidence, but to myself I wondered how much of my work with the soldiers could be applied to your situation. But now I realize it is the same. You took a very different path from my soldiers, had very different experiences, but we have arrived at the same place, haven't we?"

He drank deeply from his glass, gazed triumphantly at the ceiling. In the old man's manner, in his aura of self-congratulation, Mark felt the first intimations of dread.

"I'm sorry, Joaquin," he said, "but I have no idea what you're talking about."

"No? Then I shall tell you." He set the wineglass on the table, twirled its stem with his fingers. "The Morales Institute for Psychological Purification. A fine name, don't you think? It conveys authority, ambition, confidence. Actually, what I did there was very simple. My patients—my soldiers—came to me as lost men. They had committed terrible crimes, had done things beyond forgiveness, beyond redemption. They knew that—in their souls they knew that—and they came to me as a last hope, and I purified them. This is something Elena does not understand. To her it is very simple: These men were war criminals, they were evil, and because I treated them, I am evil, too."

He took the glass and held it in his lap, cradled it with both hands.

"But this has nothing to do with good and evil. How many truly evil men have you met in all your wars? One or two, perhaps, but I would suspect not many more. No, evil is too easy; life is far more complex. I think you would agree that most are merely weak men caught up in difficult times."

He waited for Mark to nod.

"But what happens when those men triumph, when they come to power? Once you have killed a thousand villagers, a thousand communists, why not kill a thousand more? Once you've tortured someone, how hard is it to torture again? It's easy, the easiest thing in the world, because you are a fallen angel and you have lost all hope of redemption. This is what Spain was faced with in 1939. What was I to do? Should I have let the killers continue as they were? There would have been no end to the slaughter. No, I couldn't watch that happen. So, I purified them, I brought them back to humanity. How many lives did I save? I believe I saved many."

Joaquin brought the glass to his lips and drank.

"But this is something Elena refuses to understand, refuses to even hear. That has been my dilemma all these years. She was like my own child. I was her father, she was my daughter, but for six years, ever since she learned of the institute, she has been lost to me, and that has been my challenge. I've always felt that if only I could persuade her to come home, then perhaps I could make her understand the way Spain was then, why I did what I did. But she refuses to do this, refuses to even listen."

He sighed, stared out the kitchen window. To Mark he seemed like a very old man then, broken and tired.

"I'm sorry, Joaquin," he said gently.

Joaquin turned to him and smiled. The wine had stained his teeth, given their whiteness a tint of red. "Sorry, yes, thank you, but you also wonder what possible connection all this has to you." He leaned toward Mark. "I will be plain. You have fallen, my boy. Your heart has stayed with the dead, and you can't find your way back. You try—you try very bravely—but you can't get back. You pretend to laugh, you pretend to love, but, in fact, you feel very little. A ghost, as you said. A different path—you haven't murdered, you haven't butchered—but just as despairing as my soldiers. But as I restored them, I can restore you. I can bring you home."

Mark took up his own glass, felt the bite of the wine on his tongue. He forced himself to smile.

"By purifying me?"

There was pity in Joaquin's eyes. "Yes, by purifying you."

A girl. A baby girl. The three women stood over the bed and took turns caressing Diane's cheek, stroking her hair, took turns holding her tiny pink infant in its white hospital blanket. A small, strong chain of women gathered in a hospital room, passing a baby girl from one set of arms to the next, smiling at her, cooing at her, administering soft kisses to her tiny fingers, shedding easy tears of both happiness and fear.

Elena placed a hand on Diane's warm cheek, felt a slow, deep pulse beneath her fingers, and waited for the tiny girl to reach her again.

"A dangerous place, isn't it? Especially this area you were in." Joaquin tapped a finger at the spot. "The Iraqis to the west and south, the Turks to the north, and then, over the mountains, the Iranians." He clucked his tongue. "No place for a country, is it?"

They were before the crude maps Mark had drawn on the wall,

Joaquin standing, Mark in his wheelchair. Joaquin had on his bifocals, was stooped low as he examined the first set of irregular black lines. He moved over to the second map.

"The scene of the incident," he muttered softly.

For several minutes, he studied Mark's creation: the wavering double line to signify the river, the small irregular oval of the hilltop. There were two small X's on this map, one inside the oval—where Mark had been at the time of the explosion—the other on the far side of the river, the spot where he had pulled himself from the water, where the Kurds had found him beneath the tree. Joaquin placed a finger on this second X and began a backward retracing of Mark's flight that night, along the river, across the valley, back toward the hilltop.

"Quite a journey for you. After the explosion, in your condition, it must have been arduous."

Mark shrugged. "Not too bad."

"Hmm." Joaquin's finger reached the circle of the hilltop, stopped at the small X there. "And this is you when the explosion occurred?"

Mark nodded.

"And the artillery shell, which direction did it come from?"

"I'm not sure. I assume from the west, from over here." Mark patted the bare wall to the left of the map.

"And where did it hit exactly?"

Mark leaned forward in the wheelchair, pointed to a spot just outside the circle. "Right about here."

Joaquin took the black pen from his coat pocket and gave it to Mark. "Why don't we make note of that."

Mark pulled close to the wall, added this new X to the map. He sat back, watched Joaquin's finger ponderously trail over the lines. Stooped and frowning with concentration, Joaquin seemed slightly befuddled, as if the markings were a math formula he could not decipher, a riddle in a language he did not understand.

"So you were standing here . . ." he said softly, remotely, as if to himself—and Mark watched the slow, bent finger make its journey across the wall—"and the artillery shell landed here . . . and where was Colin?"

Time stopped. Life stopped. Just for an instant, but in that instant all was white, a white of endless depth—no sound, no movement, no thought—and then he was back on the mountain, and the world was brown and quiet all around him.

He stands off the flat rock and the flower petals fall from his body. He turns away from the pool of his own blood and starts down the hill. No voice to lead him, no one to comfort him, only the wind and his own shadow on the rocks, and Mark comes to the blackened ground and there he finds him.

"Something's happened," Colin says. "I think something bad happened."

And Mark watches him for a moment, transfixed and confused, until he understands that Colin is trying to stand, that he is gripping the boulder and trying to lift himself to his feet, and Mark goes to him then and takes his arms and gently settles him on the ground, runs a soothing hand over his face, holds Colin's head down so he won't see how bad it is.

"It's going to be all right," he says. "You're going to be fine, just lie still now."

And when Colin calms, when he promises to be still, Mark walks over the shattered earth until he finds one boot and then the other, and each time he kneels down and tries not to comprehend what he is see-ing, what he is touching, as he yanks out the laces. It occurs to him how strange and unfair this is, how, on this morning, when the earth has turned to dust and shards, when a human body has been torn apart as cleanly as if by magic, the boots and the laces have perfectly survived, but when he walks back to his friend he carries the laces in his hand as if they are provident gifts, as if, at this late moment, their luck is about to change. And he sits beside Colin and ties the laces tight around his legs, an inch or two above where the ankles had been, and then he takes Colin's hand and looks into his frightened eyes.

"Save me, Mark. Save me. Take me home. Please take me home."

And through his tears, Mark nods and says over and over, "Don't worry, Colin. I'm going to save you. I'm taking you home, we're going home now."

And some time later, Colin begins to talk to his wife, to slip away, and there is nothing peaceful in this, there is a last moment of shame and nakedness in this. "Don't look, Diane. Please don't look. Something bad's happened. Please don't look."

But at the very end, Colin is transported. He opens his eyes—at last, peace and softness are seeping into them—and he smiles and reaches up to touch Mark's cheek with a blood-drenched hand and he whispers, "Oh, Diane. There was a day out there. I thought I wasn't coming back. There was a day, and I missed you so much."

And afterward, Mark lies down beside his friend and waits for the gray sky to fall, for a darkness that might shelter them as they begin their long journey, through the meadow grass and across the river, toward home.

Papa stood in the middle of the living room, his hands clasped behind his back, his head bowed like a condemned man. Elena looked past him to the empty wheelchair beneath the window.

"Where's Mark?"

"In the bedroom. He has something to tell you."

It came to her then, sharply, like a light shaft.

"It's Colin, isn't it?"

Papa nodded.

She looked at the night sky above Brooklyn. There were stars and they sparkled.

"Diane had her baby," Elena said, and in the corner of her eye she saw her grandfather come slowly toward her.

"I came for you, Elena."

"It's a girl."

"I've missed you so much."

"And now her father is dead."

"You are all I have left. You are the last thing I love."

"What is going to happen to her?"

"Come to Spain with me. Come home with me."

He had not yet reached her, but already Elena could feel his embrace, the fabric of his coat on her cheek, a comfort she had long ago lost, that she had never stopped missing.

•   •   •

[163]

He was pale with exhaustion, as pale as when she had found him on the bathroom tiles. Elena sat beside him on the bed, gently stroked his forehead, and her tears at that moment were for both Colin and the numbed pain she saw in his eyes.

"Why, Mark?"

He stared up at the ceiling, seemed very far away. He slowly shook his head on the pillow. "I don't know. I didn't want it to be true. I so didn't want it to be true. I think for a time I even believed . . ." He turned to her then, and there was such sorrow and shame in his eyes that her tears came faster. She nodded.

"What do you want to do?" she asked.

"I want to go away. With you. I want to go to Spain."

She nodded, kept stroking the face that had become indistinct before her eyes.

Diane was propped up in the hospital bed, her sleeping baby close to her chest, her mother and sister standing alongside. They all turned when he entered. Diane gave a thin, sad smile at the sight of him.

"Hello, Mark."

Without a word, the mother and sister stepped past him, left the room. He came to the foot of the bed. He didn't look at Diane but stared out the window at the gray morning sky. For a long time, neither spoke. She gently shifted the sleeping child, tucked a blanket beneath her chin.

"Would you like to see the baby?" she asked. "Would you like to hold her?"

Mark closed his eyes and shook his head. He felt his jaw begin to tremble.

"You're walking really well, Mark. But you're so skinny. You need to start eating."

He didn't say anything.

"Elena says you all are going to Spain."

He nodded.

"That will be nice, huh? Good to get away?"

Tears slipped from his closed eyes. "I didn't know how to say goodbye. I loved him. I still don't. I'm sorry."

"Oh, Mark," Diane said, beginning to cry herself now, "he loved you, too. He wouldn't want to see you go through this. It wasn't your fault. No one blames you." She reached out for him with her free hand. "Come here. I love you, too, Mark. Don't do this to yourself. Come here."

He shook his head again.

"At least look at me. Please, Mark. Please, just look at me."

She continued to beg him, her arm outstretched. But Mark would only shake his head, his eyes shut tight.

SIX

It was a still, brilliantly clear day, and when the taxi climbed the last rise, Elena touched Mark on the arm, pointed out the windshield.

"Dragons' teeth," she said. Across the fields, the glass shards atop the long white wall of her grandfather's home shone in the afternoon sun. "When I was a little girl, I called it dragons' teeth."

From the front passenger seat, Joaquin turned to her with a broad smile, his teeth straight and white. "That's right, I remember. Dragons' teeth."

Mark gazed up at the house from his vantage point in the driveway.

A mansion, really, and the small touches of dilapidation—the weeds sprouting among the roof tiles, the bare white patches where ochre paint had flaked from walls—accentuated its aura of faded grandeur. Leaning on his cane, he climbed the five stone steps to join the others at the front door.

"A fabulous place, Joaquin," he said. "I had no idea you lived in such luxury."

Joaquin, fiddling with the house keys, flipped a dismissive hand. "Nonsense. A ruin. Although I am quite pleased with the grounds at the moment."

Mark looked back at the yard. The flowerbeds and azalea bushes were precisely trimmed, the expanse of lawn the texture of a putting green.

"Ahmet," Joaquin explained. "He's from Morocco. Coming from the desert, I suspect he has a natural appreciation for the garden." He shook his head at Elena. "All those years of bad gardeners, I don't know why I didn't consider the Moslems earlier."

He unlocked the great oak door and swung it open, stood back to let them enter. He noticed Mark staring at the row of stumps along the perimeter wall. "Eucalyptus. The previous owner had them cut down for firewood in the 1920s. An act of idiocy, of course, but the owner was forever making such foolish decisions. He even built a mahogany desk too large to be moved. Can you imagine? Well, you'll see."

Joaquin ushered them through the door—Elena carrying the two small suitcases, Mark shuffling slightly on his cane—then picked up his own bag and followed them in.

Beyond an arched doorway to the left of the foyer, Mark saw a vast wood-paneled room with a fifteen-foot ceiling and a white marble fireplace. The thick beams of light streaming in from four large windows gave the room a ruby glow and revealed it to be completely bare. At the far end, open double doors let onto another room, almost equal in size and just as empty.

"Rather like your own living room, no?" Joaquin asked, peering over Mark's shoulder. "I could never decide what to do with these rooms, so I just ignored them. Come."

Leaving the luggage in the foyer, they passed through the opposite doorway, into a matching salon. Here, arrayed over a thin gray carpet, stood an assortment of modest furniture: several battered armchairs, a couch that appeared to be upholstered in vinyl, a pair of plain wood bookcases against the inner wall, their shelves bowed under the weight of books. Before one of the couches a Formica-topped coffee table supported a small television, a telephone, and an answering machine.

"Not elegant, I suppose," Joaquin said, "but sufficient for my needs." He led them through the salon to another set of double doors. One hand on the doorknob, he turned to Mark. "The ladies' parlor. My wife's little museum."

The contrast was remarkable. Here, all was elegant: ornate rose-wood furniture, antique vases on teakwood stands, a thick Persian carpet on the floor. Even the dim sunlight, filtered by velvet drapes sashed at the windows, was heavy and rich.

"It's just as I remember it," Elena said.

Joaquin gazed about the room and sighed. "Yes. Poor Violeta. I think she hoped to turn me into a Victorian." He gave Mark a tired smile. "She always said I had the aesthetic of a peasant."

They passed on into the kitchen, an airy room of pine cupboards and terra-cotta tiles, its white walls adorned with dried flowers and wreaths of garlic. A large window overlooked the back garden, and Mark saw a footpath of flagstones leading across the lawn to a small gate in the perimeter wall, a field of alfalfa beyond. In front of this window stood a dining room table with three chairs, a high stack of old newspapers and magazines on the floor.

"My reading room," Joaquin said, "quite pleasant in the morning." He saw Mark looking at the array of pots and pans and cooking utensils that hung from hooks on one wall. "Purely ornamental. I don't think they've been moved since Violeta died."

"But, Papa, what do you eat?"

Joaquin shrugged. "Fruit, cheese, serrano, whatever doesn't require preparation. I've little interest in anything complex."

Returning to the foyer, he and Elena took up the suitcases and started up the marble staircase for the second floor. Glancing back, Joaquin saw that Mark leaned heavily on the wooden balustrade as he climbed. "Take care," he said, patting the railing. "I'm afraid I haven't tested the strength of this in some time."

At the top of the stairs, he turned left and opened the door to a bedroom. It was at the northwest corner of the house, with windows on two sides, and the hard afternoon sunlight heightened its spareness: a large canopied bed in the far corner, two old dressers against an inner wall, a low desk with a chair beneath the western window, and nothing else—a bare floor, naked walls.

"I thought you would be most comfortable here," Joaquin said. "It offers a bit of privacy and is next to one of the bathrooms."

Mark stepped to the center of the room. Out the northern window, he saw a massif of treeless brown mountains with patches of snow in the upper clefts. Out the other window, the broad vega, its green fields and white villages.

It seemed so improbable to Mark just then, that all the hectic activity of the past few days should somehow lead them to this small, sunstruck room in a valley in Spain.

But, he realized, there always came this time, that strange moment of arrival, when feelings of relief at reaching one's destination merge with incredulity. He had most recently felt it in Kurdistan, on that afternoon when he and Colin had reached Rawanduz and been led to their rooms on the second floor of the guest house. After all their effort to get there, the expense, the planning, that intensely private moment when both had looked at the women they loved and tried to mentally calculate the chances they would never see them again, how improbable that those cold musty rooms on the second floor—rooms coated in blue-green enamel paint and lit by bare forty-watt bulbs—should have been their destination all along.

He turned to Joaquin. "It's perfect. Thank you."

"Rather rustic," Joaquin said, "but that appears to be your preference in any event. Come; I will show you the rest of the house."

With Mark and Elena following, he opened the next door along the walkway: a large bathroom with a white-tiled floor and claw-foot tub. He stepped to the sink and turned one of the taps.

"I asked Carmen—the ghastly housekeeper I told you about—to turn on the water for this side of the house, but . . ." There was a long hissing of air in the pipe, then a torrent of water spat out into the sink. "Voilà. For once, she remembers something."

They continued on. Joaquin rapped his knuckles on the next door—"My storage room, a shameful clutter"—then opened the next two: large bedrooms but as stripped and functionless as the downstairs salon. "All these rooms," he muttered absently, "and to what end?"

They came to the second bathroom—identical to the first but with Joaquin's toiletries spread neatly upon a shelf—and then to his bedroom at the southeast corner. It was even more spartan than the guest room: the same bare floor and walls but here the bed was narrow and on a sagging metal frame, the dresser drawers cracked and missing handles. If not for the grand windows and their view onto the valley, the room would have been as dreary as a prison cell.

"My God, Papa," Elena said, "you live like a Jesuit."

Joaquin gave a mock scowl. "No need for insults, my dear."

He led them to the next door, pulled it open with a flourish. "But now this, this is where life takes place."

Mark smelled the turpentine and paint before crossing the threshold. Here, finally, clutter: rags, discarded sketches and twisted tubes of paint on the floor, dozens of canvases—some apparently finished, others mere swatches of color—propped haphazardly against the walls, two enormous easels before the windows, and everywhere—on the floor, on the walls and window frames—speckles and smears of paint of every color.

"What a wonderful room," Mark said.

"Adequate, yes," the old man replied, "but it was better before. Here; I will show you." He led Mark past one of the easels to the eastern window, tapped a finger on the pane. "Until the 1970s, I could see the cathedral and the Alhambra from here—a glorious sight—but then they built those hideous high-rises, you see?"

In the distance, past miles of fields and tree windbreaks, were the Granada suburbs, a series of white towers rising up like tombstones. Beyond was Mulhacén, the highest mountain in Spain, its snowfields tinted soft orange in the waning day.

"Still stunning," Mark said.

As they were leaving, he stooped to examine the paintings stacked along the wall. Several were variations on a single subject—a small plaza with a ruined water fountain, a crumbling church tower beyond—and all were clearly the work of an accomplished hand, the paint thick and textured, the delicate blending of colors and sunlight and shadow creating a strangely lifelike effect. He nodded, turned to Joaquin. "I understand now why you are so famous."

Joaquin shook his head and chuckled, as if embarrassed by such praise. "Please. In a thousand years, my name will be a mere footnote."

And at last, they came to the study. As with Violeta's parlor, Mark was struck by its contrast to the other rooms, opulence amid such starkness. Atop a great Oriental carpet sat the mahogany desk, so excessively carved with ships and machinery and laurel wreaths it bordered on the gaudy, its gleaming surface bare save for an onyx inkwell from which two silver pens protruded at perfectly symmetrical angles. On the far side of the desk, a high-backed leather armchair, two standing lamps, and, on the wall between them, an old Spanish flag mounted in a glass frame. Directly above the flag, a portrait of a middle-aged and dour Francisco Franco in uniform. Except for the gallery of family photographs along one paneled wall, the study resembled nothing so much as a museum exhibit, a faithful replication of history to be viewed from behind a velveteen rope.

"The famous desk," Joaquin said. "Quite bizarre, isn't it?"

"Not as bizarre as the picture of Franco," Elena said.

Joaquin ignored the comment, turned to Mark. "During the days of the institute, I met with my patients here." He pointed to three armless chairs set along the inner wall. "Very important back then to conduct sessions in a formal setting, to maintain a professional climate—and the men did seem to respond well to it. A practice largely abandoned today, of course, what with all the hand-holding and hugging and sitting about in circles—the downfall of our profession, I'm afraid."

"And what profession would that be exactly?" Elena asked, still staring at the portrait of Franco.

Joaquin threw his head back, bayed with laughter. "Ah, *qué rico*, my dear, *qué rico*! Even with the rigors of travel, your wit, like a rapier!"

They made love slowly, lazily, their bodies fusing with sheer exhaustion, and afterward Elena looked out at the milky light of a star-filled sky, breathed in the thin scent of ancient eucalyptus. She let her mind

[171]

wander, and a number of thoughts came to her in a vague, vaporous way, drifting in, floating out again. After a time, though, one stayed.

"That was my father's room."

She wasn't sure if Mark was still awake or even if she had said this aloud, but he lifted his head from the pillow and looked to her.

"Papa's studio," she said. "When my father was growing up, it was his bedroom. After he died, Papa turned it into a shrine. He put my father's torero posters back up on the walls, hung photos of him as a child everywhere. I never liked going in there when I visited—I thought it was ghoulish—but it was even stranger to see it today and find everything gone. I wonder why Papa made it his studio. Why that room?"

Mark reached out and brushed the hair from Elena's forehead. He thought of the view from that eastern window, Mulhacén and the Granada high-rises. "Maybe it's a different way of remembering your father."

"Maybe." She gazed at the bedsheet for a moment, considering this. When she looked at Mark again, her eyes were searching, almost fearful. "But what did he do with my father's things? Do you think he threw them out?"

He stroked her hair, remembered all the barren rooms of Casa de los Queridos. "No," he said, "I'm sure he didn't do that. How could any father do that?" He leaned over, kissed her on the cheek. "Sleep now."

But some time later, Elena awoke. Moving out of Mark's heavy embrace, she read her watch face in the moonlight: a few minutes before six, not even midnight in New York. She had never adjusted to travel easily.

Slipping on her nightgown, she stepped to the window. A nearly full moon held low in the sky, just over the northern peaks, and the fields of the vega shone in a silver-black light that shimmered before her eyes, as if she were aboard a ship on a night sea. She yawned, hoping to lure tiredness, but she was fully awake now, her night over.

In the kitchen, the wall clock ticked like a metronome. She made coffee, the hissing of the machine terribly loud in the sleep-wrapped house, and carried a cup out to the front steps. For a while, she only listened. There were birds in the shrubbery, and she heard the scratching of branches, the fluttering of wings, but no song. Some distance away, a flock of sheep was being moved to pasture, their bells clapping like wooden wind chimes, the guttural bark of the shepherd coming to Elena like a cough.

It was all so eerily familiar. A place she had scarcely thought of in six years, and it was as if she had never left—the same creak to the old oak door, to the staircase balustrade, precisely the same sound of the sheep moving in the night, as if they were the same sheep she had listened to as a child, an ageless flock in perpetual search of pasture.

It had been a horrible week, the worst Elena could ever remember. Dealing with Mark, with Papa, arranging the emergency leave-of-absence from work, seeing to the myriad details that accompanied any journey, and amidst it all spending as much time as she could with Diane, consoling her as her shock turned to grief and then, in the last days, to a kind of anger.

"Why?" Diane had asked again and again. "Why didn't Mark tell us?"

It was the same question Elena had put to Mark in a dozen different ways during that interminable week. She had asked in sympathy, in rage, in tears—"Did you think it would make it easier?" "Did you think we would just forget about Colin?" "Were you ever going to tell?" And each time, he had answered, "I don't know," and each time she had answered her friend the same way: "I don't know, Diane. I don't know why Mark did it."

In all those seven days, Elena could recall only one time when her heart had lifted slightly, when she may have even managed a quick smile. It had been with Papa, when they went down to the antique shops on Atlantic Avenue to find a cane for Mark. She had found a beautiful one of hickory, its handle carved in the shape of a duck's head, and she was on her way to the counter with it when Papa took it from her hand.

"No," he said, "get a cheap one, for in a few days it will be completely useless to us." He had handed it back to her, pointed to the stand of canes at the back of the store. "The cheapest one available."

Now, sitting on the front steps of her grandfather's home, Elena found herself hoping it did not become useless too soon. Over the course of the past week, she had realized that a decision was to be made, about her, about Mark, about what future they might have. As long as there were more immediate concerns, as long as Mark hobbled about on his cheap pine cane, that decision could be postponed, thankfully pushed to the back of her thoughts.

As her eyes adjusted, the driveway and flowerbeds emerged from the dark, and she became aware of the faintest tinge of blue behind the eastern mountains. She returned to the kitchen, poured another cup of coffee, and walked through the downstairs rooms. The sky was lightening quickly, and out the windows Elena saw the bushes and hedges that had been the hiding places of her childhood.

At the top of the stairs, she listened. From the far end of the house, the snore of her grandfather. From the room where Mark slept, no sound at all. She went into the study and spent a few minutes looking at the photographs on the wall: her father as a boy, as a university student; her grandmother as a young woman, as a mother, as a dying middle-aged woman; herself as an infant, a girl, an awkward teenager.

She went into the studio. The easels loomed like giant sleeping birds, and out the window she saw that the eastern peaks were now black silhouettes on a cobalt blue sky, that a gold corona had formed over Mulhacén.

She passed along the walkway to the door of the storage room. It was the one room her grandfather hadn't opened when showing Mark around the evening before, and Elena couldn't remember now if she had ever been inside. She opened the door.

Along the inner wall were five wood boxes, their neatly packed contents indistinct under a thick layer of dust. She knelt and delicately picked through one, the dust already catching at her throat. They were her father's things: schoolbooks, toys, photographs, folded-up posters of soccer players and toreros, even some childhood clothes. All five boxes held a similar array of relics. Elena straightened and looked about the room.

At one end, a jumble of broken chairs and collapsed metal bed frames. Between the two windows, five rows of identical black footlockers stacked almost to the ceiling, perhaps forty in all. Along the opposite wall, four tall file cabinets. And over everything, the dust, a dust so thick it kicked up in little spumes with each step Elena took farther into the room.

She tapped the sides of two footlockers, lightly pushed against one of the stacks; they were empty, the column swayed. She crossed to the file cabinets.

A metal label was fastened to the top drawer of the first cabinet, and in the predawn light she made out the words: Instituto Morales. Below this label, a metal plate held a small card on which the word *ingresos*, admissions, had been written by hand.

With some difficulty, the metal grooves having rusted from years of disuse, she pulled open this drawer. Dozens of folders, each labeled with a man's name and arranged in alphabetical order. Elena lifted out several folders, carried them to a window for better light, and drew back the first cover.

A variety of official forms, all printed on crude, tissue-thin paper and emblazoned with the seal of Fascist Spain in the upper left corner. Read in order, they charted the remarkable rise and fall of one Jorge Ernesto Acosta: an illiterate seventeen-year-old farmer's son in 1936, an eighteen-year-old corporal in the Spanish Nationalist army in 1937, a field lieutenant with a commendation for bravery at twenty, a mental invalid committed to the Morales Institute at the age of twenty-one. The last form in this folder was entitled "Preliminary Observations," and here Elena recognized the tiny, pinched handwriting of her grandfather.

"Lt. Jorge Acosta is perturbed by an event which befell him on the afternoon of January 4, 1939, at a farmhouse approximately 4 kilometers west of the municipality of Santa Lucía, Valencia Province. Lt. Acosta is clearly in a state of some fragility, prone to sudden episodes of sorrow, and has been unable to find sufficient solace in either the affections of his family or the knowledge of God's everlasting love."

Elena closed the file and opened the next. The same sheaf of official forms, a similar tale of rise and ruin. She turned to her grandfather's notes.

"Sgt. José Aguilera remains perturbed by a series of events which befell him beginning on the morning of February 22, 1938, in Teruel,

Teruel Province, and which continued intermittently over the next three days of liberation activities in that city. Sgt. Aguilera displays few outward signs of psychic molestation other than a preoccupation with cleanliness and order, and a tendency toward high emotion when his exacting standards in these areas are not satisfied. He expresses deep reluctance at being reunited with his wife and children and rejects with considerable vigor any suggestion that he might find solace in the knowledge of God's everlasting love."

She read through the others. "Major Alcantara is of the belief that his mind has been inhabited by the spirits of several individuals vanquished at his hand." "Lt. Alvarado has not slept since his participation in the liberation activities of San Sebastian fourteen months ago, and spends the night hours searching for his company's mascot, a small dog that apparently went missing at that time." Each report closed with some variation on the theme of God's everlasting love, on the patient's derision or despair at ever being returned to it.

Elena replaced the files and left the storage room. In their bed, Mark still slept, his face as serene and smoothed as she had ever seen it. His cane was propped against the desk chair, and out the window the blue haze over the vega was giving way to gold, the new day coming upon them.

And now Elena realized the sorrow of war sometimes wore a very different face from the ones she had always considered, that along with the dead and the maimed and the blind, there were those who came back whole—smiling, perhaps, laughing, perhaps—but who were wholly unrecognizable to themselves and everyone who had ever loved them.

Mark moved on the bed. He opened his eyes. He saw Elena standing above him. He smiled.

The days passed with a gentle quiet. They had picnics in the mountains, strolled the Alhambra and the narrow streets of old Granada, but mostly it was lazy afternoons reading in the sunlit garden, wine-eased nights of conversation at the kitchen table.

Yet there was an element of pretense to this time. Despite his gradual physical improvement, despite the pleasured face he displayed, there were moments when Mark was wrenched back to the mountain or the river or the cave. These moments came without warning; he might be walking with Joaquin in the fields or lying in bed with Elena, and they would rise before his eyes, unbidden snapshots—of Colin's living face, of his dead legs, of the mullah giving Mustafa Karim his last kiss, of blue tags—and Mark would be gripped with a sadness that seemed ready to crush him. Afterward, he struggled to free himself, to show that he was fine and happy and better, to settle into a companionship with the living world until the next time the snapshots came.

For Elena, the pretensions were more complex. There were times when she saw the pain blossom in Mark's eyes or felt it in the tightening curl of his fingers, and she would embrace him, ask if he wanted to talk. But there were other times when she simply ignored it, looked away or talked on or let her own hand fall free, because these were times when she had to believe in normalcy, to imagine that the weight now upon them was only a fleeting state, a spell of bad weather that would pass as long as they took no notice. There were times when she wanted to close the distance she had placed between her and her grandfather, to laugh wholeheartedly at his jokes, to tell her own stories of being with him as a child, only to force herself back, remembering what he had done, that she could never fully forgive him. And each night, when the others had gone to sleep, she would go into the storage room and read through another stack of files to remember, to fortify herself for another day of remove. It was exhausting to maintain all these strategies, and Elena began to look toward her upcoming trip to Madrid with anticipation, as not just a reunion with her mother, but an escape from a burdensome house.

On the evening of their sixth day in Spain, while she and Mark walked back from Peñuelas with plastic bags of groceries, she abruptly stopped in the road to face him.

"My mother's becoming impatient; I'm thinking of taking the train up tomorrow."

He no longer used the cane, merely walked stiffly, like a man with braces on his legs, and he looked so defenseless standing there in the road, his right knee trembling slightly, his hands pinned to his sides under the weight of the bags, that Elena felt her resolve begin to slip. "I'll only go for a few days. You'll be okay here?"

He smiled. "Of course. Take your time."

That night in the storage room, she went to the last file cabinet, the one labeled *salidas*. For some time, she read her grandfather's handwritten notes, his final words on the long-ago patients of the Morales Institute.

"It is with great pleasure that I hereby certify Lt. Arsenio Castañeda as completely purified of his previous psychological molestations and returned to the embrace of God. *Por la gracia de Dios, viva El Caudillo!*"

"It is my august privilege to announce that Colonel Hector Vidalia Saenza, one of our most complex and difficult patients, has at long last been purified, having found serenity of spirit and solace in the embrace of God. *Por la gracia de Dios, viva El Caudillo!*"

In the dim light, Elena wondered if any of these miracles had actually occurred, if any of her grandfather's grand proclamations could possibly be true. She tried to imagine those ruined men walking out the institute gates, set loose upon their families, their villages, upon Spain. She thought of Mark, sleeping with such innocence in the next room, and tried to imagine what kind of miracle might be waiting for him.

They stood on the platform until the train became a small silver object in the distance, until it disappeared altogether, curving to the north in the direction of Madrid.

"So, just the two of us again." Joaquin turned to Mark with a smile. "How do you feel?"

Mark shrugged, breathed in the clean spring air. "Fine. It's a beautiful day."

"Yes, and what of your traumas? All better?"

Mark gazed down the tracks, squinted against the glare coming off the rails. "I don't know. Maybe."

"Splendid," Joaquin said. "Let's have a coffee, then."

They sat at a small table in the terminal cafe. Joaquin poured three spoonfuls of sugar into his espresso, hummed to himself as he stirred. He was in high spirits. "Well, we have the whole day ahead of us. What shall we do?"

Mark watched Joaquin's spoon go round and round in the black liquid. Everything seemed miniature, the table, the espresso cup, the tiny silver spoon. "I'm not sure this is working, Joaquin."

The old man looked up, puzzled. "Whatever do you mean?"

"The sadness, it never goes away. I'm sad all the time."

Joaquin raised the cup to his lips. "Excellent. Your recovery continues apace."

"I think maybe I need to see a specialist."

Joaquin grimaced. "Please, not this again."

"I just don't know what to do. If anything, it's worse than before."

Joaquin took a short, noisy sip from the cup. "But of course. Before you were in shock, you felt nothing. Now the shock has worn off, you are healing, and healing is always painful. The mind is exactly like the body in this regard."

Mark remembered Talzani's words—pain is always preferable to numbness. "But I don't feel like I'm healing. It's not getting any easier. Every morning, it's the first thing I think of. Every day—"

Joaquin silenced him with a raised hand. "And a specialist will put a stop to that? What is a specialist going to do for you?" He leaned forward. "Don't you see? No one can make this easier for you, because no one can know how you suffer—not me, not Elena, and not some specialist. Pain is the most private thing in life. If you don't understand this, if you continue to believe someone else holds a solution, then you will never be cured." He sat back, saw the confusion rise in Mark's eyes. "Ah, you sense a contradiction: You are thinking to yourself, 'So why am I here? He said he could help me.' Well, I can help you. As much as anyone, I can help you." Joaquin drained his espresso in one gulp and rose from the chair. "We go. I want to show you a place."

They drove east out of Granada and turned onto the road leading to the ski resort on Mulhacén. For nearly an hour they climbed, the road an endless series of hairpins, their surroundings becoming steadily more barren and wintered until finally there was only snow. At the summit, they drove past the lodge and parking lots to a narrow service road. It cut through deep snowfields before ending alongside a ski-lift pylon at the crest of a ridge. Joaquin stopped the car, and they stepped out into the cold air, walked to the edge of the precipice.

The world spread vast and tranquil below them. Nestled amid the mountain peaks was Granada and, carving a course to the west, the broad green basin of the vega. Along with a light wind came the regular clank of empty ski chairs passing through the machinery over their heads.

"You see there?" Joaquin pointed to a highway and cluster of buildings at the southernmost tip of the Granada plain. "It is called El Suspiro de Moros, 'the Sigh of the Moors.' When the Moors were forced from Granada, the sultan stopped at that spot to look back at his Alhambra palace one last time. He cried, and then he turned and began his journey into exile."

Joaquin's finger trailed a course through the southern mountains, and Mark saw the shadow of a deep ravine there, a winding path that cut through a tangle of rock and brown earth all the way to the Mediterranean, a low wall of blue in the hazy distance.

"That is how most people believe the Moors left, that they went to the coast, boarded ships, and set sail for Africa, never to return."

Joaquin dropped his hand and turned to Mark with a smug look.

"Not true, of course. Come."

He led the way a bit farther along the crest. The land to the southeast opened up as they walked, until Mark saw that another valley lay directly below them. It ran parallel to the coast and was far deeper and more rugged than the vega, only a thin ribbon of green fields in its very depth, small white villages clinging to the sides of steep slopes.

"The Alpujarra," Joaquin said. "Few Spanish history books make mention of it, but that is where many of the Moors went in 1492. The sultan signed a treaty with Queen Isabel, and in return for surrendering Granada they were given this valley. The Moors turned it into a garden—terraced the mountains, established a government, developed a sophisticated irrigation system. They remained there for eighty more years and would still be there if the Spaniards hadn't betrayed the treaty. In the 1560s, the Catholic king decided there was no place in Spain for nonbelievers, and the Moors were forced to either convert or leave. The last Moorish resistance was in the Alpujarra."

He laughed. "And what do you think happened? The valley was

resettled with peasants from Galicia and Asturias—good Catholic Spaniards—and it immediately went to ruin. The terraces crumbled, no one knew how to operate the irrigation system, and the Alpujarra became one of the poorest regions in the country. And so it is still. Many of the villages down there didn't have electricity or schools or even roads to them until the 1970s."

Joaquin put his hands in his coat pockets to warm them, continued to gaze down at the valley.

"What is remarkable, though, is that there are no regrets. I doubt you could find a person in the entire Alpujarra who would say that life would have been better if the Moors had stayed. You see, we Spanish hold to the idea of national purity—far worse than the Germans on this matter. Better to be poor, better to live like animals, than be tainted by outside influence." He looked to Mark with an arched eyebrow. "And how does a nation achieve this purity? By cleansing, by *la limpieza*. That is the history of Spain: the Moors, the Jews, the Christian heretics of the Inquisition, the Civil War Republicans, Spain cleansed itself of them all, and after each one, the Fatherland was restored, returned to splendor, returned"—he motioned toward the valley—"to the purity of ruin. Interesting, no?"

Mark nodded. "Tragic."

"Tragic?" Joaquin pondered for a moment, shook his head. "I don't know. It appears to be what the Spaniard wants, what pleases him."

They looked out at the view, at the changing shadows the scudding clouds cast on the land and sea. After a time, Joaquin pointed to a cluster of peaks on the far side of the Alpujarra, perhaps fifty miles to the southeast.

"On the other side of those mountains is Almería. That is how I came. When the war started, when the blood squads started, that is how I came." He lowered his hand. "Terrible. Terrible and so pointless, because Almería could have easily escaped that war—at least the worst part of it, those first days. It was a very liberal city, the communists and trade unions quite powerful, but when Franco ordered the Rising, the military garrison there obeyed the call. They were quickly crushed, of course, and then the Republican mobs went wild, hunted down anyone they considered unreliable—priests, landowners, conservatives. Terrible. I was away from home when it started, but my family was prominent—good monarchists, very outspoken against the left—so I knew they would come for us, I saw what they were doing in the streets, but there was no way I could . . ."

Joaquin stared at the distant peaks, hunched his shoulders against a windburst that came over the ridge and laced them with powdered snow.

"So, I fled. I had to flee. I hid in a friend's home for almost a month, and then I climbed up into those mountains. When I reached the top, I didn't know what to do. The Alpujarra was like a slaughterhouse then, blood squads from both sides roaming everywhere, so I continued along the crest until I could go no farther." Joaquin's finger slowly traced the ridge of the coastal range before stopping at the mountain directly across the valley from them. "Then, no more choices; either I stayed up there and starved or I came down into the Alpujarra." The finger charted a course down the far slope, over terraced fields, and past white villages. "It was difficult. I moved at night, hiding whenever I saw or heard someone else. During the days, I stayed in the forests or up in the rocks. But at last, I reached the river there"—he pointed to the ribbon of green at the heart of the valley—"and then I started up this side, crawling, running, hiding, all the way up until I came to here."

The finger pointed down, to the ground on which they stood.

"And it was only when I was here and saw the Alpujarra behind me, saw Granada before me, that I knew I was safe, that I had escaped."

He turned to Mark. In the strong wind that had risen, the ski chairs above their heads swung violently from side to side, screeched against the wire line that held them. Joaquin dug at the snow with his shoe.

"And it was on this very spot that the most astonishing thing happened. It was dawn. I stopped here for a moment to glance back, to see the world I had escaped, and I looked over there"—he motioned to the southwest, to the Mediterranean—"and I saw something far out at sea shining like gold. I didn't know what it was. It wasn't the sun, obviously, because the sun was to the east, but it was almost as bright, as if there were a second sun on the horizon. And because I couldn't make sense of it, I decided it was a miracle—I was still a Catholic then—a divine sign that God was offering me a new life. But this was not a pleasurable moment—I suspect miracles rarely are—because to take this new life meant I would be alone, that I would have no one, that my family, my friends, all were lost to me. But what choice did I have? There was no choice. Either I accept this new life or I die. And so . . ."

Joaquin turned on his heels until he faced Granada. For a long time, he stared in silence at the city and the vega. Suddenly, a grin came to his face. He wheeled to Mark.

"And do you know what it was, my miracle? It was sand, the sand dunes of Africa. Incredible, I know, because Africa is maybe two hundred kilometers from here, but that's what it was. I'm told it's still possible to see it on a very clear day." He laughed. "Sand!"

The two men faced each other, the wind whistling past their ears in gusts. Joaquin's grin slowly waned, and he stamped his feet against the cold.

"You think I am cavalier, but that is not true. I understand that what happened in Kurdistan is very difficult for you. But you cannot let it ruin you. You have to turn away from the past. All of us, we have to turn away. It is the hardest thing a man can do, but we must do it. Not only a necessity, but an obligation, because no one has the right to waste their life. Whether or not you believe in God, no one has this right."

Mark looked out at the Mediterranean. " 'Forget the dead,' " he muttered, " 'the dead don't need anything from us.' A doctor in Kurdistan told me that."

There was no golden light today, no sand dunes of Africa, only a white film that made the meeting of sea and sky a gradual blending.

"His name was Talzani, Ahmet Talzani. I didn't realize it then, but he knew Colin was dead. It's why he said that to me. They'd found his body down by the river and brought it up to the hospital— in bad shape, unrecognizable—and I didn't tell Talzani it was Colin, lied to him the same as everyone else. But he knew the truth." He looked to Joaquin. " 'Forget the dead.' "

Joaquin nodded.

"But how do you do that? I don't know how to do that."

"Only partly a matter of will, I'm afraid," Joaquin said. "But at least with will we can hope to recognize the terrain when we come upon it."

Mark was baffled. "Terrain?"

"Oh, I don't think it's for us to decide—we're far too small for that. No, redemption can only come from something greater—faith, usually, but it seems nonbelievers such as ourselves must rely on the land." Joaquin waved a hand at the view. "Earth, sea, sometimes just sand: It will deliver us from all manner of sorrows if we allow it."

The wind had eased slightly, the ski chairs settling back into a gentler rocking motion. Joaquin stepped to the cliff edge and peered into the rugged folds of the Alpujarra once more.

"A cruel land. They say we Spanish are a cruel people because we were born on cruel land, but that is not so." He motioned at the valley with his chin. "We made it cruel. That was a garden at one time."

He smiled sadly at Mark. "I think you might find the Alpujarra an interesting region to explore. Once you leave the main road, the villages are quite unspoilt and traditional, very photogenic."

Mark seized upon this advice with ardor. Each morning, he carried his camera bag to the car, drove out the gate of Casa de los Queridos, and turned east.

The first hour was only to be endured, the vega farmland quickly supplanted by junkyards and grimy industrial parks, then the first bleak high-rises of the Granada suburbs. When Mark connected up to the southern highway at Suspiro de Moros, it was much the same except more traffic, more billboards, more ugly gashes in the hills for roads and apartment complexes. It was only after he had descended halfway to the coast and turned onto the Alpujarra road, after he had negotiated the narrow, tourist-clogged streets of Lanjarón and emerged on the other side, that he began to feel content, the great, quiet valley opening before his eyes.

More than a valley, the Alpujarra was a massive ravine. At its western confluence, it was quite wide, the Guadalfeo River at its heart broad and slow-moving. Driving inland, the land grew more rugged, the valley floor giving way to a jumble of hillocks and rock screes, the

Guadalfeo diminishing to a narrow, twisting snake of fast water. The flanking walls of mountain drew closer and steeper, then became irregular, sliced by the deep creases of side valleys. And everywhere on this landscape were tiny whitewashed villages: in the shadow of gorges, on tors of rock, on windswept meadows just below the snow line. To Mark, it seemed quite possible that their locations had been chosen as some ancient form of punishment, places where the inhabitants would be eternally deprived of some essential need: water, sunlight, soil.

Each day, he stopped the car in a different corner of the Alpujarra, took up his camera bag, and set off into the hills. Occasionally, he would venture into one of the villages, walk its crooked streets, but mostly he stayed to the periphery, to the terraced fields and olive orchards and forests of stunted pine. He climbed. Each day, a little higher. He would climb without stopping, feel the pleasant burn in his legs as they regained their strength, breathe in the damp of the spring earth, listen to the bells of distant sheep, and eventually he would come to a place—a rock outcropping, a field of meadow grass—where he was alone at the top of the world, and there he would sit and watch the valley and villages and river, would hear nothing but his own breath and the wind shuddering down from the snow peaks, and there he would feel happy as he talked to Colin.

"Do you like it here?" he would ask. "It's beautiful here, isn't it?"

Sometimes he would ask Colin's opinion on photographs he was considering—"Should I tighten down the F-stop, should I use the tripod?"—or complain about the haze in the far reaches of the Alpujarra. Sometimes he would ask about Diane or reminisce about one of their trips. "Remember that birthday party for the mujaheddin commander in Peshawar? That was surreal, wasn't it? Remember the hand-grenade fishing trip with the Tamil Tigers?" And Mark would laugh, shake his head. "Crazy times, some crazy times we had."

And in the late afternoons, as the villages began to slip into shadow and the Guadalfeo became lost in the murk of dusk, Mark would stand, brush his pants, and feel suddenly chilled. "Well," he would say, "I guess we should head home."

But at some point during the long walk back to the car, Colin would start to lag behind, would finally stop following altogether, and

Mark would glance over his shoulder, maybe give a quick wave. "Don't worry," he would call, "tomorrow."

Once back at Casa de los Queridos, Mark and Joaquin would eat a simple meal of cheese and bread and serrano ham and talk about pleasant things—Moorish architecture, the techniques of oil painting—and then they would take a bottle of wine and sit together in the garden. No snapshot images rose before Mark's eyes, no shaft-rays of sadness, and he would lean back in his chair, feel the wine on his tongue, and follow Joaquin's finger as it traced the star-filled sky.

"Look, Cassiopeia. And over there, Ursa Major. An exquisite night, don't you think?"

And in Madrid at that moment, Elena would be at a dinner with relatives or sitting in a smoke-thick cafe-bar with her college girl-friends. For her, this was a time of enforced lightness and pleasantry. With her aunts and uncles and cousins, she talked of the excitement of living in New York but not of the somberness of her work, listed the exotic places Mark traveled to but not the horrors he witnessed there. Never mentioned was why she and Mark had come to Spain at this time or why he had remained behind in Granada. All the relatives knew why—Elena could see in their solicitousness and grave expressions that her mother had informed them all—but at each gathering the play of manners was upheld, and all pretended that nothing was amiss with Elena, the golden child of the family, the intelligent and ambitious girl who had set an independent course and found success beyond all imaginings.

But it could not hold forever, and at her Uncle Javier's house on the fourth night, it ended. It was late, nearly midnight, and they were in the living room with coffee and brandy when her younger cousins, Ana and Luisa, began begging to see photographs of Mark. Elena was reluctant, already sensing the fraying within her, but she finally relented, reached into her handbag, and handed the billfold to the girls. Ana and Luisa huddled on the couch to study the small glassine-encased photos.

"*Qué guapo!*" Ana giggled. "And so strong!"

Luisa, the fourteen-year-old, looked to Elena earnestly. "He must be very brave."

Elena stared at the girls, unable to speak. "Yes," she thought to herself, "he's so strong he doesn't need to laugh or cry, he's so brave he can watch his best friend die and pretend it never happened." She began to cry, fled the room.

Later, during the taxi ride home, her mother held her hand. "I'm sorry, Elena, I should have realized this would be torture. It's just that everyone was so anxious to see you."

Elena nodded, stared out at the rain-swept street. "It's okay."

Her mother leaned across the seat, turned Elena's chin toward her. "Tell me."

"I want to know why, Mama. It's not what Mark did so much but why. I've tried so hard to understand. Was he in shock? Was it guilt? Until I understand, I feel I don't know him at all."

Her mother nodded, stroked her hand. "But you will never know," she said quietly. "*He* will probably never know. People are inscrutable even to themselves. You can go mad looking for reasons. We must accept that people do inexplicable things."

"But there's always a reason. There has to be a reason."

Her mother shrugged. "And what reason could he give that would make you feel better? You see? It's pointless. The important thing is for Mark to become healthy again."

Elena stared at her mother's caressing hand. " 'Returned to the embrace of God.' " She looked up. "That was Papa's phrase when he decided his patients were cured."

"Really?" Her mother smiled, drew back a little in surprise. "I always thought your grandfather was an atheist."

Now Elena smiled, too. "Not back then, I guess. I don't think an atheist would have been very popular with the Francoists."

Her mother laughed lightly, but a careful, inquisitive look came into her eyes. "And how are you getting along with Papa?"

Elena nodded. "Okay. I know I've been very harsh with him. And in a way I can't figure out, I do think he is helping Mark. Still, it's hard. When I think of what he did, those horrible men he helped . . ."

"It was not so black and white as you imagine, my dear. Both sides did unspeakable things in that war. And, remember, your grandfather lost everyone. He was a young man, and he lost everyone."

"I know," Elena said. "I know I've been harsh."

They rode in silence for a time. The taxi turned off Avenida

Castellana onto Calle Legazpi, and Elena gazed at the dark windows of her old primary school, Santa Filomena's, as they passed. The three-story stone building looked drearier than she remembered.

"I think you should go back to Granada."

She turned to her mother. "What?"

"I know this is an ordeal for you, Elena—all these family parties and having to be so pleasant when you're preoccupied with Mark. You should go back."

"But I want to spend time with you, Mama. Besides, Mark is ashamed; I think in some ways it's easier for him to not have me there."

Her mother patted her arm. "Then go for your grandfather. I will be here for a long time, but your grandfather is nearly eighty. You always loved him so much, and you were like a daughter to him. It would make him so happy to be reunited with you before he dies."

Elena laughed softly. "I don't think he's going to die anytime soon, Mama. Sometimes I think Papa will live forever."

Her mother smiled but kept her hand on Elena's arm. "Please. Do this for me. I will come to New York this summer and we'll have a nice visit, but right now, be with your grandfather."

Elena looked at the streetlamps and shuttered storefronts of Calle Legazpi, the business street she had passed along so many times in her youth, where she had once known the names of every salesclerk and grocer. She nodded.

As she lay in her bed that night, Elena thought of how far she had moved away from Madrid, how the people and streets she had once known like her own hand had receded to strangeness. Then she tried to remember Mark's face, his old face, before the pain settled in his eyes. She had always found this difficult in the past, but this time his face came to her, slowly, one feature at a time, until it was complete. Then she remembered the words her grandfather had written to set his patients free, and she whispered them to herself as if in prayer.

Mark leaned over the steering wheel and stared at the roadside sign.

He was on the south flank of the Alpujarra, on a back mountain road he hadn't taken before, and he had almost missed the tiny sign as he came around the curve. The black letters on the white background were partly obscured by rust, but enough remained of the single word—Olía—to have caught the corner of his eye, a moment later to register in his mind. He had braked, reversed the car back to the turnoff.

The engine idling, he sat and tried to remember where he had heard the name, kept staring at the sign as if it might reveal the answer. Finally, it came to him; the lost patient of the Morales Institute, Perez something, the Beast of Olía.

He looked along the dirt road, followed its zigzag course up the barren mountainside, but saw no sign of a village, no sign of habitation at all. Mark knew from his time in the Alpujarra that even if the town were only a few kilometers away, just over the first ridge line, it could take twenty minutes of driving to reach it. He glanced at his watch.

Elena's train was coming into Granada in a little over an hour; already he was late. With great reluctance, he put the car in gear and pulled away, watched for landmarks to guide his way back to this lonely stretch of road.

Elena led Mark across the back garden, swung open the small gate, and went with him into the field of alfalfa. They held hands, and she talked of her days in Madrid, leaving out the difficulties, relating instead funny things her mother had said, family gossip he might find amusing.

"And how has it been here?"

"Good," he said. "Relaxing. I've been driving down to the Alpujarra every day, hiking up through the hills, taking some photos. It's quite stunning there."

Elena nodded, stooped to pluck a poppy flower by her feet. "I knew you'd like the Alpujarra. Rugged and out of the way, the sort of place you like."

They walked a few more paces—the red of the poppies was everywhere among the green plants—and then Mark stopped, turned to her excitedly.

"I forgot. I passed by the village where that patient was from, the one who went missing from the institute. Olía. The Beast of Olía, remember?"

Elena searched his face. There was something about his animation, the sudden burst of enthusiasm, that puzzled her. She nodded. "Carlos Perez."

"Right," he said. "Well, I was thinking of going up there tomorrow, just asking around, see if he ever did show up again. You want to come along?"

Elena started walking again, staring down at the furrowed ground as she considered.

She, too, had remained curious about Perez. During one of her nighttime visits to the storage room, she had looked up his name in the records cabinets and, just as Papa had said, found his file gone. Where the other folders had been thick with papers, that for Captain Carlos Miguel Perez had consisted of one half-sheet of thin yellowed paper, two short sentences noting the date of his admission to the institute, the date of his termination, the forwarding of his records to the military command.

But Elena had met the son, she at least had a simple reason for remaining curious. Mark's interest was harder to grasp. She remembered having been disquieted by it back in New York, and now she was again.

"Sure," she said, "I'll go with you."

From the window of his study on the second floor, Joaquin watched them walk hand-in-hand over the alfalfa field.

On the wall beside him was a gallery of framed photographs, perhaps thirty in all. They were not arranged in any pattern as to chronology or subject, but together they formed a chronicle of much of his life.

In the center of the arrangement was a small black-and-white photograph, dulled to grays with age. It was a formal portrait of Joaquin as a young man of twenty-three, on the eve of the war. He sat stiffly, his back straight, hands folded in his lap. In almost every respect he seemed the embodiment of a young Spanish aristocrat— the black suit against the ivory-pale skin, the waxed moustache, the hair pomaded and combed back from his brow. It was the oldest photograph on the wall.

The other photographs surrounded this one. For the next several years, they remained black-and-white and posed. There was Joaquin in an overcoat on the ramparts of the Alhambra, taken soon after the civil war had ended, his hand on the shoulder of his best friend, Arnulfo Benavides, Arnulfo already looking forlorn and wraithlike in his black Falange uniform, already ravaged by the lung cancer that would eventually take him. Joaquin in a doctor's coat standing proudly beside a bronze plaque with the words "Instituto Morales para la Purificación Psicológica" at the gateway to his home. Joaquin in a wicker chair in the front yard, flanked by patients in civilian clothes and priests in black robes.

There was the first one of Violeta, a remarkably beautiful young woman in a white summer dress and pinned-back hair, before a painted studio backdrop—a coastal village, the sea; another one from their wedding in 1942, Joaquin clean-shaven now, looking dashing and severe in a high-collared tuxedo, Violeta's tender face obscured by a bridal veil of white. Here, the background was of a church altar—surfaces of polished gold glowing from the shadows, stained glass windows blanched to columns of light—and alongside Joaquin and Violeta stood a priest, members of her family, military officers, and Falange party officials. A pleased Joaquin holding Victor, his infant son, on the front steps of Casa de los Queridos, a matching one of Violeta cradling the boy.

In the 1950s, the black-and-white became tinged with pastel colors delicately applied by studio painters. Arnulfo Benavides was gone, and so too were the patients and priests and doctor's coat. Now, there was only family: Violeta and Joaquin, their arms intertwined, posing in Madrid's Plaza Mayor, mother and father flanking Victor at his confirmation, at a school awards ceremony. Gradually, the photographs gave over to full color—more true to life, perhaps, but also more cruel, for in color it was impossible to conceal the slow fading of Violeta, the vibrant woman shrinking into a specter of herself, her skin becoming sallow, the hard, frightened light growing in her eyes. Cruel to Joaquin, as well, as the once-smooth face took on creases of worry, the pleasant curl of his lip becoming a grimace as he watched over the long, slow death of his wife. Then there was only father and son, the father's body thickening, becoming stolid in middle age, the son growing into a young man, a husband, and then a father himself.

At one end of the wall, set slightly apart from the others, the first photograph of Elena: Joaquin, his hair graying now, holding her in the garden of Casa de los Queridos as he had once held Victor, his hands huge against her three-month-old body. Then one of Elena with her parents in a Madrid park, Elena almost three now, adorable in a flowered dress, held aloft in the arms of her father. This photograph was of poor quality, a bit unfocused, but it was the last one of Victor, taken just two weeks before his accident. After that, all were of Elena: Elena as a small child asleep on her grandfather's lap; Elena at seven or eight, walking in a field of poppies with her grandfather, holding his hand; and then one of Elena as a teenager, gangly, self-conscious, but still affectionate, still leaning into her grandfather's embrace in the garden, and that was the last one. There was no photograph of Elena at university, no visual record of the day she opened the textbook on contemporary Spanish history and came to a page that described her grandfather and his vile institute. The chronicle of Joaquin's life stopped before that. It stopped with that last embrace of his granddaughter in his garden, in the light of a sun-drenched day, on the eve of her education.

With the sun slipping toward the western mountains, Mark and Elena started back to the house. The villages in the far hills were already in shadow, but the vega was struck by a last, pristine light. It shone off their skin, off the petals of the poppy flowers, and in this light, Casa de los Queridos—its ochre walls, its windows and glass shards—shone as if wrapped in a wreath of gold.

On the second floor, Joaquin watched the two lovers come over the field toward him, wishing the sight might never end, held by a happiness that was almost unbearable.

SEVEN

"Ah, good morning, my dear," he called. "I thought I heard you rustling about."

Thick beams of sunlight slanted through the eastern windows of the studio, making the paint spatters on the floor shine as if freshly spilled. Joaquin was before one of his easels, a thin brush in his hand, and Elena made her way toward him, avoiding twisted tubes of paint on the floor, to kiss him on the cheek.

"Morning, Papa." She stood alongside to see his painting: a grove of almond trees, a ruined farmhouse, a pallid sky. "It's very nice."

He snorted. "Don't tease, child. An abomination. Only morbid curiosity compels me on." With his fine brush, he added tiny spots of deeper blue to the sky. "So, you two are off to the Alpujarra?"

Elena nodded. She watched her grandfather's ministrations for a time, the way the slight tremble of his hand stopped whenever he raised his brush to the canvas. "Do you think this is a good idea?"

Joaquin turned to her, puzzled.

"Mark wanting to look for this Carlos Perez. There's something about it that bothers me a little."

"How so?"

"I don't know. He was so excited when he brought it up yesterday, more excited than I've seen him since . . . It's almost like he's trying to make up for Colin in some way." She gazed about the studio, then back at her grandfather. "What do you think?"

Joaquin flicked his brush through the blue paint on his palette. "Very difficult to say. You're probably right about his motives, but maybe that isn't such a bad thing. It will depend on how much he takes the disappointment to heart."

"Disappointment? You mean you don't think he'll find out anything?"

Joaquin peered at his granddaughter over his bifocals. "No." He returned to his painting. "In any event, I think sometimes we concern ourselves too much over whether a decision is the right or wrong one. For someone in Mark's situation, perhaps it is merely the ability to make a decision, to take some action, that is key. A crucial difference, one often overlooked by those of us in this field."

Elena moved to the side to watch him paint, felt the sun rays on her body. "And that would be the field of fraudulent psychiatry?"

Joaquin turned to see his granddaughter watching him with an arched eyebrow, the trace of a sly smile. Never before had she attempted a joke on this topic. She had never spoken of it except in anger, and he savored the silence that held them. Then he threw his head back and laughed.

"Ah, Elena, how I've missed your little witticisms! Fraudulent psychiatry? *Qué rico!*"

"But it's true," she protested, laughing herself now. "You were a fraud."

"Oh, stop, please," he said, seized by fresh fits of laughter. "You are simply too funny!"

A few minutes later, as she was leaving, she turned at the door. "I found your old patient files in the storage room. I've been reading some of them. I'm sorry, I probably should have asked your permission, but I think it's helped me understand Mark a little better."

Joaquin looked at her across the expanse of the room, slowly shrugged. "No need to ask permission, my dear. Whenever you like." He dabbed his brush in the paint again. "And you've found things of interest?"

Elena nodded. "But you were right about the file on Carlos Perez. It's gone—just a little note in it saying that he was dishonorably discharged, his papers sent on to military headquarters. I showed it to Mark."

Joaquin gently set the brush on the palette, gave a deep sigh. He didn't look at her but at the painting before him, and when he spoke his voice was very soft. "Terrible. A terrible thing we did to those men, the incurables. After what they had been through, expendable"—he flicked his fingers in the air—"*basura.*" He turned to her. "I had no control over it, Elena. There was nothing I could do for them."

"I know that, Papa. I know." She leaned against the doorframe, gazed over the room.

From what she had seen, her grandfather spent most of his waking hours here. The rest of the house felt almost uninhabited; this room held even the smell of him.

"Why did you make this your studio? I understand about the view and the sunlight, but after the way you had it before, with all my father's things in here, what made you change it?"

He appeared to ponder for a time, as if it were a question he had never considered. "I'm not really sure," he said. "There just came a day when it seemed right."

"Mark said it was probably your way of remembering him."

He gave a slight smile. "Yes, maybe so. I suppose that was it."

Downstairs, Mark was still at the dining room table, the file open in front of him, staring at the single sheet of yellowed paper as if there were not just two terse sentences written there, but a great volume, an entire story. He turned up to see Elena in the doorway and smiled.

"Not much, is it?" she said.

His smile broadened. "No, but at least it's something." He looked at the paper again. "And I feel good about this. I think we're going to find him."

Mark turned the car onto the lower road out of Lanjarón and descended toward the Guadalfeo River. The valley floor lay in shadow at midmorning, and a lingering dew gave the fields and trees a milky sheen. They slowed to cross the narrow steel bridge over the river.

"Do you know what Guadalfeo means?" Elena asked, gazing down at the churning brown water. "It means 'ugly river.' *Feo* is Spanish, obviously, but *guadal* comes from Arabic, from the Moors." She looked to Mark. "I guess it was ugly even back then."

They turned east, the road snaking into side valleys and around headlands as it skirted the southern mountain wall. This part of the Alpujarra was arid, the slopes bare—very different from the northern side of the valley where Mark had spent most of his time. There, on the watered and sun-exposed flanks of the Sierra Nevada, there had been rushing streams and forests, there had been meadows. Here were only naked hillsides, the thick brown ribbon of the Guadalfeo slipping in and out of morning shadow.

After an hour, they came to the small, rusted sign for Olía and turned onto the dirt road leading up into the mountains. Within several miles, they entered a tortured landscape of rock tors and great chasms, cut across a seemingly endless series of vertical cliff faces. Mark took to counting the crude roadside memorials to drivers who had made mistakes, trying to match them up with the ancient wrecks resting hundreds of feet below. Elena clutched the doorhandle and stared out, mesmerized by the yawning canyons just past her window.

On a hillside bluff, Mark saw a tiny white house surrounded by pine trees and, just below it, several stone terraces upon which olive trees grew. It was the first building he had seen since leaving the main road and, from that distance, he couldn't tell if the place was inhabited, if the fat, twisted trunks of the olives were growing that way by design or neglect. There was no road leading to the house, not even a path from what he could see, but the building appeared cared for, the stone terraces in good condition, and Mark realized they were entering a world where it was never easy to determine what was living and what was dead, where the cycles of generation and decay had so slowed as to be imperceptible to the stranger's eye.

Closer in, it was easier, the familiar sharp line between life and death restored. Even if they were the only ones upon the road—they had not passed another car since leaving the valley—there were the traces of those who had come before, the memorials of crucifixes and plastic flowers and photographs, the metal husks on the rocks below. On this land, even the garish relics of death could be a comfort.

They left the eroded canyons, emerged onto a high pastureland, and finally came to the crest of the coastal range. Behind them was the Alpujarra, its far wall of snowcapped peaks, while ahead the mountains began their long tumble toward the sea, an indistinct pale blue in the distance. The road began to descend steeply, and Mark eased the car along at a crawl, turning the wheel back and forth to avoid the deepest ruts, listening to the weeds and rocks scratch at the undercarriage. As they rounded a hillock, a few stone buildings and terraced fields came into view on the slope ahead, and then a sight that momentarily startled him, caused him to bring the car to a stop. Tucked into a recess just beside the road was the village cemetery. It resembled a small fort, a rectangle of high white walls open to the sky, and in the wall facing the road was an archway crowned by a metal crucifix.

"Shall we go in?" Elena asked.

Mark peered out the windshield at the first houses of the village, just a few hundred feet on, then back at the cemetery. He nodded.

They walked through the thick weeds and under the arch. The dead were interred in compartments stacked four high in the walls. Most of the crypts were sealed, faced with marble on which names were engraved, but enough remained empty to remind Mark of a partly abandoned honeycomb. Small metal vases were mounted beside each crypt, and here and there he saw the remnants of old flowers: a bundle of bare stalks, the black petals of a dessicated rose.

They walked together around the enclosure, Mark carefully checking each name they passed. Everywhere were Perezes—Ernesto Emilio Perez, Lucía Chamorro Perez, Infanta Perez—on every wall that surrounded them, but none bore the name he was seeking. When they had finished, about to leave through the archway, he stopped to look back.

In the center of the enclosure was a crude shrine, a concrete column supporting a small alcove fronted by clouded glass. Mark crossed the flagstones to it. On a narrow ledge were the remains of more dead flowers, the stumps of burnt candles. From behind the smoke-blackened glass, the eyes of the Virgin Mary stared dolefully out at him. He turned to see Elena watching him from the entryway.

"Maybe it means he's still alive."

She didn't answer.

The road ended just before the first buildings. There were no cars, no sign that cars had been there recently. They parked beneath a tree, followed a stone path leading down into the village.

It appeared abandoned. Rotted doors hung lopsided from their mounts, and the cracks in the walkway were filled with thick white powder, remnants of the stucco that had once covered the rock homes. They went slowly, peering through open doors and broken windows, looking for some sign of habitation, but there was only rubble, shafts of sunlight piercing collapsed ceilings. The path led to a flight of stone steps, and they paused to gaze over the lower part of the village, waited for the sight or sound of a person, but there was no one, only the soft scream of metal twisting in a light wind.

They came to the plaza. There was a small fountain that had cleaved in two, a shade tree, and a single concrete bench upon which an old man sat. He wore a cap and was hunched low over a cane, perfectly still. For a moment, Mark's heart leapt at the thought that it might be Carlos Perez himself, dessicated and preserved like the roses in the cemetery.

They were only a few feet away when the man suddenly looked up, a motion so quick and startling they froze in midstep. He was ancient, with a dark, deep-lined face, but his brown eyes gradually widened with amazement at the sight of them. For a long moment, no one moved. Then, the old man rose from the bench and, with a certain courtly flourish, removed his cap.

For some time on that long morning, Joaquin stood before the easel and attempted to work on his pleasant landscape, but his concentration failed him. It had been shattered by Elena's questions.

He went to his study, took up one of the simple wood chairs, and

[198]

carried it back to the studio to place before a window. For several hours he sat there, his elbow resting on the sill, watching the changing shadows on Mulhacén.

Of all the terrible things he had been forced to do in his life, there were only two that still haunted him. One had taken place on that mountain. The other had occurred in this room.

A miracle. That was how he had described it to Mark. Well, why not? The boy needed to believe in miracles. In any event, Joaquin was not able to think of another word to describe the sorrow of that day.

He had reached the ridge at daybreak, the Alpujarra still wrapped in night below him. Far away to the southwest, the sand dunes of Africa struck like gold, like a second sun rising. To the other side of him, Granada, cloaked in haze, tiny glows of orange from morning fires. And he had stood there, on that ridge line of the highest mountain in Spain, exhausted, cold, and hungry—dying, in fact—but still unable to leave, a last hesitation at the decision he had made. Behind, blackness and ruin and everyone who loved him. Ahead, warmth and life and a loneliness that would never end. And he had waited until the last possible moment, clasping one final time to the company and comfort of his parents and brothers and sisters—to the faces he knew better than his own, their voices, the sound of their laughter—had waited until the cold and hunger that had followed him like a shadow was replaced by a great warmth, until the sleep of the dying was nearly upon him, and then he had risen and begun his descent toward the city, drawing up the very last of his strength to cry like a lost child.

After a long period of time, Joaquin turned away from the window and Mulhacén to gaze at the paint-spattered walls of the room in which he sat. That other day of parting had been just as terrible. It had cost him every shred of his courage to strip this room bare of all that remained of his only son. Because, in truth, he had not made this room his studio for the reason that Elena imagined, that he had let her believe. It had not been to honor his son's memory but rather to finally say goodbye to him.

He rose from the chair and passed along the second-floor walkway to the storage room. He eased open the door and saw Elena's footprints, small and delicate, through the dust. Standing at the thresh-

old, he saw how the footprints crossed the empty expanse of the room
to the footlockers, then over to the file cabinets, how the floor before
the cabinets and the far window was almost free of dust, brushed away
by the bare feet that had remained there for many hours. Poor Elena.
So trusting in what paper might tell her.

He looked down at the five large boxes arrayed along the wall,
Victor's things. He saw that some of these had been examined, the
dust unsettled, clean portions of posters and books and photographs
exposed. Joaquin could not bring himself to look closely, to touch
anything. Instead, he walked across the room—gingerly, so as not to
kick up the dust—to the jumble of metal cot frames. He brushed off
the corner of one as best he could and sat. Leaning on his knees, he
gazed across the room, at his wall of file cabinets, at Victor's boxes.

If he had been imprecise in his talk of miracles with Mark, he had
been even more so in his talk of God. To be sure, he had been an
atheist—for nearly thirty years, in fact—but that was no longer true.
Now, Joaquin fervently believed in God, thought of Him often. The
difficulty was he hated Him, and this had seemed a needless complication to impose on the boy in his condition.

If he had chosen to be forthright with Mark, he would have told
him how he had lost his faith on those first days of the war, how, with
all the indignant rage of youth, he had decided that no God would
stand by in the face of such evil, that any God would surely take
vengeance. He would have explained how his faithlessness had
stayed with him through the years of the institute, even through the
long, last days with Violeta—cancer, after all, was random, as coinci-
dental as birth.

Joaquin reclined on the cot frame until his back rested against the
wall, listened to the old, rusted springs screech beneath him.

But if he had told Mark this, he might also have felt compelled to
tell of how his faith had returned, to describe that cool, overcast afternoon in November 1965 when he had received Isabela's call and
learned of Victor's accident outside Burgos. Joaquin had understood
then, as he understood now, that here was a cruelty too exquisite, a
vengeance too precise, for him to doubt God's existence ever again.
But explaining this, to Mark or to anyone else, was something he
could not do. It was pointless for him even to try. If Joaquin had

learned one thing in his long life, it was that each person had to find his own way back to God.

As patriarch of Olía, as well as discoverer of the strangers in the plaza, eighty-one-year-old Antonio had assumed the role of host. Leading Elena and Mark to his home, he dispatched one of his grandsons to summon the other villagers and set the younger one to arranging tables and chairs on the veranda. Bowls of olives and bottles of wine were placed on the wood tables, and within minutes the last fourteen residents of Olía had gathered to meet the visitors in their midst.

Other than two elderly couples, everyone in Olía was a relation of Antonio: his wife, Marta, a middle-aged daughter-in-law, the two grandsons and their wives, three great-grandchildren. Like a master of ceremonies at an official function, the old man stood alongside Mark and Elena, held a tumbler of red wine aloft, and waited for silence.

"Don Mark and Señora Morales," he said stentoriously, in the thick-tongued, truncated accent of Andalusia, "a great honor to have you among us. A long time, many years, since we've had visitors here in Olía. Welcome." All the adults drank in toast, then Antonio turned to the others. "Our friends here have come to inquire after Carlos Perez."

To Elena's surprise, a ripple of excitement passed through the small group. Even the youngest children seemed familiar with the name.

"So you remember him?" she asked.

"Of course!" the old man cried. "Everyone remembers Carlos Perez! He married Julia Castañeda. They had a son."

Elena glanced at the others. Marta, Antonio's wife, nodded insistently, as did the eldest of the other couples, a man and woman who appeared to be in their late sixties. "Is he . . . is he here?"

This sparked soft, amused laughter from Antonio's grandsons but not from the old man. Shaking his head wearily, he sank into the chair beside Mark and leaned his elbows on the table. "No. Unfortunately, he isn't here any longer. His is a sad story, one of many sad stories we've had in Olía." He absently ran the base of his glass over the rough wood, producing a slow, steady sound like tearing paper.

"Carlos was a very good friend to me," he said quietly. "Two years younger than myself but, Olía being a small place, all of us boys were friends together. A very intelligent boy, always getting us into mischief of some kind, and I also remember he helped build the new well, that he worked down inside because he was small. Julia was a few years younger again and, of course, back then the boys and girls did not mix as much as now, but I remember she was a very pretty girl—clever, as well. But if I was to say one thing about Carlos, it would be his intelligence. He was the best student at the school we had here then, very quick with numbers and figures, and we all knew he would not stay in Olía, that he would leave here to make something of himself. And so he did." Antonio glanced up. "You know that he joined the military, became an officer?"

Mark and Elena nodded.

"He was posted at the barracks down in Bermez—this was during the war, the civil war, shortly after he and Julia married—and then he was promoted to Granada. We had a party for them here before they left for the city. A great party, all of Olía was there. Julia was pregnant at that time, and Carlos was very excited—I remember him saying he was sure it would be a boy, that their first child would be a son—and some time later we saw this had been the case. After the war, Julia came back for a time with the boy—Luis, I believe his name was, or maybe Alejandro."

"Luis," Mark said. "And Carlos didn't come with them?"

Antonio clicked his teeth, shook his head.

"No. We never learned the full story, but of course in a small village you learn enough. It seems that after the war ended, Carlos became ill." He paused, toyed with his glass again. "*Pues*, if the truth be told, he went mad. He was put in a hospital, but then he went missing. For a long time, maybe five or six years, Julia and his relatives—his cousins and uncles—looked for him. Along the coast, in the Alpujarra, all over Andalusia. Nothing. Gone."

With a sigh, he reached for the jug of wine, refilled Mark's and Elena's glasses and then his own. "In the end, Julia and the boy left. There was no future for her here, of course, a widow, unable to remarry, and so . . ." He gave a slow wave of his hand. "We later heard they had gone to America, and that was the last we ever knew."

For the next few minutes, Elena told the villagers what she knew of Julia Perez and her boy, that Julia had died recently, that the son was now a successful American businessman, a banker. The news seemed to dispel some of the pall that had settled over the veranda, and the conversation veered off into questions of what America was like, what Mark and Elena did for a living. More wine was poured, and the women took turns slipping into the house, returning with plates of sausage and cheese, a bottle of homemade brandy.

"And what of Carlos's other relatives?" Mark asked during a lull. "Are any still here?"

Antonio looked to him, his smile easing away. "I'm sorry, Don Mark. At one time, there were many here, but now they have left. All of them, they have left." The old man motioned to the ruins of the village beyond the veranda. "At one time, we were almost three hundred people here. Now, as you can see, we are very few. We have had war, drought, insects, and each time, some of us . . ." He fluttered his hand in the air again. "Most left in the 1950s, some more in the sixties. I believe the last of the Perezes left in 1957, the Castañedas in the early 1960s—the exact dates I can't remember."

"Do you know where they are?"

Another heavy sigh from Antonio. "Impossible to say now. All over Spain. Madrid, Malaga, maybe even Barcelona. A few came back to visit—only to visit, of course, not to live—but that hasn't happened in some time, maybe ten or fifteen years, so where they would be now, I couldn't say."

Mark calculated in his mind. The exodus from Olía had begun over thirty years ago, but there was still a palpable note of hurt in Antonio's voice, as if it were a very recent event, one that still puzzled and pained him. Mark thought back on the isolated house they had passed on the road; here, time was measured differently.

He rose from the chair and stepped to the edge of the veranda. Antonio's home was at the edge of the village, perched on high ground, and Mark gazed over the rooftops of Olía. In the cleft of two mountains, he saw a triangle of the Mediterranean and the shoreline, studded with the hotels and condominiums of the Costa Tropical. Between Olía and the sea were perhaps fifteen miles of mountains and ravines, but it may as well have been a thousand, as vast a gulf as that between the Spain of 1939 and now. Such a strange place, where the passage of time could mean so little, where the past and present lived within sight of each other.

He became aware of Antonio standing alongside him, looking out at the same view. After a time, Mark turned to him. "And what of his reputation?"

The old man was perplexed. "Reputation?"

Mark tried to remember the Spanish word for "infamous" or "notorious" but couldn't. "Carlos Perez. I heard he had a bad reputation during the war."

Antonio's frown deepened, then gradually cleared. "You mean with the blood squads?"

Mark nodded.

"Yes, in the first days of the war, Carlos was doing that. He formed a squad with some of the other soldiers, some of his friends from here. They carried out activities all over this area—over to Orgiva, as far away as Cadíar, as I recall. That is what you mean?"

"He had a nickname, didn't he?" Mark asked. "Didn't they call him the 'Beast of Olía'?"

"Yes, that's right, the 'Beast of Olía.'"

Antonio said this so matter-of-factly, so without emotion, that Mark wasn't sure how to respond. He stared out over the ruined homes of the village. "And did he kill people here," he asked softly, "in Olía?"

"Oh, yes. Very many!" Antonio raised his cane, pointed to a collapsed house just below the veranda, its windows gone, the roof caved in at one corner. "The schoolteacher, Roberto Molina. And over there"—the cane swung out to point at another abandoned dwelling—"Alberto Serrano and his brother Gustavo." He pointed farther down the hill. "And then down there, just by that path you see . . ." He slowly lowered the cane. "Well, so many—fourteen, I think, here in Olía. And in the other towns, many more, too many to know. Oh yes, Carlos and his blood squad, they killed a lot."

Mark looked into the old man's kind, solicitous face. He felt as if he were gazing across some great unbridgeable abyss. "And that was not a bad thing, the killing was all right?"

Antonio appeared confused by the question. Mark turned to see the other villagers; they, too, were looking at him as if mystified.

"But, Don Mark," Antonio said, "it wasn't a question of right, of good or bad. We were having a war then. Those of us here, we were like lambs between the wolves." He raised his cane again, waved it over the mountains to the east. "There, the Republicans." He pointed his cane to the west. "Over there, the Nationalists. We were between them. All of us here were innocent, none of us political in any way, but we were between the wolves, so we had to choose. Some had to be sacrificed so the others could live, so that those who could be saved were saved. That is what happens in war. Carlos helped us choose and, fortunately for us, he chose well."

The old man rested a hand on Mark's shoulder. He leaned close, and when he spoke again, his voice was barely a whisper.

"But, sadly for him, Carlos made a terrible mistake. Do you see now the mistake he made?"

Mark saw the trace of a smile on the old man's lips. He shook his head.

"Olía protected us. In his impatience, in his ambition, Carlos forgot this. He forgot that when you leave your people, you are alone and anything can happen to you. When he left this place . . . Well, as I say, we were like lambs between the wolves, and none of us, not even Carlos, could know what sorrow waited out there."

The old man looked away, toward the ravines and the sea.

He left the storage room and wandered past the upstairs rooms to his office. He stared at his leather armchair, the great mahogany desk, at the two simple chairs along the inner wall, and then he slowly crossed to his gallery of portraits. He studied one in particular, the paint-enhanced photograph of him with his friend Colonel Arnulfo Benavides, taken on a spring day in 1944 on the ramparts of the Alhambra.

A thick mist had covered Granada that day, and from the Alhambra walls they caught only brief glimpses of the city—a rooftop, an intersection, an apartment building—before the vapors came together again and there was only whiteness. In the breaks of white, they saw cars moving below. Normally, it was quite possible, given a certain condition of wind, a certain clarity of air, to stand on the ramparts and hear the horn of a car ten kilometers away, but no sound reached them that day. Joaquin had never before been enveloped in such a mist, in such a silence, and it had made him feel anonymous there on the ramparts.

They had gone into the palace and leisurely toured the rooms, gazed at the Ceiling of Stars, admired the intricate woodwork, the flecks of ancient blue paint that still clung to the deepest niches of the portals. They strolled through the gardens, the gloom causing them to speak in hushed tones, their voices and footfalls smothered in an absorbent stone. Other visitors appeared and receded indistinctly, like phantoms. Nervous phantoms, for there was the peculiar sense that if one explored too remote a corner, ventured too far from the well-traveled paths on this day, one might just disappear.

"Let's go to the Sevilla Tower," Arnulfo said, and there had been a trace of a dare in his voice, as if this would be an adventure.

The Sevilla Tower was away from the main route of visitors, perched above an eastern ravine, and they had climbed the slick stone steps to the rampart. Looking over the precipice, they saw only the outline of trees in the mist, the spill of rocks below. And then the mist had suddenly thickened, curled up from below to enshroud them, so dense Joaquin could not see his own feet.

"Good heavens," he heard Arnulfo call excitedly from somewhere in the cloud. "This is truly remarkable, isn't it?"

Joaquin had not answered. He felt the damp on his face, on his chest, and he stared into the whiteness, waiting for it to end, and in that time of waiting, he knew he was absolutely invisible in the world.

"Joaquin? Joaquin?"

He had seen his friend's disembodied hand, raised, the fingers groping for him in the mist, and Joaquin had stepped back, suddenly shocked by the thought that it would be so simple to take that hand, maneuver his friend to the edge of the tower, and fling him onto the rocks below, that it all could happen in a mere instant of whiteness.

"Joaquin? What has happened to you?" Arnulfo's voice became strained, a little nervous, and still he did not answer, had continued retreating from the hand that reached for him. And then Joaquin had understood why it would not happen, why it was so terrible when it did happen. Because what he had learned from looking into the faces of men whose lives were passing before their dying eyes was that it was not to their mothers or children or lovers that they were returned in the last moments but, rather, to their crimes. If nothing more, it meant men should choose their crimes with care.

"Joaquin, please!" Arnulfo became distraught; his fingers grasped at the air.

"Here I am," Joaquin had said finally, reaching out to take his friend's hand. "I was only teasing. What a child you are."

They barely spoke during the long drive back, their moods matching the desolation of the land. There were times when Mark assumed Elena had fallen asleep, so long was her silence, but whenever he stole a glance away from the road, he saw her staring out at the mountains. It was late when they reached the main Alpujarra road. In the depths of the valley, the light hung like smoke.

"So I guess that's it then," she said at last.

Mark looked across the valley, at the snowfields and whitewashed hamlets high on the northern slopes. "I think maybe tomorrow I'll go up there, check around some of the villages, their cemeteries. You can come along if you like."

Elena didn't answer.

The road began its descent toward the bridge. The river came into view, curving around the flank of a mountain to run alongside them.

"Why is this so important to you, Mark?"

At the bridge approach, he pulled the car to the shoulder and stopped. He stared out the windshield, at the steel girders against the darkening sky, then stepped from the car. He walked to the center of the bridge and looked over the railing at the water. The river ran fast and high and brown in the spring runoff, and it had spilled from its course to flood a grove of birch on the far bank.

He wanted to remember the river, the other river, just this way: swollen, impassable, a current that would sweep a man down in an instant. But his memory was too good. It should have been easy to cross—slow water, barely hip-deep. Only his haste, a misstep on a rock, had caused him to fall.

He heard Elena breathing beside him. "Ugly river." He chuckled. "I guess it is pretty ugly, isn't it?"

He turned to rest his back against the cold railing and gaze into the eastern reaches of the valley. Now, even the heavy half-light of dusk had left the lowlands. Shadows were creeping up the slopes of the Sierra Nevada toward the snowfields.

He thought of her question, the answer he could give her, and he understood then the futility of it, that he could tell her everything and it would still bring him no closer to an explanation. Joaquin was right, there was no way to share any of this. Everyone was alone with their burden.

"A cruel land. That's how Joaquin describes this." He looked to Elena and smiled. "But I suppose it's the same everywhere. The world, after all, is a very old place."

Elena searched his face, reached out to touch his arm. He looked into the darkening valley and tried to find some answer to her question. "I would just like to find him, that's all," he said, because he could not think of anything else to tell her.

"Ah, Schliemann returns!" Joaquin cried as Mark entered the kitchen. He tossed his magazine onto the table, pulled out the chair beside his. "And what treasures did the expedition unearth?"

With a bemused frown, Mark settled into the chair. "Schliemann?"

Joaquin looked aghast. "Heinrich Schliemann? The great archaeologist? Discoverer of Mycenae and Troy?"

"Sorry. I went to American schools."

Joaquin laughed. "Your excuse for everything. An absolute disgrace you people were ever allowed to become a world power." He reached for the bottle of mineral water and an empty glass on the table, poured some for Mark. "So, any luck?"

"Not really." Mark told him about Olía, the cemetery, their long conversation with Antonio and the other villagers. "I was thinking tomorrow I'd check up around Lanjarón, some of the larger towns."

"Hmm." Joaquin glanced up to see that Elena was now standing in the doorway, somberly watching Mark from behind. "Come in, my dear, come in and join us. There's water here or cognac on the counter."

Elena gave him a thin smile. "Maybe in a bit. I'm going to go clean up." She glanced at Mark's back once more, then slipped away.

Joaquin reached for his water glass, took a small sip. "So, expanding the search, eh? You think that's wise?"

Mark frowned. "What do you mean?"

Joaquin saw a peculiar light come into his eyes, a certain poised wariness. He had seen it once before in Mark, on that night at the kitchen table in New York, just before he had led him to the maps on the wall for the last time. Joaquin looked at his own hands on the table, picked at a fingernail.

"To be frank, Elena is a bit concerned about all this. She thinks you've taken on this little project as a way to make amends for Colin. Atonement, if you will."

"That's not true. I just feel like, I'm here, I don't really have much to do, so if I can find out something for the son, well . . . Is that what you think, too?"

Joaquin shrugged nonchalantly. "Oh, I suspect there's an element of that, but I'm afraid I take a rather laissez-faire approach to these matters. I don't see much harm in it as long as you remain realistic."

"Realistic?"

Joaquin looked into Mark's eyes and saw that the watchful glint was still there. "You're not going to find him. You do know that, don't you?"

Mark turned away, his gaze traveling over the table to the large window, his reflection there. "I don't know, Joaquin, I feel confident about this. Actually, I think I will find him."

Joaquin studied his profile, listened to the ticking of the wall clock, the wind rustling the bushes outside. "No," he said at last, "no, you won't." He reached over, clasped Mark's forearm. "I'm sorry. I just don't want you to suffer any illusions about this." He squeezed his arm to compel him to turn, but Mark sat stiffly staring at his own reflection, his eyes blinking rapidly.

EIGHT

"I saw in the paper yesterday that it's in the midforties in New York," Mark said with a smile, "midforties and raining. A shame to be missing that, isn't it?"

He steered the rental car through a tight curve on the mountainside. Through breaks in the trees, he caught glimpses of white buildings on the slope ahead. He motioned with his head. "Lanjarón."

The town was quiet at midmorning, the vacationers still in their hotels, the day visitors still en route, and Mark trolled slowly along the main street to peer up the side roads, searching for the cemetery amid the homes and surrounding hills. From his explorations in the Alpujarra, he had noticed that a town's cemetery was usually located on its outskirts, on some piece of land chosen for its uselessness, but he wasn't sure this would hold true in Lanjarón; the village had become famous for its artesian spring water—supposedly pristine, supposedly therapeutic—and grown into an unpleasant sprawl of cafe-bars, souvenir shops, and small health-spa hotels, the new overwhelming the old.

A thought came to him, and he pulled to the side of the street, scanned the shops that were just opening for the day. He strummed his fingers on the steering wheel.

"Maybe we should get some flowers," he said. "Not like a grave bouquet, just some nice spring flowers." He considered for another moment, still strumming his fingers, then nodded sharply. "Yeah, that'd be good."

He stepped from the car and started along the sidewalk. In a few minutes, he returned carrying a great bouquet of wildflowers—reds and whites, golds and violets—wrapped in green tissue paper. He placed the bouquet on the rear seat, got back behind the wheel.

"Now all we have to do is find him," he muttered, easing the car into the traffic again, quickly glancing up the side streets he passed. It was at the far eastern edge of town that he spotted the fortresslike walls on a hillside. "Voilà."

He turned onto a tree-shaded dirt lane. It was deeply rutted, causing the car to lurch and dip. The road climbed out of the trees onto the bluff, and then the high, whitewashed walls of Lanjarón cemetery were directly ahead, painfully bright in the mountain air. Mark slowly braked to a stop, gazed at the walls for a time, then turned to the passenger seat.

"I'm sorry, Colin. I tried. There was nothing I could do."

Joaquin swung open the kitchen door, stepped down to the flagstones. "Elena, my darling, I thought you'd gone with Mark." There was surprise, even alarm, in his voice. "You've been out here alone all this time?"

At the table in the back garden, Elena smiled. "It's not like I was trapped or anything, Papa. I knew I could always scream for help."

Joaquin chuckled, slid into the seat beside her. "Still, if I'd known you were here, I wouldn't have spent all this time up there destroying a perfectly good canvas." He smiled at her. "So, you've resigned from the search party?"

Elena shook her head wearily. "I don't know what Mark is doing." She thought back on the day with him at the Cloisters, his strange exuberance on the bluff. She had seen it again that morning as he got ready to leave for the Alpujarra. "I think he's getting worse again." She looked at her grandfather. "What do you think is going on with him?"

Joaquin shrugged. "Who can say? Perhaps his own way of finally accepting what happened in Kurdistan. People find very different paths to take in these matters. Anyway, I really don't feel it's something to be too concerned about."

Elena nodded, gazed out at the garden of Casa de los Queridos, at the glass-sharded wall, the alfalfa field beyond the gate. She listened to a songbird in the brush, allowed his words to make her feel better. "Maybe when you're finished with your painting, we can go for a picnic in the hills."

Joaquin grinned, slapped the table with his hand. "A splendid plan." He thought of his canvas, the same one he had labored over the day before. "In fact, I've already done enough damage to that thing; we'll go now. Let me just close up my paints." He rose, started for the kitchen door.

"What if he does find him?" Elena called after him. "I mean, there's always that chance, isn't there?"

Joaquin stopped and turned to his granddaughter, sitting there in the sunlight. Such a beautiful child she had been, such a happy child, there had been moments when he had found his love for her almost heartbreaking. For the first time in many years, he found himself on the edge of tears. "Yes, my child," he said, "there is always that chance."

The sun had ascended far enough into a cloudless sky to bleed away the bright colors of morning. It reflected off the glossed marble and made even the stone path leading into the heart of Orgiva cemetery shimmer before Mark's eyes.

He had spent nearly an hour vainly searching among the graves in Lanjarón, then driven the six miles on to the larger lowland town of Orgiva. At least here there was an attendant, Francisco, a wiry old man in a threadbare blue jacket and matching blue cap, and he hurried ahead of Mark, leading him into the farthest reaches of the walled compound. He stopped before an area where the tombstones were less ornate, the pathways unkempt, and waved a hand over the sprawl.

"Here, this is the oldest section. And the name again?"

"Carlos Miguel Perez."

"Yes." Francisco nodded emphatically. "We have some of those here."

With great purpose, he strode down a side path, and Mark watched him circle among the graves, stooping to read a name, moving on, stooping before another. He soon straightened, waved a beckoning hand. Mark went to him in a fast walk, and crouched to read the tombstone inscription: Carlos Miguel Perez, 1881–1942.

"It's him, yes?" Francisco asked.

Mark shook his head. "No. No, he's too old. The one I'm looking for was probably born around 1910, 1912."

The old man sighed with disappointment but immediately set off to resume the search. After several minutes, he whistled, again waved Mark over to where he stood. He was near the perimeter wall, and he continued to point to the grave by his feet, as if it might vanish if not closely supervised.

"A child?" Francisco asked hopefully, as Mark reached his side. "He was a child?"

Mark looked at the grave. Carlos Miguel Perez, 1913–1919. Five or six years old, a little boy. "No," he said. "No, it's not him."

For a time, they both stood at the foot of the child's grave, staring at his stone, as if through sheer will they might change what was inscribed there. Finally, Francisco clicked his teeth.

"I'm afraid that's it, then. I know all of them here, and there are no Carlos Perezes like the one you want."

They turned away in silence.

He led the way to a promontory, a small bluff of meadow grass and young pine that overlooked the vega. The pastures below them were radiant with spring grass and wildflowers.

"Adequate?" Joaquin asked.

"Perfect," Elena said.

Joaquin unfolded his light aluminum chair, while Elena spread the blanket on the grass. She stretched across its length. In the valley, the towns glistened as if newly painted.

"I'd forgotten how beautiful it was here," she said. She plucked a grass shoot to chew on; it was young, a brilliant emerald green, the color of a lizard's belly. "Not a matter of forgetting, exactly. I think I just assumed I'd exaggerated it in my mind over the years. It's been a long time since I last visited, you know."

In his chair, Joaquin nodded. "Yes, I know." He stared over the vega. The noon sun was nearly hot, making the snowfields of the far-off peaks seem fanciful. "But quite humbling, don't you think? Quite impossible to ever master such beauty, to comprehend its intricacy."

"But if it were easy, you would quickly lose interest."

Joaquin smiled. "Too true, but I don't mean only painting. No, it takes different forms, but the land holds the same lesson for all of us. A reminder of our artlessness, our fall from grace."

Elena squeezed the grass shoot with her teeth. It tasted sweet, slightly milky. "You're sounding like a Catholic again, Papa."

Joaquin laughed. "Worse, a Catholic philosopher."

She sat up and reached into the picnic basket, withdrew the paper wrappers of cheese and serrano ham. They ate with leisure, picking at the various things they had brought, letting their wine warm in the day's heat.

"I feel sorry for Carlos Perez's son," she said after a time, "the man I met in New York."

The comment lifted Joaquin from his quiet thoughts. He sipped at his glass. "Why so?"

"What a terrible choice he has. To never know anything about his father, or to learn what kind of man he really was. I don't know which would be worse."

"Yes," Joaquin said, "a burden, I should imagine."

Elena plucked another grass shoot from a tuft beside the blanket. "I wonder what he was like," she said softly. "The Beast of Olía."

Joaquin propped his chin on a hand, watched a bee flitter over a spread of clover. "Probably normal in most every way. Probably courteous, a good husband, a good father. Religious, no doubt—they all were back then."

Elena peeled away the leaves of the grass shoot one by one,

watched how the color slowly diminished until she came to the last leaf, the most protected one, white and tender. "How did you cure them, Papa?"

Joaquin laughed gently. "Oh, I didn't cure them, my dear. They thought I did, and that was the important thing, but there was no cure for how those men suffered. I suppose if I taught them anything, it was to forget history, to revile it."

Elena sat up, shielded her eyes against the sun to look at him. "What do you mean?"

"The worst invention of man, history—if one were religious, it could be called his greatest sacrilege—because it tries to explain why things happen. 'This war started because the communists were taking power.' 'This soldier killed this family because his best friend had died at the battle of Guadarrama.' You see? We invented history for the same reason we invented God, because the alternative is too terrible to imagine. To accept that there is no reason for any of it, that we are only animals—special animals, maybe, but still animals—and there is no explaining the things we do, that happen to us—too awful, no? So we make history. Other animals can build, can communicate, can even kill each other, but only we have history. It is our greatest luxury, the price we pay for being special."

He dropped the empty glass onto the thick grass by his feet, clicked his teeth in disgust. "*Dios*, I'm so tired of hearing about history! But look how they do it today. Look how they talk of Israel or Ireland or Africa—centuries of conflict, tribal hatreds . . ."

He leaned over the arm of the chair, animated.

"Our war, Elena, was not caused by religion or politics or agrarian reform or anything else you may have read about in your textbooks. It was caused by nothing. If we must have a reason, let us admit it was boredom, that we went to war because peace had become tedious for us. We slaughtered each other without mercy because we wanted to see how blood ran, because it seemed an interesting thing to do. We killed because we could. That was the reason."

"But, Papa, it's always more complicated than that."

"You think so? Where was the grand reason when the Nationalists murdered four thousand innocents in Granada? When the Republicans threw five hundred people off the bridge in Ronda? What does history have to teach us about these things? To hell with history. If there is anything to be learned from any of it, it is only that civilization is fragile, that in war it takes nothing for a man — any man, fascist, communist, schoolteacher, peasant, it doesn't matter — to become a beast."

Joaquin stared at his granddaughter for a long moment. His eyes gradually softened, and he slumped back in the chair.

"But that's not very satisfying, is it? Makes for a rather thin textbook. Much easier for the professors and historians to talk of constitutional crises, economic disparities. 'We murdered Spain's greatest poet, we threw five hundred people off a bridge, because we were suffering a constitutional crisis.' Well, to the Devil with them."

Elena watched her grandfather's profile, the way his cheek pulsed as he ground his teeth.

"But the institute," she said at last. "If you thought this way, why did you help them?"

Joaquin shrugged. "Precisely because I thought this way. Once I saw there was no reason for it beyond savagery, I saw how it would continue. Because when a man falls into savagery, he continues to fall. Kill once and killing again is easy, it becomes routine — eventually, it even becomes a cure for the spiritual torment, a cycle without end. This is what happens in war, any war. But eventually one side of killers will win, and what happens then? I will tell you: The slaughter continues as long as the killers remain separated from their consciences. That was the situation we faced in 1939. Nationalists, Republicans, it no longer much mattered who won, for both sides had their beasts, and their days of blood were not over. Should I have stood by in silence and let them proceed? No. I couldn't do that. With the institute my hope was to restore those men so that the killing might stop, that Spain might find peace again."

Elena leaned back on the blanket, propped herself on her elbows. "But it didn't work, did it? The killing didn't stop. Franco killed thousands — tens of thousands — more after the war. He was still ordering executions in the 1970s."

All at once, Joaquin seemed tired, his eyelids heavy. "Well, that's where it failed," he said softly, "with Franco, with El Caudillo." He stretched out each syllable with contempt. "It is this matter of conscience. That is what all the men who came to my institute had in common—what, in fact, had caused them to fall ill. But Franco had no conscience. Death, killing, it meant nothing to him." He chuckled, low and bitter. "You know, after the war he was given lists of all the Republicans who had been captured, all these thousands and thousands of men in the prison camps. Franco spent months going through those lists, late at night after his other work was done, making little check marks beside the names of those to be executed. He finished his other work, he had dinner with his wife and children, and then he went into his office and began making his check marks. Just items in a ledger book to El Caudillo . . ." Joaquin tilted his head back, gazed up at the sky. "And I've often wondered, how did he decide? There could have only been files on a tiny fraction of those prisoners— the commanders or the most notorious—so how did Franco decide the fate of all the others? Did he send men to the firing squads because he didn't like the sound of their names, or the name of their home village, or because his stomach was irritated that night? I'm sure he did, I'm sure he did—and I'm sure he never lost a moment's sleep over any of it." He slowly shook his head. "A diligent shopkeeper totaling up his accounts . . . yes, with Franco there was no hope. Without a conscience, there is nothing to restore."

He looked to Elena with a quick grin.

"And did you know it was quite by luck that he came to power at all? If Calvo Sotelo hadn't been murdered, he would have been *caudillo*. If Sanjurjo's plane hadn't crashed in Portugal, it would have been him—and if the Republicans hadn't executed Primo Rivera, it would have been him. None of those men would have inflicted such cruelty on Spain. Only Franco." The grin stole away and Joaquin shrugged. "Well, was it just luck, who's to say? The historians have found reasons enough."

A car passed along the road above them. It was the first vehicle to pass since they had been there, and Elena watched it until it slipped from sight, until the sound of its engine was gone.

She had listened to her grandfather with growing bewilderment, the source of all her anger and shame of him over the years suddenly turning vaporous. "If you hated him so much, Papa, why do you have his portrait on your wall?"

Joaquin stared into the grass. "I don't really know. Maybe as a warning. A reminder of how normal, how dull, a beast can appear. Or maybe it is a kind of revenge." He chuckled. "To be honest, the one aspect of history I quite enjoy is this careless way it chooses its heroes, how the vanquished always have the chance to come back and triumph in the end. It doesn't happen too often—usually, history is dictated by the winners—but it happened in our war. Even though we won, we Nationalists became the forces of darkness and evil, the Republicans the fallen angels of freedom, all goodness and light. Oh, I suppose one could have predicted it. After all, they had La Pasionara and Picasso, a thousand paintings and poems and books for the faithful to cry over. What did we have? We had Franco and his Blueshirts and his little fawning priests—hopelessly outmatched, you see?"

He chuckled louder, but to Elena it sounded strange, hollow and hard.

"And I, of course, became the 'Fascist Father Confessor,' the protector of torturers. Well, so be it. A small price to pay for the comfort of knowing the *caudillo* will suffer worse. Even now, I can sit in my office and look at his portrait and think to myself, 'I shall be forgotten, but you, Francisco, you are immortal; in a hundred years, they will still be spitting on your grave.' "

Elena rose from the blanket and walked slowly over the bluff. The grass felt cool and damp beneath her bare feet, and there were flowering dandelions growing in clumps. She picked several of them, watched the white, thick liquid seep out the hollow stems onto her fingers. "Purified," she said, "returned to the embrace of God. That was what you wrote in the files of the men you released."

"Really?" Joaquin feigned astonishment. "I'd quite forgotten. How embarrassing!"

Elena smiled, came back over the grass toward him. "But what did you do? How did you help them?"

Joaquin thought for a moment. "I suppose I stripped them. I took them out of their uniforms, I refused to recognize them by their rank. I made them see what they had done. I wouldn't listen to their excuses. I was angry with them, appalled by them, and I think they respected that, that it was what they needed. And then I clothed them again. For most, the simple ones, it didn't take much. A little soul-searching, a few tearful episodes, and then the priests came in, burned some incense for them, muttered some Latin words over their heads, and they felt better. For the smarter ones, it was a bit more sophisticated—philosophical debates, maybe some discussions about morality and free will, but, still, nothing too profound. The power of myth, the need to believe. I convinced them they could be cured, so they were."

"But what of the ones like Carlos Perez, the ones who wouldn't be cured?"

Joaquin looked out over the vega, and he seemed saddened at the question. "Fortunately, there were very few like that," he whispered. "Very few. Perhaps it was only egoism on my part, but I didn't want to give up on any of them, I tried very hard with them all. But, of course, there came the time, there always came the time. They were not recovering, there were so many more waiting, and one reached the point . . ."

He lifted his arm from the chair, gave a slow, backward sweep of his fingers in the air.

"Cast out," Elena said, "purified from history."

"Just so," Joaquin said.

Mark reached for the glass of mineral water on the counter before him. He gazed over the rows of bottles on the far side of the bar and thought of how far away he was from anyplace he knew.

He had gone to five cemeteries, and then he had given up. Returning to Orgiva, he had taken the lower road that led toward the river, pulled into the dirt parking lot of the cafe-bar just before the bridge. It was midafternoon, and the bar was empty save for the young girl behind the counter, a yellow hound sleeping by the door, four old men playing cards at a corner table. The men smoked strong, blond-tobacco cigarettes, and the gray smoke hung densely in the still air. Their low conversation was punctuated by the occasional shout of triumph or disgust as their game wore on.

Mark hunched over the counter, absently ran a finger through a small pool of spilled water. The futility of it had struck him all at once. He had been in the cemetery of one of the small villages on the northern flank, and as he walked back to the car, he had stopped to look out at the panorama of the Alpujarra. Standing there, seeing all the small villages tucked into hillsides, all the isolated farmhouses, he thought to himself, "Why did I come this way, choose this cemetery? Why not east, why not west, why not anywhere? Carlos Perez could have wandered off and lived or died anywhere." At that moment, Mark had realized he could search through cemeteries for the next five years—in the Alpujarra, in Andalusia, in Spain—and come no closer to finding anything.

He set a hundred-peseta coin on the counter, nodded to the girl. *"Gracias."*

"Adiós."

He stepped over the dog, through the beaded entryway. It was only midafternoon, but already the valley was taking on shadow. He looked at the bridge, a hundred yards farther along the road, and decided to walk down to it. He stood where he had the day before, leaned over the railing to stare into the rushing water.

One night, while they had lain in bed in their corner room of Casa de los Queridos, Elena had asked him about Colin's grave.

"What does it look like?"

And Mark had told her of the view from the hillside above the hospital cave, the mountains, the valley, how the sounds of sheep bells and street vendors and playing children floated up from the town below. He told her how he had marked his grave, the small pyramid of stones he had placed there, the old Indian head nickel he had set in the earth.

"We should go there sometime," Elena had said, "when the situation settles, when you're feeling up to it. We could bring him home."

And Mark had lain there, his arm holding her close, and tried to imagine how he could ever tell her, why he ever should. How to tell her that already there would be hundreds more men buried on that hillside, hundreds more anonymous pyramids of stones? How to tell her that in Kurdistan all the dead of one day went in together, in a ragged trench carved out by an old diesel-driven backhoe, that to find Colin now would mean searching over an entire mountainside for a small, dulled coin buried beneath an inch of dirt?

He had leaned to her, softly kissed her hair. "Yes," he had said. "That would be good."

Mark rested his back against the bridge railing and looked into the eastern reaches of the Alpujarra once more. Amid the southern flank of mountains, he noticed a low, barren peak some five or six miles off. It stood apart from the others, far away from any villages or farmhouses or terraced land, and its crest was a cascade of rock that shone in the late sun. He began walking toward it.

Clouds had begun forming over the Sierra Nevada in early afternoon, and they were now drifting westward, over the vega, casting the towns and fields in alternating pools of sunlight and shadow. There was still some day left, but the evening's chill had already begun, the dry air thickening.

"What is Almería like?" Elena was lying on the blanket, her head on her arms. Joaquin turned to her slowly, as if awakening from a nap.

"Why do you ask, my dear?"

She lifted her head. "I'm just curious. I realize I've never been there. I don't know much about it."

In his chair, Joaquin looked down at his folded hands. "I don't know what it's like now—I imagine it's grown a great deal—but I can tell you it was a very pleasant place at one time. High cliffs over the sea, the sierra behind, old Moorish walls, some of the finest flamenco singers to be found in all Andalusia . . . Well, what can I tell you? It was once a very pleasant city."

"You've never been back?"

"No. Oh, right after the war, of course, to see if I could find anyone, if there was anything left of our home, but . . . No. Since that time, I haven't been back."

Elena sat up, tucked her legs beneath her. "Why don't we go? We could go down tomorrow, spend the day there."

Joaquin looked to her. His gaze was hard, cold even. "And why would we want to do that, my child?"

"I'd like to see it. I want to see where you grew up, where that part of my family lived. You're not interested in seeing how it's changed?"

"No," he said. "I saw enough of how it changed."

Elena studied the blanket's crosshatched design. She nodded slowly, as if to herself.

With a grunt of exertion, Joaquin hoisted himself to his feet, teetered slightly after so many hours spent in the chair. "It's getting late; probably we should go." He turned to her. "Anyway, that was a long time ago, not important now. We should talk of pleasant things."

She gathered up their belongings, returned the glasses and food wrappers to the picnic basket. She shook out the blanket, spread it cleanly over the bluff, kneeled on the grass to fold it.

"I'm sorry, Papa," she said. "But you have to remember, I was young, a college student. You know how self-righteous college students can be."

"I've heard tell." He stood alongside, holding his collapsed aluminum chair in one hand, and watched her fold the blanket in half, in quarters.

"I didn't know how much I was hurting you." She looked up at him. "I'm sorry."

Joaquin shrugged. "A trifle, not worth another thought. You came back. That's what is important. You're back now."

They drove through the twilight, night settling as they turned into the driveway of Casa de los Queridos. There were no lights on in the house, no sign of the rental car.

"Odd," Joaquin said, as they came up the pebbled drive. "Mark isn't home yet."

Elena gazed up at the house, at the shine of its windows in the reflection of the headlights, and was gripped by a sudden thought — that Mark was staying out there, somewhere in the dark, because it was all he knew anymore, that he wouldn't be coming back.

He sat upon the rock, arms hugged around his knees, and watched the blackness close on the valley. It became a very dark night, overcast, with no moon. From his vantage point on the hilltop, all the small villages and remote farmhouses of the Alpujarra were obscured, hidden behind the surrounding peaks, and the only lights Mark saw were those of an occasional car passing on the valley road far below.

The only sound was of the wind and his own breathing. It became cold, and he held himself tighter.

He had stood off the flat rock, and the flower petals had fallen from his body. He had turned away from the pool of his own blood and started down the hill. No voice to lead him, only the wind and his own shadow upon the rocks, and he had come to the blackened ground, and there he had found him.

"Something's happened," Colin said. "I think something bad happened."

And he had administered to him as best he could, comforted him as best he could, and then they had come to the time when there was nothing more to be done, when the dying had to end, and finally Colin had slipped away, and Mark had lain down beside him and waited for the gray sky to fall, for a darkness that might shelter them as they began the long journey.

Mark stood up. The wind buffeted him, made him feel small and fragile. He could barely see his feet in the night. He started to walk, slowly, gingerly, down the hillside, toward the valley and the road and the river.

As he walked, Mark tried to remember the feel of that other night, the weight of Colin on his back, the crush of him when they fell, the sight of Colin's dead hands, tied together with one of the bootstraps, dangling over his shoulders, rhythmically swaying with each step they took down the mountain. "I don't want to die here." He tried to remember the slice of the sawgrass on his fingers, how the wind sounded like soldiers' voices, the terror that had risen in him until all he could utter was the last chant of the dying. "I don't want to die here."

After a long time of walking—two or three or four hours, Mark didn't know—there came another sound, the deep, steady roar of the river. He stepped onto the road, deserted at this hour of the night, and began walking along its shoulder, down toward the bridge, listening to the roar of the water in the darkness below him. Rounding the last curve, the lights of Orgiva appeared in the near distance, and they illuminated the steel girders of the bridge. On the far bank, he saw his car parked before the shuttered cafe-bar, its hood gleaming beneath the glow of a single streetlamp.

He started along the bridge approach, but then changed his mind. Leaving the road, he carefully picked his way down the embankment until he reached level ground. Maneuvering through the jumble of rocks and bushes and garbage, he finally came to the water's edge. The river flowed past, so violently that he felt its mist on his face.

Standing there, he tried to remember the feel of that moment, the chill of the water, the slip of his foot on the rock, and then the clutch of the strap on his throat, pinning him, sending him deeper, sending him colder. And what he couldn't forget was that none of it should have happened that way. It was a little mountain river, barely hip-deep. It should have been easy.

Mark looked down at his feet. In the faintest light being cast from the distant streetlamp, from the reflection off the bridge's steel girders, he saw that he was before a small eddy of the Guadalfeo, that the water that gently lapped against the rock on which he stood was black and calm.

"Don't worry," he whispered. "I'm taking you home, buddy. I'm taking you home."

They sat at the table in the back garden, gazing out into the darkness, their conversation sporadic. They heard the breeze riffling through the young alfalfa in the field beyond the gate. After a time, Joaquin lightly slapped the edge of the table, rose from his chair.

"Well, my dear, I'm beginning to suspect he became lost some-how—maybe had trouble with the car. Still, no reason to worry; Mark is certainly resourceful enough to find a pension, fend for himself for a night."

It was an assurance that neither of them truly believed, that failed to explain why he hadn't at least called. Joaquin leaned over Elena, placed a hand on her shoulder, kissed her on the top of the head, the way he did when she was a child. "You will be okay?"

She took his hand, held it against the warmth of her neck. "I'm fine, Papa, thank you. You should get some sleep."

Some time later, she, too, rose from the table and went into the house. At the top of the stairs, she looked down the long walkway. Her grandfather's room was dark. The office was just before her, the double doors thrown open, and Elena stepped over the threshold, turned on one of the standing lamps. In the light, the mounted Spanish flag appeared blanched, Franco's portrait almost invisible behind the shine of glass. She leaned against the desk to gaze at the gallery of photographs on the side wall.

In the center was the formal portrait of her grandfather as a young man, twenty-three or twenty-four, posing stiffly before the studio backdrop, a handsome aristocrat—delicate hands, white skin—on the eve of his ruin. There were photographs from the days of the institute, of her grandmother, Violeta, of her father as a boy, a young man, a father himself. She saw that the most recent one, the last one Papa had chosen to preserve, was of her, standing with him in the garden, an eighteen-year-old girl held in the embrace of her grandfather on a sunny day. There were no photographs of his family, of his parents or brothers or sisters or aunts or uncles, and Elena understood that sometimes it was a terrible thing to be the one who lived, that this could be a weight in your heart that never left.

And on the other side of the house, Joaquin lay on his narrow, military-issue cot trying to will sleep on. Finally, he gave up and rose, stepped to the bedroom window to gaze out at the night. Beyond the glass-sharded wall and dark fields were the lights of Peñuelas, but above there was nothing, no moon, no stars, as if a black blanket had been placed over the vega.

He pondered where Mark might be at that moment, if he was cold, the thoughts he might be having. Because as he lay on his cot, Joaquin had realized that he and Elena had been wrong. Mark's search for Perez wasn't really about Colin. Colin was right beside him. Colin had never left him. Mark was looking for himself, still trying to find his way back from the dead.

He returned in midmorning. Elena heard the car come up the drive, and when she stepped out the front door, she saw him sitting on the steps, his hands clasped around his knees, looking out at the lawn. His trousers were stained, caked with dried mud, his socks and shoelaces studded with burrs. She saw that his arms and hands were laced with small cuts, the kind thorns and sawgrass made. She placed a hand on his back, twisted a lock of his hair around a finger.

"I just wanted to find him," he whispered. "That's all."

Joaquin came out. Rubbing his paint-smeared fingers with a rag, he stepped past them, down the five stone steps to the driveway. He looked at the two of them. Elena gazed up into his face, desperate, beseeching. Mark continued to stare off across the garden, as if not really seeing anything at all. Joaquin turned, started down the drive. He passed the rental car and saw a large bouquet of wilting flowers on the backseat.

He walked to the front gate. He stood there for a long time, rubbing his hands with the rag, alternately examining his fingers for spots he'd missed and gazing in either direction along the empty country road.

It had never been about the boy. It had always been about Elena. And, if the truth be told, it had started out as a mere strategy, the best one—the only one—ever to present itself. But he had grown fond of Mark. He did want to help him. Even more, Joaquin saw that they came together, that if Mark were lost it would mean losing her again as well.

He looked at his hands; all the paint was gone now. With a sigh, he set the rag down beside the gate and started back up the drive.

He came alongside the rental car and saw that they still sat on the steps just beyond. He stopped, pulled open the driver's-side door, looked over to them.

"Come on, then," he said. "I will take you to Carlos Perez."

NINE

They drove deep into the Alpujarra, over the Guadalfeo bridge, and turned onto the narrow little road that led to Olía. They climbed up through the canyonlands, past the first series of cliff faces, and then Joaquin pulled the car to the side and stopped. Mark looked out to see the farmhouse he had noticed the other day, the white building perched on the bluff above its terraces of olive trees, the grove of pine beyond.

Joaquin led the way up the hill. As they approached, Mark saw that the olive trees had long since reverted to wildness, weeds clutching at their trunks, limbs split and dead. The house was nothing more than a small stone shepherd's hut, its windows gone, one corner of its roof sagging in. They walked on, into the grove of trees, and the land opened up into a small meadow, where Joaquin stopped. There was only the sound of the wind whispering through the pine needles, the occasional creak of a bending branch. Standing in the middle of the clearing, Joaquin gazed up at the swaying trees.

"What I can tell you about Carlos Perez," he said, as if to the pines, "is that he was a man of conscience. Hard to believe, perhaps, considering the things he did, but it is true. A devout conscience. It was what doomed him." He looked to Mark and Elena, standing a few feet away, and gave a weak smile. "And the truth is, I liked him. I liked him very much, but there was nothing I could do to save him."

His smile crept away, and he looked to the ground before his feet, absently ran a hand through his thinning hair.

"He came to me as a ruin. He had done terrible things in the Alpujarra, killed hundreds, him and his little blood squad. In the villages they conquered, anyone who was a Republican sympathizer, even the suggestion of it, that was the end of them. A horrible slaughter—one of the worst histories of any of my patients. Well, the generals saw this differently, of course. 'Such a good killer, we should make him an officer, bring him to Granada where he can kill more.' So, they took him to Granada, Carlos and his wife, and he was assigned to the cleansing squads, rooting out the last of the enemy."

Joaquin stopped stroking his hair, let his arm fall to his side.

"But then they had a child, a son"—he glanced at Elena—"the man you met, apparently—and in a curious way, this proved to be Carlos's undoing. Quite suddenly, he found he could not kill anymore, that what he had done tormented him. He was transferred to an administrative unit at the Granada headquarters, away from the shooting, but even this didn't help. It was there that he had his collapse. He was brought to me. In fact, he was in the very first group of patients to be brought to the institute."

Joaquin began to pace slowly, four or five steps in one direction across the clearing then back again.

"He was very intelligent. That, too, was a problem. Always, I found my smartest patients were the most difficult, and I think maybe Carlos was the smartest one of all. Very difficult. There were times when it seemed he was recovering, times when he was happy, eager to be reunited with his wife and child. Bright signs of progress. But then the blackness would come over him, a despair that was overwhelming."

He stopped pacing, peered into the trees.

"The child, the boy, was crucial in all this. Carlos loved that child, he was the world to him. He had a small photograph of the three of them, just after the boy was born, and Carlos would always talk of him, show the other patients the photograph, talk about what a good father he would be when released, what he and the boy would do together when he was older." He looked to Mark and Elena. "But it was a love of desperation, you see? A dangerous thing. In Carlos's condition, a very dangerous thing."

He hunched his shoulders against the chill, began to pace again.

"God, the hours I spent with him! And there were many times when I was almost ready to let him go, but then the blackness would come again, and he would descend. A kind of madness. He would rant about killing himself, his wife and boy, his family, his village, everyone he knew. He believed he was evil, thoroughly evil, beyond redemption, that this evil had infected everyone around him, and the only solution, the only atonement, was to eliminate all of it, everyone. At these times, he had to be restrained, tied into his bed day and night. He was inconsolable, a danger to himself, to the other patients, terrible times . . ."

Joaquin stopped, stared into the trees for a long time in silence.

"And always the pressure to release him. So many others waiting to come, always the administrators pushing me to discharge him. Again and again, I said he wasn't ready, that he needed more time, until finally they ordered me. That is when I learned of their little system with the problem cases—discharge them from the army, seal their records, throw them out the gate. Wash your hands of them. That is what they told me to do with Carlos.

"But I couldn't do it. For weeks, I delayed, tried to think of what to do. He was in one of his good periods, eager to leave, to see his wife and son again, but I knew he wasn't better, that another dark time would come, and there was no doubt in my mind that when it came, he would do what he had promised: kill his family, kill as many as he could before killing himself. I knew this would happen, I was certain of it, so what was I to do?"

He looked to Mark and Elena, fixed them with his sad, tired smile. "Well, of course, you know what I did."

They didn't answer, merely watched him. At the edge of the meadow was a pine stump, a tree shorn long ago, and Joaquin walked to it, gingerly sat upon it. He leaned his elbows on his knees, his eyes on the pasture.

"I brought him here. On that day he was released—September 15,

September 15, 1939—I brought him here, in the staff car. I was taking him home. I had no choice. We were driving along, just the two of us, talking pleasantly—he was so excited to be going home, he thanked me over and over, he cried with happiness—and the whole time I was thinking to myself, 'What are you doing? You can't do this, you can't do this.' And then I saw this place—the only place anywhere around, even then it was abandoned—and I saw what I had to do. I stopped down by the road and told him that we couldn't drive any farther—I made up some story that the road ahead was washed out—that it had been arranged for us to come up to this house, that someone would be waiting with horses to take him the rest of the way to Olía. Well, a peculiar story, but Carlos didn't think anything of it—after all, we had a good rapport, he trusted me. And so we came up here. We saw that the house was in ruins, and I remember Carlos said, 'This is the place, you're sure this is the place?' And I saw the trees, the pine forest, and I said, 'Yes, but I think maybe in there, maybe they said to wait in the forest.' And so, we came on, Carlos walking very quickly— he was impatient, anxious to get home—and we came out to here, to this meadow. I remember he stood right there"—Joaquin pointed to the far end of the clearing—"and he looked all around, down into the trees for some sign of the horses, and he was getting confused, a little upset. 'Here?' he asked me. 'You're sure this is the place?' When he turned around, already I had the gun raised to him."

Joaquin wearily rubbed his jaw, took a deep, ragged breath.

"He was shocked, of course, but only for a moment, a split-second. And then he did something that I was not prepared for at all, that I've never forgotten. He knew what was about to happen, but he didn't protest, didn't try to beg or attack me. Instead, he just put his face in his hands and began to cry. I cannot explain this, and maybe you won't believe me, but he was not crying for mercy or because he was about to die. It was something else. I believe he was crying out of a kind of relief, that he understood it had to end this way, that he had tried to come back, that I had tried to bring him back, and it hadn't worked, that it was hopeless. I think this was the crying, the relief of knowing he did not have to try anymore, that the burden of hoping was gone.

"And then he looked at me. Still he cried, but he took his hands away and looked at me. I asked him if he wanted to say a prayer, and

I remember he stared up at the trees for a moment, as if I had asked him to see a bird there, and then he turned back to me and shook his head. I asked him if he was ready, and he nodded."

Joaquin stared at the spot of ground where Carlos Perez had stood.

"He went over backward, flat onto his back. He didn't make a sound. I went up to him to make sure he was dead. His eyes were open, and there were still tears coming from them. I hadn't expected that. I had never seen that before, didn't know it was possible, but tears were still coming from his eyes."

He scratched his cheek with a trembling hand.

"So I buried him," he said. "Right over there." He pointed into the pines at the far end of the clearing. He lowered his hand, curled it into his lap.

Mark was leaning against a tree, gazing into the swaying branches. Elena had settled on the ground, gently touched the spring grass beside her.

"What was I to do?" Joaquin asked softly, slowly looking from one to the other. "If I had let him go . . . What was I to do?"

There was a long quiet in the meadow, intruded on only by the wind.

"Was he the only one?" Elena finally asked, touching the grass, not looking at him.

Joaquin shook his head. "No. The first one, the most difficult one. Eight more. Three here, the others in different places. All the ones who couldn't be saved, too dangerous to set free."

Elena turned to him then. "But how did you know that, Papa? How could you be so sure?"

Joaquin gazed at his granddaughter. "But I wasn't sure, my dear. I had to guess. That's all any of us can do. Guess."

"And that was enough? It gave you the right to decide?"

He shrugged. "Who else? I was there. There was no one else. I had to decide."

After a time, he rose from the stump, slowly crossed to the far edge of the meadow, gazed down into the trees where he had buried Perez. There was no sign of the grave anymore, no indication that the earth had ever been disturbed. He turned to them, saw that Mark still stared into the trees, Elena at her clump of grass. He started back toward his granddaughter, realized that, even against his will, his lips had curled into a slight smile.

"So, something of a complication, no?" he called gently. "What to make of old Papa now? Not just the 'Fascist Father Confessor,' but the killer of killers. Better or worse? I'm afraid our old history textbooks aren't going to be much help here—more of a philosophy question."

He stopped with a few feet between them, waited for her to look up at him. In her eyes was a numbness, an exhaustion, but Joaquin didn't see revulsion there. His smile was tentative. "Too bad Franco didn't seek my services, hmm?"

She didn't return the smile but gazed back down at the grass by her hands.

He turned to Mark. "And what of you, my boy? You know, I did this for you. I hope it was worth it."

Mark wouldn't look to him. He continued to stare into the distance, and Joaquin took two or three careful, slow steps in his direction. The wind, picking up in the early afternoon, made the rustling of the pine needles sound like running water.

"Fraud though I am," Joaquin said, "I knew the truth about Colin from the first moment I heard his name and saw your face." He waited for some reaction, but there was none. He shrugged dramatically, casting his empty hands out to either side. "But, as a keeper of secrets myself, my first thought was to respect your silence, reasoning you would tell when the appropriate time came." He chuckled softly. "Well, with a little prodding from me, the appropriate time came."

Again, he waited for some reaction. There was none.

"Look at me."

As if it were painful, Mark turned. Tears were welling in his eyes.

"I've also known from the beginning that there was more, that there was something you weren't telling, and, again, I tried to respect your silence. But now it's time, my boy. You have to tell. You can't go any further." He gave him a tender smile, waved a hand over the meadow. "I won't tell you it's easy or that you'll instantly feel better. What I'm telling you is that you're not as tough as me. You cannot carry this any longer." He glanced over at Elena, saw that she was watching them. "You have to come back to the people who love you."

Mark leaned his head against the trunk of the tree, and tears began to slip down his cheeks.

"He wouldn't stop dying," he whispered. "He begged me to save him, but there was nothing I could do. I tried, I tried for so long, but I didn't know what to do, and he was just dying, dying forever. I couldn't watch it anymore, I just couldn't watch him die anymore."

And he had lain down beside Colin and held him in his arms, kissed his face, and then he had reached down, felt along the trembling leg until his fingers touched the bootlace, the knot he had made there, and he had taken the lace between his fingers and gently pulled it free, and then he had reached over, felt for the other lace, and gently pulled it free. And as the blood had flowed out, forming small pools before seeping into the earth, he had held Colin close, stroked a hand along his cheek, and looked into his eyes—at last, peace and softness were coming into them—and he had said over and over, "Don't worry, I'm taking you home, we're going home now."

"And I tried," Mark said, his voice still a whisper, his head still resting against the trunk of the pine. "I tried, but he was on my throat, and I was in the water. I kept saying, 'Don't worry, I've got you, I'm taking you home,' but he wanted to go, he wanted me to go with him, and he wouldn't let me breathe, and I finally let him go, I had to let him go. What was I supposed to do?" He looked to Joaquin. "What was I supposed to do?"

Joaquin stepped to him then, smudged away his tears with a rough thumb, put an arm around his shoulders, and pulled him away from the tree to hold him to his chest. "There was nothing you could do. You did everything you could. It's over now. It's over."

They stopped by the bridge over the Guadalfeo. From the backseat, Elena handed Mark the bouquet of flowers, and he stepped out of the car, made his way down the embankment to level ground. He walked along the edge of a field, toward the flooded grove of birch trees. He came to a place where he could go no farther, and he sat there, rested his back against a tree, and watched the brown water just beyond his feet.

"It's nice down here, don't you think?" he said. "Too bad the water is so dirty, but it's the spring runoff, always pretty dirty then. Still, it's nice to be around water. Always nice to be around water."

He undid the tie around the stalks, and the flowers tumbled out to form a heap on the ground beside him. He picked up one stalk. It held four white flowers that resembled buttercups, and he leaned out to place it on the water. He watched the flowers drift away, floating placidly through the grove until meeting the main current, and then they disappeared quickly, propelled down over the rocks, on their way to the sea. He picked up the next stalk and placed it on the water.

From the bridge, Joaquin and Elena gazed down at him. There was a chill in the afternoon air, and the steel railing was cold beneath their hands. Elena moved closer to her grandfather, slipped under the arm that reached out for her, leaned into his embrace.

He came to the last stalk of flowers and held it for a time. It was a kind of flower he did not know—a wiry, brown stem, a profusion of tiny orange blossoms with petals that felt like paper. He leaned forward to place it on the water, and as he watched it slip away among the birch trees, he felt Colin ebbing—the look of his face, the sound of his voice. And this was a difficult moment, one of the most difficult, but along with the flowers and his friend, Mark felt something else leaving him, the tether on his throat, the night water on his temples. He watched the flowers drift until they were suddenly yanked into the main current, swept down over the rocks, and gone.

"Goodbye, then," he said softly.

And as Elena watched him pick his way back through the flooded grove, she saw for the first time how this day and journey might end. It would be in the corner room of her grandfather's home, and she would lie down beside Mark and reach up to cradle his head in her hands. She would run her hands through his hair and she would feel only the faintest ridge of a scar beneath her fingertips, and she would look into his eyes and they would not be green stones but eyes lit with longing and sad hopefulness and the promise of future laughter, and that light would stay with her, even as she lay her head on his chest and listened to his beating heart, even as she slept, entwined with him, enveloped by the dark of a moonless night.

TRIAGE

DISCUSSION QUESTIONS

1. Initially, Elena is "able to live with the worry by telling herself that what Mark did was important, even noble." Is a war photographer's job admirable? Or could it be considered exploitive? How do Mark's experiences highlight the difficulty of being an observer—instead of a participant—in war? Compare and contrast Mark's career with Elena's job as a refugee program coordinator at the UN.

2. Is it wrong for Colin to travel into a war zone and endanger his life while Diane is pregnant with their first baby? Discuss the impact of dangerous careers on spouses and children. Why do you think Mark is so adamant about wanting to have a baby with Elena when he returns from Kurdistan?

3. When did you begin to suspect that Mark might know more about Colin's fate than he first admits? Do you think he deliberately withholds his knowledge of Colin's death or subconsciously blocks it from memory?

4. Joaquin Morales is disdainful of traditional psychotherapy and dismissive of Elena's suggestion that Mark see a "real" doctor. Yet Joaquin's "cure" helped patients at his institute and seems to work for Mark as well. What do you think of "Dr." Morales' unique approach to therapy? How would you describe his methods? What does the book as a whole seem to say about the field of psychology and the nature of expertise?

5. Joaquin Morales says: "There is no salvation, Mark. There is no God to forgive you and there is no psychiatrist who can cure you. This Western idea that we can pass over our pains, how absurd! You never pass over them. You carry them with you forever. That is what it means to live." Do you agree with him? Does traditional therapy seek to eliminate pain instead of helping people accept it?

6. "Triage"—the prioritizing of who will get medical treatment under extreme circumstances—seems rather ruthless as practiced by Dr. Talzani in the Harir cave. Discuss the ethics of this selection process and how it relates to fate and the randomness of war. Why did Anderson choose *Triage* as the title of his book?

7. Compare and contrast Dr. Talzani's mercy killings of the "blues" in the Harir cave with Dr. Morales's murder of dangerous "incurables" at his institute. How does each man justify his dual role as healer and murderer? Do you find their reasons compelling or repugnant? Compare their killings with Mark's hastening of Colin's death. Can murder—or euthanasia—be a moral act?

8. After revealing the secret of Carlos Perez's fate, Joaquin says to Elena: "What to make of old Papa now? Not just the 'Fascist Father Confessor' but the killer of killers. Better or worse?" Answer his question. Why does Elena finally forgive her grandfather for his past? Do times of war require unique or altered ethical codes?

9. Dr. Talzani says: "There is no pattern to who lives or dies in war. Some live, some die. It's the only way to view it. Anything else is just self-torture and arrogance." Dr. Morales says: "We invented history for the same reason we invented God, because the alternative is too terrible to imagine. To accept that there is no reason for any of it, that we are only animals and there is no explaining the things we do, that happen to us—too awful, no?" Do you agree or disagree with these statements? Are both men fatalists? Compare and contrast their philosophies about life and war.

10. Do you think that Mark Walsh will continue with his career as a war photographer after his traumatic experiences in Kurdistan? Why or why not?

NOTE FROM THE AUTHOR

While I've never thought of *Triage* as an autobiographical novel, the fact is I started writing it in circumstances quite similar to those facing Mark at the beginning of the book. I had just returned to the United States from a war zone—Sri Lanka—where I had gone through a rather traumatic experience, and found that I was incapable of talking about it to any of my family or friends. Instead, I moved to a city where I knew no one—Baltimore—holed up in a squalid little apartment, and spent four months feverishly writing the first draft of the book.

That was eleven years ago, and that first draft, frankly, wasn't very good. The problem, I gradually realized, was that I was writing with the same sort of emotional numbness that I felt. It took a long time, and many more drafts of the novel, for me to be able to articulate what I truly felt about my experiences in war and to bring what I hope was a deeper emotional honesty to the novel.

Now, if I had to try to describe what I think *Triage* is about, I would say it is about searching, a search for redemption and a search for belonging. In their own way, the main characters of the book are war-orphans, either physically displaced from their homeland or emotionally displaced from their loved ones; in their own way, they are trying to return to what existed before. What they ultimately discover is that redemption and belonging are part of the same thing, and this discovery holds out the hope that there is a path they might follow to better, happier lives.

Discover more reading group guides on-line!
Browse our complete list of guides and download them for free at
www.SimonSays.com/reading_guides.html